The Proposal

ADRIANA LOCKE

The Proposal
Copyright © 2023 Adriana Locke
All rights reserved

Paperback ISBN: 978-1-960355-09-6

Cover Design: Kari March, www.karimarch.com

Special Edition Paperback Cover Design: Staci Hart, www.stacihartnovels.com

Photo: © Regina Wamba, www.reginawamba.com

Editor: Marion Archer, Marion Making Manuscripts

Copy Editor: Jenny Simms, Editing 4 Indies

Proofreader: Michele Ficht

Books by Adriana Locke

My Amazon Store

Brewer Family Series
The Proposal | The Arrangement

Carmichael Family Series
Flirt | Fling | Fluke | Flaunt | Flame

Landry Family Series
Sway | Swing | Switch | Swear | Swink | Sweet

Landry Family Security Series
Pulse

Gibson Boys Series
Crank | Craft | Cross | Crave | Crazy

The Mason Family Series
Restraint | The Relationship Pact | Reputation | Reckless | Relentless | Resolution

The Marshall Family Series
More Than I Could | This Much Is True

The Exception Series
The Exception | The Perception

Dogwood Lane Series
Tumble | Tangle | Trouble

Standalone Novels

Sacrifice | Wherever It Leads | Written in the Scars | Lucky Number Eleven | Like You Love Me | The Sweet Spot | Nothing But It All |

Cherry Falls Novellas

608 Alpha Avenue | 907 For Keeps Way

For a complete reading order and more information, visit www.adrianalocke.com.

To Rachel Brookes
There should be more people like you in the world. I'm grateful to have you in mine. With love.

A Note from Adriana

Dear Reader,

I've wanted to write this story for a long time, but it never fit into my schedule. Things moved around a little this year, and I decided to plug it in. I hope you love these characters as much as I do!

This story is meant to give you a break from reality—to fall in love with the idea of love. If it distracts you from your everyday life for a few hours, I've done my job.

Thank you again for giving me the chance to do that.

I know you have endless choices when you sit down to read. I'm so grateful you chose The Proposal.

Happy reading,
Addy

Synopsis

The Proposal

Breaking News: Rugby's bad boy marries his best friend's little sister
If Renn Brewer would've asked me to marry him, I would've said no.
Why?
One, his reputation precedes him. His name is in the headlines at least once a month. Two, he's not just my brother's best friend. *They're teammates*. And three, I'm in my self-care era.
Unfortunately, a version of me equates self-care with bad choices.
The cocktail in my hand—similar to the one that got me into this situation—is the prettiest shade of pink. It's almost the same color as the giant rock on my left hand. And instead of discussing an annulment, I'm considering a 90-day marriage of convenience to the man I accidentally married in Las Vegas.
Renn didn't propose marriage. But he does deliver a proposal I might be unable to turn down.

USA Today and Amazon Charts Bestselling author Adriana Locke delivers a **"spicy & sweet!" forbidden sports romance with a marriage of convenience** that will make you swoon!

CHAPTER 1

Blakely

"Could you die quietly?" Ella sighs, pulling her sunglasses down and squinting into the sunlight. "And maybe do it over there, please?"

Two quintessential frat boys, a label I'd bet my life on yet feels like a disservice to fraternities everywhere, cease their constant complaints about being hungover. Their whining is a show, a pathetic effort to gain attention, and one we're over—especially Ella.

They fire a dirty look at my best friend. She cocks a brow, challenging them right back, and waits.

Lying on the chaise next to her, I smirk. *How many seconds will it take for them to realize they're outgunned by a five-foot-three pistol with bubble-gum pink toenails?*

Eight ... Nine ... Ten ...

They gather their things quietly, watching Ella like she might toss them into the pool if they don't act quickly enough.

I wouldn't be shocked if that happened, either.

Ella St. James doesn't surprise me much anymore. She carried a tray of freshly baked snickerdoodle cookies when she rang my doorbell three years ago. She was adorable, wearing an apron with embroidered cherries and a white silk ribbon in her hair while welcoming me to the Nashville neighborhood. It starkly contrasted with the following weekend

1

when she took me out so I could *get acquainted with the city.* That night ended with Ella jacking some guy's jaw for trying to grope me on the dance floor and me picking her up from the police station in an Uber at three in the morning.

"Thank you," she says, sliding the glasses up her nose and returning to her book.

Las Vegas is sweltering. Blue water sparkles just inches from our feet, and I swear it only amplifies the sun's rays. We should probably get a massage or go shopping to beat the unbearable heat, but I didn't fly for almost four hours to stay inside.

I could've celebrated my new job and birthday like that in Tennessee.

"How do you think I would look with red hair?" I ask, stretching my legs in front of me. "Not bright cherry red, but a more purple-y, crimson-y red."

"No."

I furrow my brows. "That wasn't a yes or no question."

"I was cutting to the chase." Her fingertip trails along the bottom of the paperback. "That's not the question you were really asking."

It wasn't? I settle against my chair. *Yeah, it wasn't.*

It was a last-minute attempt at being young and reckless before I turn thirty tomorrow.

This whole birthday crap has been a bit of a mind fuck.

I've lived the past ten years with little abandon. I've traveled, dated, and swam with sharks. Went on a ten-city tour with a rock band. Attended a movie premiere, got engaged (and unengaged), and ate pizza at the world's oldest pizzeria in Naples. *Check that off the bucket list.* And with every year of fun, I assumed I had nothing to worry about—that I would have my shit together before I turned thirty and became a real adult.

That was an incorrect assumption.

By all accounts, I should be in a stable relationship and burdened with a mortgage and enough debt to bury my soul until Jesus returns. Appliances should excite me. I should have a baby. *I should understand life insurance.* Instead, I just broke up with *another* bad boy with commitment issues, re-upped the rental contract on my townhouse, and refilled my birth control.

But that all ends in six hours. I have to turn over a new leaf when the sun comes up. It's time.

Ella's book snaps closed. "This is not a tri-life crisis, Blakely. It's just a birthday."

"I know that."

"But do you?"

"*Yes, I do,*" I say, mocking her. "I'm not in crisis mode. I'm just transitioning into this new era of buying eye cream and freezing my eggs, and it's a little … terrifying."

She sighs. "You've been buying eye cream for years."

"Yeah, as a hedge against the future. This *is* the future."

Ella rolls onto her side, brushing her dark hair off her shoulder. "While I can't relate because I have a solid two years before I'm thirty—"

"Was that necessary?"

She laughs. "You're freaking out for no reason. Tomorrow is just another day."

"I know. *I really do.* There's just this pressure to get my ducks in a row and start making serious progress, or else I'll be fifty with no husband or kids. And I want both."

"All I ask is that you be a little more selective on the husband part because the last few guys you've dated …" She whistles. "Not good, Blakely."

Yeah, I know.

"I know you feel your biological clock ticking or whatever it is, but you *have* been doing big things," she says. "You're the new artist manager assistant at Mason Music Label. Remember, you little badass? That's impressive."

I shrug happily at the reminder. That's true—a dream come true, really. *And even more of a reason to get my shit together.* "But would I be even more impressive as a redhead?"

"The answer is still no."

I groan. "*Come on.* I want to go out on something big. Something fun. Something wild that I'll remember while I'm taking vitamins and going to bed before ten."

Ella reaches for her water. "Fine. But let's find something else. Red doesn't suit your skin tone."

"Like what? I'm not getting anything pierced, and I don't think I'm ready to commit to a tattoo."

"You've been wanting a tattoo since the day I met you. As a matter of fact, weren't you looking at tattoos when I brought over those cookies?"

I laugh. "Yes. But it's so permanent. What if I don't want it next week?"

She rolls her eyes.

"What else is there?" I ask. "Let's think."

"Well, you could find a man with money and get a quickie wedding on the Strip."

I laugh again, turning over onto my stomach. "At this point, that's the only way I'll get married—inebriated and to a stranger." *The guys I date aren't marriage material. I'll probably be alone forever at this rate.*

"Hey, people find love in all sorts of ways."

"True, but the odds that I'll find a marry-able man in the next few hours is incredibly low." I fold my arms under my head. "In lieu of sexy strangers with an engagement ring in their pocket, what else do you suggest?"

She taps a finger to her lips. "We could go to a show tonight. A male striptease or something like that. It might be a way to get your juices flowing—"

"*Ew!*"

"*While lacking permanence.* Then just see where the night takes us. Be free-spirited."

"You just want to go because it's one more way to needle Brock."

Her grin is full of mischief. "So? What's your point?"

Ella and my brother have been *a thing* for almost two years. *What kind of thing?* I'm afraid to label it, although I'm fairly certain they're exclusive without declaring exclusivity.

On the one hand, Ella is a lot to handle. She's smart, opinionated, and doesn't need a man—and she knows it. She also has a propensity to make decisions and weigh the risks after. That drives Brock nuts.

On the other hand, dating Brock would be a nightmare. Women throw themselves at him wherever he goes. Men stop him for autographs and to *man-swoon* over him. And during the season, he's focused and mostly unavailable. That doesn't always work for Ella.

I watch this back-and-forth and vow never to get into a relationship with a player—an athlete or otherwise. *Again.* I've done that before, and it didn't end well.

"I'm taking it you two are still fighting," I say.

"We aren't fighting. There's nothing to fight about." She lifts her chin to the sky. "I'm right, and he's wrong. That's all there is to it."

"I agree. You're right this time."

Her eyes widen. "*You're damn right I'm right.* I'm not putting up with him taking off to Miami with his friends and not even mentioning our anniversary."

"How can you have an anniversary if you aren't in an official relationship?" I snicker. "Isn't that what you always tell me? That you aren't in an official relationship with him?"

She waves a hand through the air, dismissing my question. "It's a prelationship, but that doesn't change anything in this circumstance."

"A *what?*"

"A *prelationship.* The formative stage where boundaries and expectations are established so you can determine if the other person is willing to abide by them." She pauses. "*Brock isn't.*"

I roll my eyes and let it go. They'll settle this before Brock returns from Miami and we're home from Vegas. I've seen it too many times to count.

"Then fine," I say, sitting up. "Let's go to a show. But if my brother asks whose idea it was, I'm not taking the blame."

"Tell him it was mine. *I want him to know.* A little competition never hurt anyone."

"Competition for your non-boyfriend?" I ask, grinning.

"Precisely."

I shake my head as a bead of sweat trickles down my face. I wipe it away with the back of my hand. "I'm ready to go in and grab a shower."

"And I need to make reservations for dinner." She sits up, slipping on her flip-flops. "You owe me, you know."

"What do I owe you for?"

"For depriving me of my right as your best friend to throw you the most outrageous, amazing birthday party that Nashville has ever seen." She stuffs her water bottle in her bag. "I'm known in certain circles as the girl who throws the best bashes. I can only wonder what everyone is thinking about this."

I laugh at her ridiculousness, slipping my cover-up over my head. "You've thrown me a huge birthday party every year I've known you. You can miss this one. It won't hurt."

She frowns. "Maybe it won't hurt *you*, but it pains *me*. I have a reputation to uphold."

"You'll survive."

I drop my phone, towel, and water bottle into my bag. I skim the area around me to ensure I have everything.

"Ready?" she asks.

"Yeah." A bubble of excitement fills me. *Let the birthday festivities commence.* "Let's go find trouble."

Ella shares my smile as we slide our bags on our sun-kissed shoulders. I spot my book under her chair and grab it. *How did it get there?*

As I stand, my gaze falls on Ella. Her wide eyes are twinkling. I've seen this look enough times to know things are about to get real.

"What?" I ask, frozen in place.

Her grin pulls wider. "I think trouble just found us."

Oh no.

CHAPTER 2

Blakely

T his could go so many ways.

"What's happening?" I ask, afraid to look.

Ella grins, returning her gaze to the object of her attention. *And desire from the looks of it.*

I mentally prepare myself for all possibilities—stripper, policeman, *mobster*. It's Ella and Vegas. *Anything is possible.* But despite my attempt at preparation, I'm unequipped for what's coming our way.

Conversations fall into hushed whispers as I turn around. Eyes widen. Mouths gape. There's probably drool trickling down chins too, but I can't look close enough to tell. I'm too busy bracing for impact.

I clutch my bag and watch two men walk toward us.

My brother is oblivious to the energy swirling around him. The man beside him is not.

In Renn Brewer's defense, it would be impossible not to know the effect he has when he walks into a room. *Or a hotel pool area.* Even if he didn't observe the heads turning, proverbial pants dropping—people scrambling for a writing utensil and scrap paper on the off chance he stops for an autograph—he must look in the mirror at some point.

God favors him.

Perfect symmetry. Deep brown eyes beneath heavy brows. Full lips and a jawline that evokes primal, throw-you-over-my-shoulder vibes.

The way Renn fills out a plain white T-shirt should be illegal. Couple that with the Tennessee Royals hat sitting backward on his head, hiding his trademark *almost* too long, tobacco-colored locks—it's downright felonious.

"Hey, cutie," he says, the words reaching me moments before the smooth, warm notes of his cologne toy with my senses. He slides his Aviators off, his lips twisting into a smirk.

A flurry of goose bumps rushes over my skin, intensified by the slight Australian accent he picked up while playing rugby there for the last few years. Somehow, it makes him more attractive, more desirable —*an absolute dream.*

Before I can reply, I'm bumped by Ella's hand going to her hip.

"What are *you* doing here?" she asks Brock.

My brother doesn't break his stride. Without missing a beat, he wraps one arm around her waist and hauls her into his chest. She starts to protest, but the words are quieted with a long, deep kiss.

I shake my head. "That didn't take long."

"I'm still mad," Ella says through the corner of her mouth. The words are garbled, making us all laugh.

Renn removes his hat, stopping beside me. It's as if he woke up, grabbed a shower, and tucked the strands under the cap without a second thought. The unruliness makes my fingers itch to comb through the tangled mess, digging my nails into his scalp until he moans.

He watches me intently as he tugs the brim over his head again.

Despite knowing him for nearly ten years, adjusting to his presence always takes a moment. I've wondered if being around him regularly, not just by chance when he's with Brock, would make it easier. *Could you ever get used to a man like this?*

Everything about Renn is overwhelming. *His stature*, coming in at over six feet and two hundred thirty pounds. *His body*, which is nothing short of muscled, primed perfection. *His confidence*—a magnetic, *main-character energy* that makes you feel like a part of a larger story when he notices you.

I'm not sure this could ever get old, but I'd give it a try.

As if he reads my mind, he winks at me.

"I'm feeling left out," I say, pretending to pout.

"Why?"

"Well, it's *my* birthday, but Ella gets all the attention." I grin. "How is that fair?"

His eyes brighten, and he closes the distance between us. "*Say less.*"

"Don't even think about it," Brock says, pulling away from a giggling Ella.

Renn holds my gaze but stops in his tracks. "You're such a buzzkill, Brock."

"Better than killing *you*, isn't it?" Brock asks.

The playfulness of his words is cut with a sharp warning—to tread carefully. It's a message heard loud and clear.

Brock is a bit overprotective. He was only nineteen when our mother died, and the court system made him my guardian. He left his rugby scholarship, moved into our childhood home, and ensured I graduated from high school the following year. Made sure I had dinner. Helped me grieve. Kept me out of trouble. And then somehow managed to settle Mom's estate, get me into college, and himself back on the rugby pitch.

We're close—more like friends than siblings. But there's one murky, muddy line that we haven't cleared. That line is Renn Brewer.

I blow out a breath and gather my wits. "What are you guys doing here, anyway? Just a happy coincidence?"

"Because *he*," Renn says, rolling his eyes, "couldn't manage to get his—"

"I didn't want to be away from my baby sister on her thirtieth birthday," Brock says, smiling facetiously.

Ella smacks his shoulder. "Oh, *that's why*? Good to know because apparently, I was under the wrong impression."

Brock sits on the chaise, pulling Ella down on his lap. "That's not the only thing you'll be under when we get to our room."

Our room? "I—"

"I'm not getting under you, on you, or around you until you tell me why you're here." Ella shifts until she's looking at Brock. "And you better come up with the right answer this time and enunciate it clearly."

Brock sighs. "El—"

"Wait a minute," I say, setting my bag on my chair. Sweat drips

9

down my spine. "Let's back up. There is no *our room*. We have one queen bed, Brock. You know that. *You* made the reservation."

My brother looks at me warily.

"What?" I ask, unsure where this is going.

Renn's hand slides across the small of my back. He slips behind me, lightly brushing his body against mine, before sitting beside my pool bag.

I force a swallow before chuckling, shaking my head at him.

His lips press together as if to hide a smile. *Bastard*.

"No need to worry. I took care of it," Renn says.

"*Took care of it*?" I ask. "What's that mean?"

He rests his elbows on his knees and looks at me through his long, thick lashes. "A suite has been secured, birthday girl."

A suite? He booked us *a suite? Us? As in the four of us?*

"Brock is going to be *making up* with Ella since he pissed her off. Her ass will be in his bed all weekend, and you know it. So either stay with us too or sleep alone." Renn smirks. "Or I can give them the suite and sleep with you in your room. Your call."

I suck in a breath, the heat of his gaze melting me quicker than the desert sun.

"You two better knock it off—" Brock starts, but Ella springs to her feet.

"*Since he pissed me off*?" Her hands go to her hips again, her eyes narrowing at Renn.

I groan. *Here we go.*

Brock tugs on Ella's arm, but she shrugs him away.

"Choose your words wisely because I'm already pissed at you," she says to Renn.

"*Oh no*," he deadpans. "You're pissed? How will I survive?"

I cover my mouth and try not to laugh.

"You won't if you keep it up," Ella says. "I know you talked him into going with you to Miami. He went, so it's his fault. But you're the freaking Pied Piper of bad decisions."

Renn sighs, turning on his playful smile. "Look, El, I'm sorry. I should've consulted you first. *Of course*. But my brother Tate scored tickets to a Beau McCrae concert, and they're impossible to get. Can you really blame us?" He bats his lashes. "Please forgive me."

Ella growls at him as Brock pulls her back onto his lap.

"Tickets to Beau McCrae? Sounds like I need to meet Tate," I say.

Renn turns slowly toward me and lifts a brow. "Tate's boring."

The sentence sounds harmless, a vague description of a sibling being altogether uninteresting. *But it isn't.* There's a challenge embedded into the casualness of those two words—and I'm not sure why it's so damn hot. But the fire he lit inside me earlier has been doused with a bucket of gasoline.

"Really?" I ask, smiling sweetly. "Because Tate sounds *super* interesting to me. *And impressive.* Beau McCrae tickets? *Wow.*"

Renn's jaw sets into a hard line. *That's the real wow here.*

"Oh, he's impressive, Blakely," Ella says, goading Renn. "You should follow Tate on Social. It's a good, shirtless time."

Brock buries his head in her neck, making her squeal.

"*Ooh,* will do," I say.

"Do you even follow *me*?" Renn turns his palms to face the sky, annoyed.

"I don't know." *Absolutely, I do.* "Do *you* follow *me*?"

He drops his hands to his thighs. "I follow three people, and two of them pay me to."

"Okay, so the short answer is *no*, you don't."

"Let's get back to the suite subject," Brock says. "It's hot as hell out here."

I drag my eyes from Renn's and face my brother. "I don't know why you think you can just barge in and take over my birthday party. It's rude."

"Because I'm me."

"This was a girls' weekend." *And my last chance to be wild and free.* "You weren't invited."

Renn stands, stretching his arms over his head. It takes everything in me not to watch the hem of his shirt slip up his abdomen. "I invited him."

What? "Um, you weren't invited either."

"I saw your face light up when you saw me coming," he says, his smile smug. "Don't pretend you want me to leave."

I'll ignore that. "We have plans tonight. Don't we, Ella?"

She snickers at the memory of our earlier conversation—when she was adamant that Brock could kick rocks. "Yeah. That's true. We do. Or we did."

"*We do.*"

"So incorporate us into your plans." Renn takes a step closer. "I'm a good time. Promise."

I bet you are. Not that I'll ever find out.

"Careful," I say, tilting my chin to look up at him towering over me. "You've promised me that before and never followed through."

His eyes blaze. "Tell me when, cutie."

Our gazes slam together. The air between us crackles.

And this is where the ambiguity begins.

Our attraction is undeniable. It's no secret. We flirt ruthlessly, fill conversations with sexual innuendo, and unnecessarily touch whenever we're together.

But that's where it ends.

That's where it has to end.

Renn is the epitome of *mistake.* He's the personification of the type of man I'm drawn to—the same type that is wrong for me.

Gorgeous. Charismatic. Skilled. *And a bad-boy reputation.*

He's even taken it further than most by getting kicked out of rugby in Australia for excessive suspensions, disorderly conduct, and a social media error that will live in infamy.

Besides that—or because of it—Brock would lose his shit if anything happened between his friend and me.

And I promised myself I would make better decisions going forward anyway. My best decision is to keep a barrier between me and the sexy, chiseled, *I can only imagine what he's like in bed* athlete.

I know that. I'm determined to stay safe in my self-care era. *But damn, it's hard.*

He bites his lip.

I bet it's really hard.

"We have a three-bedroom suite," Brock says, side-eyeing his friend. "It'll be safer up there, too."

"No one paid any attention to Ella and me until you two arrived."

Renn looks me up and down. "Doubt that."

I ignore him. "If you wanted us to relax in peace this weekend, you shouldn't have come."

My heart squeezes as my brother pleads with me to acquiesce.

I appreciate that he wants to be here even though some of that has more to do with Ella than me. But even if she weren't here, he would be.

Brock goes out of his way to ensure I don't feel alone. We're together every holiday, and he calls or texts me daily. I think my seventeen-year-old emotions when Mom died haunt him—my fear that we had only ourselves—because he does his best to make me feel safe and loved.

And that's part of why he puts up with Renn's and my antics.

Renn might be many things, but he's loyal. Brock knows if I needed anything, I could call Renn, and he would come with no questions asked. *I know that too.* So if we keep things transparent, Brock gives our flirty behavior a pass.

Barely.

Brock sighs. "I want to spend the weekend celebrating you, and the fact that I get to use that time making up with Ella is a bonus. But if I'm here, we gotta take some precautions, B. You know how it is. I'm sorry."

I frown.

"If you don't want to hang out with them, we won't," Ella says. "I'm here *for you*, Blakely."

"*She wants to.*" Renn picks up my bag and tries to slip it on his shoulder, but his tattooed arm won't fit through the loop. Instead, he dangles it at his side. "Come on. We'll let you have the biggest bedroom with the tub that overlooks the Strip."

"That does sound nice ..."

He touches my side, sending a bolt of energy through me. "Then let's go."

"If I agree to this, I want a birthday cake. *A big one*," I say, shivering as Renn's fingers press gently through my cover-up and into my bare skin.

"You got it," Brock says, standing.

"A chocolate one." I look up at Renn. "With ice cream."

"Anything else?" Renn asks. An ornery grin settles on his kissable lips.

His fingertips press a touch harder, searing my body with his gentle yet purposeful touch.

I turn my back to my brother and settle my gaze on Renn's. His jaw flexes, his eyes trained on my mouth. This is one of those moments where the line between *playing* and *foreplay* blurs.

Anything else? Such a broad question, Mr. Brewer.

Our eyes lock as I run through a litany of things that qualify as *anything else*.

His tongue caressing every part of my body. His hand wrapped around my ponytail, pulling my head back while he slams into me from behind. The taste of him as he comes in my mouth.

I grin. "That'll be all."

A low, throaty chuckle is his response.

I enjoy the mischief in his eyes before turning and following Ella toward the hotel.

CHAPTER 3

Blakely

"We need fifteen minutes," Brock says, waiting for me to open the door.

Ella is tucked under his arm, her pool bag in his other hand. She gives me a look of victory, saying my brother is about to apologize to her in ways I'd rather not envision.

I touch the key card to the pad above the handle. *They give me a headache.*

"What do you want us to do?" I ask. "Stand in the hallway?"

"Fuck that. Take your fifteen in the suite, and I'll help Blakely get their luggage," Renn says.

Brock stares at him, unblinking.

"What? I'm being helpful. Do you want to fuck Ella in private or not?"

"Just announce it to the world, Renn," Ella mumbles as a couple walks behind us. Unfortunately, her attempt at discretion fails.

"Uh, excuse me," the man says, lightly tapping my brother on the shoulder. "Are you Renn Brewer and Brock Evans, by any chance?"

Ella slips away from Brock and follows me into our room because we know the drill. Fanboying, pictures, and a rehashing of the guys' stats. An inquiry into the proposed expansion of the American Rugby League will follow this. A handshake so long that it's painfully awkward will close the encounter—*if* they manage not to draw a crowd. If they do, it's rinse and repeat.

"All of our unpacking for nothing," I say, surveying the space.

"This room is a mess." Ella sits on the edge of the bed. "I'll tell Brock I'm helping you, and then we'll go up together. I'm not leaving you to deal with this crap."

"No. Go with him. It'll be fine."

"I can't, with a clear conscience, leave you to do the work on your birthday trip, Blakely. Come on."

I snort, swiping my Kindle by the lamp and tossing it into my carry-on. "Oh yes. *Poor me.* Leave me with Renn all alone. *Boo-hoo.*"

She laughs.

"I'm kidding." Glancing up, I spot her lifted brow. "Okay, I'm not *totally* kidding. Things could be worse."

"May I make an observation?"

"Sure."

"That man is *so* into you, Blake."

I fight a smile. "That man is into *everyone*, El."

She rolls her eyes.

"You know it's true," I say, venturing to the window.

"Okay, he's a bit of a playboy. I'll give you that. But I highly doubt he looks at every woman like he looks at you."

"It's just his vibe, Ella. It's a part of his charm."

"He doesn't look at *me* like that."

I laugh. "Because Brock would kill him."

"And he wouldn't kill him over you?"

Point taken. I don't look at her, or else she'll see the dopey grin on my face.

It's an ego boost to pretend that Renn is seriously into me. *Who wouldn't want to think that the man who could have any woman he wants chose them?* His face sells magazines. His body sells apparel. He carries such confidence, such swagger, that *the idea of him* sells cologne. But pretending is a trap—one I can't fall into.

Even if I was his type and Brock somehow got on board with it, Renn can't give me the things I need in this stage of life. *Love. Stability. A family.*

16

And I deserve those things. I'm determined for my thirties to be my self-care era. *Screwing around with Renn Brewer would certainly be self-sabotage.*

The door creaks open.

"Come on, Ella. Let's get the fuck out of here before we're pinned down," Brock says as Renn strides past him.

She gets up and dashes for the door. It slams behind her.

"Are we going to have a fan club out there when we leave?" I ask Renn.

"We mentioned that we aren't staying on this floor. So I hope not."

"The downfalls of fame."

He grins. "It can't be as bad as over the weekend."

"How was Miami, anyway?" I ask.

"Aside from getting a police escort to leave the concert, we had a good time. Met up with Tate and Ripley—my other *boring* brother."

I look at him and laugh. "How many brothers do you have again?"

"Too fucking many."

"Are they all boring?"

"They're all overrated." He shoves off the wall and takes his phone out of his pocket. "Can you excuse me for a second? Or I can take it in the hall?"

I shrug. "Take it here. It's fine."

"Thanks." He puts the phone to his ear. "Hey, Dad," he says, then pauses. "No, *I did not say that.* Ask Tate." His forehead wrinkles as he listens. "I don't know where you're getting your information—*wait.* I do. Gannon told you that, and he can fuck right off."

Yikes. I go into the bathroom to give him some privacy.

I try not to eavesdrop as I repack Ella's and my toiletries. It takes a lot of effort to block out the richness of Renn's tone and focus on the cream bottles and hair ties instead. His voice raises, then softens. It's gruff, then smooth. I can only gather that someone, presumably his father, isn't too happy.

As I zip the last cosmetics bag, I hear him end the call.

"Everything okay?" I ask, shoving a curling wand under one arm and picking up the bags. "Sounds like you've been a bad boy."

I turn the corner, and my feet falter.

Renn is standing next to the dresser with a pair of my yellow panties dangling from his finger.

"I'm always a bad boy. Want a demonstration?" he asks, smirking.

I drop the bags and wand into Ella's open suitcase before snatching my panties from his grasp. My cheeks burn as I tuck away the rest of my lingerie.

"Actually," he says, "I wasn't being reprimanded. Only *reminded*."

"Of what?"

"To be on my very best behavior. I promised my dad I would be as good as gold."

I glance at him from the corner of my eye. "So you lied to your father?"

He chuckles, taking the clothes hanging in the closet off the hangers. "*No*." He draws the word out as if he's thinking it through. "I endeavor to be on ... probably not my *best* behavior, but I don't plan to ruin my contract terms or his business deal."

I hum.

Renn's suspension from international rugby was worldwide news. Even if I didn't follow the sport, I would've known. *Renn transcends rugby*. So when he returned to the States, the big question was *would he sign with a team here*? It was touch and go for a while, and he sat out last season. But a few months ago, he signed with the Tennessee Royals to play with Brock.

"What kind of deal? Anything interesting? Or is it boring like Tate?"

He lays the clothes on the bed next to the suitcase. Then he sits beside it. "Dad is in the process of purchasing the Tennessee Arrows."

"The baseball team?"

He nods. "All owners have to vote and approve any team purchases or transfers. It's a fail-safe to preserve the league's integrity. Apparently, they're concerned about our family's reputation—mine specifically— which is all kinds of bullshit considering we've owned a pro hockey team for twenty years and a dozen corporations without a problem."

Wow. What kind of first world problem is that?

"It's really just a campaign by another shareholder to keep us out because Dad pulled strings they didn't want pulled on a business deal in the nineties," he says. "So they use my ... *spirited behavior* as ammo. And the fact that the Royals made me sign a *good boy clause* in my contract didn't help."

"That seems kind of unfair."

Renn shrugs. "It's how it goes. Baseball is much pricklier than other sports, it seems."

He hands me a dress. I avoid his fingers and take it.

"So why baseball and not rugby?" I ask. "Or soccer?"

"I don't fucking know. It's all Gannon's doing, I think."

I take another dress from the stack. "Another brother, right?"

"Yeah. The biggest prick of them all."

"So he's not boring like Tate?"

He narrows his eyes playfully and gets up from the bed. "*Stop thinking about Tate.*"

I laugh and lay the dress on top of the other.

Renn moseys around the room while I finish folding the things we'd hung up in the closet. *Ella completely overpacked.* The sunlight creates a muted warmth in the room, making it feel cozy and calm.

Besides his looks, this is what I love most about Renn. Sure, he can be frustrating and, at times, self-centered. And it's almost impossible to have a genuine conversation with him if people are around. But when it's just the two of us—*when he's not Renn Brewer, Superstar*— it's almost possible to forget what a player, figuratively and literally, he is.

"Give me those," I say, taking a pair of my shoes from him. "Did you come here just to go through my stuff?"

"Yup." He removes a silver heel from my bag, ignoring my sigh. "These are fucking hot."

"Well, I do get a lot of compliments when I wear them."

His eyes flip to mine. He tosses the shoe beside the other. "So who are you seeing these days, anyway?"

With my back to him, I grin. "No one."

"Such a shame."

I laugh.

"What's the problem?" he asks. "Just haven't found the right guy?"

I pull a phone charger out of the wall. "I have a tendency to pick the wrong ones. What about you? What starlet's heart are you in the midst of breaking?"

"I'm keeping my options open. Much to my mother's dismay."

He rolls his eyes, but there's also a gentle, affectionate smile for his mom. *Lucky woman.* "Rory Brewer believes that her six children should all be married and producing grandchildren. And as far as I care, she can shove that up her ass."

"Renn!"

He whisks his phone off the bed and glances at the screen. "I had to make sure Dad wasn't still on the line." Satisfied, he shoves it in his pocket. "I did that once—thought I'd hung up but hadn't and said some shit I shouldn't have. That didn't end well."

I point at him. "That's why you shouldn't say anything about someone you wouldn't say to their face."

"Oh, I've said as much to Mom's face ... *every time I talk to her.* She thinks I'm playing with fire with my scandalous, bed-hopping ways. According to her, I should settle down, find a nice woman, and start a family before I retire."

I zip my suitcase while Renn works on Ella's.

"Does she pressure all of your siblings?" I ask.

His hand pauses in the air. "Now that I think about it, it's mostly me."

"She probably thinks it'll get your name out of the tabloids." I pull the suitcase onto its wheels. "Think about how good that would be for your image. You, winning a championship, with a blushing bride and bouncing baby boy at your side." I laugh. "What would the baseball guys say then?"

He makes a face that has me laughing.

For someone with the nickname *Renegade*, Renn is surprisingly dutiful regarding his family. His respect for his father is evident. His love for his mother is written all over his face, and he's always mentioning his siblings, making it obvious they're close. So his apparent disdain for wanting a family is odd.

"You don't want to get married someday?" I ask.

He licks his lips. "I'm too busy. I can be selfish. To be honest, I like my independence. I can spend my money on whatever I please. But probably the biggest thing is that I don't have to wonder about hidden motivations."

I nod. I can understand that. I've seen Brock deal with similar things.

"It makes it difficult to have a real relationship with someone when you're wondering in the back of your mind if they see dollar signs, you know?" he asks, his voice softer. "I've seen way too much—with me and my family. I don't think I could ever trust anyone that much."

He forces a swallow.

"Makes sense." It's also one of the reasons Ella and Brock work. He trusts her. And he doesn't trust easily.

He grins. "Your turn. What's in Blakely Evans's future?"

"*That* is a good question."

"Do you want a marriage someday or no?"

"Oh, I do. Definitely. It's just something I've never prioritized. But now that I'm thirty—or will be in a few hours—I need to stop dating men with no husband potential." I brush a strand of hair out of my face. "If I don't find a decent guy, I'm going to wind up with an anonymous sperm donor. You and Brock will have to be the cool uncles who spoil my baby with male attention."

He chuckles.

"I'm not joking. I've seriously considered getting a sperm donor someday. Think about it—it has its upsides. No man to deal with and no pressure to settle with one just to start a family. No in-laws to loathe. I can do it on my own terms and timeline."

"I have an idea," he says, grinning.

"That scares me."

He pulls Ella's suitcase across the room. "Have a baby and tell my mom it's mine. Think about it—you get a kid with a built-in babysitter and college fund, I get the media boost, and my mom is happy. We all win."

"*Oh, okay.* That sounds like a great idea," I say, looking at him like he's lost his mind.

"What do you mean? It's perfect."

I laugh. "Renn Brewer, that might be the most selfish thing you've ever said."

21

"Selfish? You mean *selfless*?"

"Nope. I meant selfish."

He pulls the bright green suitcase to a stop by the door.

"Oh, wait. We forgot Ella's carry-on." I grab it off the chair and attempt to finagle it onto my arm. "I need more hands."

"Here. I can get it."

I cross the room and hand the satchel to Renn. My foot bumps my suitcase. It rolls behind me, effectively blocking Renn and me in the small corridor beside the door and bathroom.

The room around us shrinks, and the air thickens. Suddenly, I'm aware of the rise and fall of his chest beneath the thin layer of cotton stretched across his torso.

His Adam's apple bobs as he looks down at me.

We're *almost* too close. *Almost* touching. His exhales fill the small space between us with small blasts of wintergreen.

"Does this make you uncomfortable?" he asks, taunting me.

"Should it?" I smile coyly back at him.

He widens his stance, a playful smirk ghosting his lips. "Would it make you uncomfortable if I kissed you?"

My stomach pulls tight, and my lips part, begging for air ... and a kiss. The movement catches his attention, and his gaze drops to my mouth. His tongue swipes across his bottom lip.

A shiver snakes down my spine, reminding me of all the things that tongue could probably do.

We've been here before—one wrong move away from starting something I'm pretty sure we wouldn't, *couldn't*, stop. Lucky for us, we both know better than to go too far.

That doesn't mean we won't go as close as we can. It's a carefully choreographed dance that we've perfected over the years.

"Is that what you want to do?" I ask, lifting a brow. "You want to *kiss me*?"

He grins, his eyes hooding. "No. I want to fuck you."

God.

My palm sweats around the suitcase handle. I try to look away from him—needing as much distance as possible to think straight. But as I attempt to pull my gaze from his, he refuses to let go.

"If only there weren't so many reasons that can't happen," I say, as much a reminder to myself as it is to him.

"Refresh my memory."

I laugh. The sound breaks some of the tension, and I clear my throat. "For starters, my brother would kill us both."

"I can take him."

"*Okay.*" I laugh again. "Second, we're friends."

"You'll like me even more when I make you come. Promise."

My face flushes. "*Stop it.*"

"What other reasons do you have?" he asks. "You gave me two shitty ones."

My head scrambles, trying desperately to remember why I can't grab his face and bring his mouth to mine.

He reaches for me, pressing his thumb against my lips. "Just think about it—I'd bring your birthday in with *a bang.*"

Fucking hell. I struggle to catch my breath as I imagine that scenario in detail. *His calloused hands roaming over me. His tongue circling my nipple. His cock—*

He laughs, pulling his finger away from me. "All right. Come on, cutie. Let's get out of here."

"*What?*"

He grabs the door handle and leans toward me, lowering his voice. "We better get up there before your brother beats me up."

I shove his chest. He grabs me, wrapping his hands around my wrists and jerking me into his chest. I pant, staring up into his handsome face.

"Remember something," he says, eyes sparkling. "*You* said no."

"*No*, I didn't. *We* said no."

He releases me slowly, smirking. "I didn't say shit."

Dammit.

My blood heats, pinking my cheeks. I can't hear anything over my heartbeat thumping in my ears. I fight myself from reaching for him, from taking him to bed and fucking him like an animal.

He pulls open the door and props it open with his foot. "I only get turned down once." He watches me pass by him, smiling ruefully. "If you ever want this dick, you're gonna have to beg for it."

"Ha. Not going to happen. I *never* beg."

"Then I guess there's nothing to worry about."

I know him well enough to know he's struggling to keep his amusement off his face. And he knows me well enough to know I know that.

"You're an asshole," I say, heading down the hallway. *Thankfully without a crowd.*

The door closes behind me, ending the moment.

CHAPTER 4

Renn

"It's been fifteen," I shout, holding the door open until Blakely and her suitcase get through it.

She uses a few colorful words to get the behemoth over the threshold.

"You could've just let me pull it," I say, repeating the offer I gave her no less than twenty times since we left her room.

"I'm capable."

"Barely."

She jams her elbow into my stomach. I humor her by groaning.

Her cheeks are still pink from our conversation a few minutes ago. The rosiness makes me wonder what she looks like after an orgasm—something I've wondered too many times to count.

How could I not think about that? Blakely Evans is a wild mix of beautiful, pretty, and sinful.

High, sculpted cheekbones. Delicate, soft shoulders. Dangerously wicked curves.

A gold fleck shines in her eyes when she's turned on. She nibbles her bottom lip when she's nervous. She smells like cinnamon and oranges and tucks her hair behind her ear when she's feeling self-conscious.

Her looks got my attention many years ago, but her personality kept it. And if she wasn't my best friend's little sister, and *if* I was a man who wanted a girlfriend, I might risk asking her out. But it would be a risk because it's Blakely. She might be the only woman who would turn me down. *She's also the only woman I've ever considered as the elusive what-if, too.*

"*Oh my God, Renn,*" Blakely says, abandoning her bag in the foyer and hurrying into the suite. "This is *incredible.*"

"I really hoped you'd be saying that in a different capacity right about now, but whatever," I mutter loud enough for her to hear.

She looks at me over her shoulder and grins.

Damn her.

When Brock suggested that we fly to Vegas this morning, I was on board immediately.

Being around Blakely always feels like a vacation—like a break from reality. She doesn't treat me like I'm anything special. With her, I'm not a professional athlete who can further her career with my contact list. She doesn't give a damn that my family is one of the wealthiest in the country. *Does she even know that?* I don't have to worry about ulterior motives, or if I say or do something dumb, she will send it to the tabloids.

Or, worse, an attorney.

I lean against the wall and watch her take in the space.

"Have you stayed here before?" she asks, her fingers trailing along the wet bar. "Or did you just luck into this?"

"I've stayed here a couple of times." *Like the time I bought it.*

She hums, strolling through the sitting room and past a spiral staircase that sold me on the property. I didn't need, or want, a place in Vegas—or anywhere for that matter. But Dad kept chirping at me to secure a place to relax. *"You need a getaway, son. You can't be a wanderer forever."* And Gannon was on my ass about investing my money in real estate to *diversify and hedge against inflation,* whatever that means.

So I did the one thing that I could think of that would be taking their advice while also irritating the fuck out of them. I found a new hotel selling penthouse suites and bought one. *In Sin City.*

"Holy shit. *Look at this,*" Blakely says, getting to the other end of the sitting area.

The far side opens into an airy atrium. The ceilings are high, opening to the loft above it, and it's enclosed on two sides by floor-to-ceiling windows overlooking the Strip. A long white marble table sits in the center of the room. I have no idea its purpose because the kitchen is on the far side of the suite, but it came with the place.

Blakely stops at the glass wall and stares across the sea of buildings and flashing lights.

"Wait until it's dark," I say. "It's even more impressive then."

"I don't know how it could be. *Just look at that*." She motions toward the outside, eyes sparkling. "It's like you're in a castle up here. It's incredible."

Her excitement delivers a satisfaction that knocks me sideways.

When I first met Blakely, she was dating Edward fucking DiNozzo —a giant asshole who didn't deserve her. *We've played on the same team a couple of times. He's the worst.* I sat across from her at dinner that night, trying not to stare.

She was timid that evening, anxious even. It was like she was a woman dying to contribute more to the conversation but was afraid the world would burn down if she did. It was a challenge that night to get her to laugh. Granted, I wanted to make it happen to piss off a haughty DiNozzo just as much as I wanted to hear it for myself. But once she gave it to me—a bright, head-thrown-back giggle, I made it my mission to get her to respond like that as often as I could.

And it got easier every time we saw one another. Granted, it was only a few times a year. After she ended things with DiNozzo, being around her on my trips home was even better. She was fun, inquisitive, and so fucking sweet. We could sit and talk all night long and have it feel like an hour.

Things might've gotten interesting back then if I hadn't been working halfway across the world. Now that we're both in Nashville? *Things could get interesting.*

"Come on, cutie." I motion for her to follow me. "There's a lot more to see."

"Nah, I'm good. I'll pull a chair up to the glass and sleep here. I'm easy to please."

"Good to know. I'll note that for later."

She grins. "I thought you were waiting on me to beg."

Fire shoots through my veins, and it takes every ounce of control I can muster not to lay her on that fucking table and tease her until she gives in.

"Keep it up," I say. "I'll have you doing it on your knees."

Her flush deepens. The color staining her face and neck makes my cock throb.

"You wish," she says, smirking.

Damn right, I do.

If Brock overheard this conversation, he'd murder me. No questions asked. And if I went through with it? He'd hurt me so badly that he'd end my career. There's not a doubt in my mind about that either.

The worst part? I can't blame him.

I like to think I'm not as bad as the media makes me out to be. The headlines make it sound like I'm cold and callous, blowing through women with no care in the world. And while I never feel attached to any of them, I do remember they're someone's daughter.

But sometimes respect isn't what they want.

And what they want is something I won't give them. *Any of them.*

Keep it moving, Brewer.

"I'm staying in this bedroom," I say, clearing my throat and pointing at a door on the other side of the table.

"Great." Blakely fixes the knot of dark hair on top of her head. "Where am I sleeping if I'm banned from the chair?"

"I'll show you. Let's get your bag first."

She follows me into the foyer. "I think I'll let you carry it this time."

"Gee, thanks for letting me. You're so nice."

She laughs. "I have lactic acid in my arms, okay? I'm not used to that much physical exertion."

"That's your fault. I tried to get it for you." I grab the handle of her suitcase and point at the closed doors with my other hand. "Powder room. I have no idea if there's food in the kitchen. Brock and Ella's room is down that hallway."

Our footsteps pad softly against the stone floor. It fills the suite with a warmth I've yet to feel here.

"After you," I say, sweeping my hand across the steps.

She looks at the landing above our heads. "My room is up there?"

"If you want the giant bathtub, it is."

"I do want that." Blakely starts up the steps, looking at me over her shoulder. "Good luck with that suitcase. Bet you wish you gave me a downstairs bedroom now, don't you?"

Her ass cheeks peek out from beneath her cover-up.

"Nah, I'm good," I say, gripping the banister.

I think she's going to cover herself. Instead, she pulls the back of the fabric up to her waist and gives me a full view of the curve of her cheeks. Her bikini bottoms barely cover anything, showcasing the roundness of her behind, the deep dip of her hips, and the soft glow on her skin left from the sun.

My cock pulses so hard that I grimace. *Fuck.*

"Careful," I warn. "That looks a lot like begging."

She gets to the top of the staircase and drops the fabric, hiding herself from me again. A coy grin slides across her lips. "Oh, that wasn't begging, Renn. I can be *a lot* more persuasive than that."

"I bet you can." I yank her suitcase up with a thud. "Wanna show me?"

She feigns surprise. "That looks a lot like you asking me twice."

"That's called giving you a chance to get what you want."

Her grin is full of mischief. "Do you even know what I want?"

I take a step toward her, watching gold flecks sparkle like stars in her eyes. "Tell me so I'm sure."

She leans forward, giving me a clear view of her cleavage. Her bikini top has slipped. A line curves across her round tits, displaying a tan line just above her nipples.

My. God.

I'm not going to make it. I'm going to die a death by blue balls. No one will believe it. It'll be the only true headline ever printed and the only one no one believes.

"I want a giant bathtub," she whispers.

And I want to join you in that giant bathroom, you little tease.

"Go," I say as she laughs. "Put some distance between us. *Now.*"

29

She giggles but does as I ask. She rounds the corner beside the wet bar that gives the main bedroom privacy from the staircase. As soon as she's out of sight, I hear her shriek.

"*Renn!*"

I smile at the sound, adjusting myself as I head toward the bedroom I use when I'm in town.

The view from this floor *is* amazing. It's the best view in the entire suite, but also in the entire hotel. The loft is open to the atrium. But, with a push of a button, a wall descends from the ceiling, creating privacy and a shield against the morning sun ... or visitors below.

My cheeks split into a wide smile as I watch her enter the attached bathroom and squeal again. *I knew she'd love it.*

Her head pokes around the corner, eyes wide as saucers. "Okay, this tub is *massive*. And did you see the view from there?"

I chuckle. "I saw it."

"I might live here. Seriously. I might never leave."

"*Where are you?*" Brock calls from below.

Blakely jumps. *Yeah, I forgot they were here too.*

I jam a thumb over my shoulder and exhale. "I'll see what they're up to while you get situated. Was this worth staying with us? I don't want to disappoint you."

She hurries to me and presses a soft kiss against my cheek, careful not to make further contact. "You're the best. Thank you, Renn."

"You're very welcome. Happy birthday."

She takes her suitcase and wheels it into the closet.

This will be one long weekend.

I'd be lying if I said I didn't love Blakely's affection. Coming from a large, tactile family, hugs and kisses are par for the course. *Except with Gannon. Fuck Gannon.* But outside the family? I don't trust anyone's touch ... or agenda.

Usually. Blakely is an exception.

"Renn!" Brock shouts.

"Hold on, dammit," I shout back, shaking my head. *Give me a second so you don't see me hard over your little sister, please and thank you very fucking much.*

I descend the stairs and then head toward the kitchen. Brock is opening a bottle of water when I enter.

"I thought you forgot how to tell time." I take a bottle too. *Maybe this will help cool me off.*

"Sorry. Ella was *really* mad."

"Bet you hated that." I take a long drink, my adrenaline beginning to ease. Ella bounces down the hallway. "Hey, El. What's the plan tonight? Don't the two of you have something you want to do?"

"Kinda." She laughs. "But not anymore. I'll talk to Blakely and see what she wants to do. She ruled out tattoos and piercings, so those are a no-go."

Brock and I exchange a curious glance.

"Nice suite, Renn, by the way," Ella says, poking her head through the doorway. "Where's Blakely?"

"Upstairs."

She pivots on her heel and heads that way.

"That girl is a ball of energy," I say.

Brock chuckles. "You have *no idea*. She just bit the fuck out of me." He clasps a hand over his shoulder. "Not complaining but *fucking hell*. It hurt."

I laugh.

"So about tonight ..." He yawns. "I just want to make sure my sister has a good time and is safe. She's been stressed over this birthday, and I want her to start it off on the right foot."

"Stressed? About what?" I ask, taking another swallow of water.

He shrugs. "I tried to follow along. But all I got was wrinkles, calcium pills, and a sperm bank."

I cough, water spewing across the kitchen. My words from earlier echo through my brain. *"I have an idea ... You can have a baby and tell my mom it's mine."*

"Are you all right?" Brock asks, concerned yet curious.

"Yeah." I suck in a breath before coughing again. My voice is raspy, my throat burning. "I'm fine."

"Okay ..."

I sputter until I can breathe easily again. Just as I recover, Ella comes bopping by again.

"We decided on dinner, and we're leaving in an hour, boys," Ella says, heading back to her room. "Brock, can you grab my luggage? I need to shower. And do one of you two think you can pull your magic *I'm famous* card and get us a reservation?"

"I'll do it," Brock says. "I'll grab your suitcase, and you can tell me where you want to go."

"Thanks, babe."

"See ya in an hour, I guess," he says to me.

Judging how long "fifteen minutes" is in his book, will we even see them again tonight?

"See ya," I say.

I empty the water bottle and then toss it in the garbage. *I need to stop with the single-use plastics.* I also need a shower—and a blow job, but that looks out of the question.

Irritated, I head toward my room. I pull my phone out of my pocket and check my texts.

> Ripley: You didn't wind up with my sunglasses in your bags, did you? The ones with the gold frames that I wore to the concert.

> Me: Nope. Did you ask Tate? It would be a very Tate thing to wind up with your glasses.

> Ripley: Funny. He said the same thing about you.

I roll my eyes, bumping my room door shut with my hip.

Ripley: Remember Carly from the Beau McCrae after-party?

Me: I'm bad with names.

Ripley: Of course. Let me try again. Red hair. Ginormous ass. Black leather skirt. Hung out with us for a while.

Oh, yeah. I grin.

Me: Turns out I'm great with adjectives.

Ripley: Well, she wants your number. Said she hit you up on Social but didn't know if you'd ever see it.

Me: I never check that shit. It's a sea of sharks.

I move away from the text app and open Social instead.

Ripley: I figured.

My eyes bulge at the number of unread messages in my account.

Me: The last time I responded to a girl on Social, it cost me a cease & desist.

Ripley: <laughing emoji>

"There was nothing funny about that," I mumble, hitting my profile picture. I find my followers list and click it. My stomach swirls as I type in Blakely's name.

Ripley: So, Carly? Yes or no on the number?

Blakely Evans follows you.

"That's my girl." I open her profile page, entirely too satisfied by this revelation. "*Holy fucking shit*. Why have I never looked at this before?"

Each picture provides a deeper insight into her world.

I sit on the edge of my bed and swipe through her posts. Blakely with Ella. A stack of books—romances, maybe. A cup of coffee. Blakely with Brock when they were younger, posted with a story about Christmas morning.

Ripley: Don't ignore me, asshole.

Me: I'm busy.

I type Tate's name in the search bar. Once I'm on his profile, I ignore the plethora of shirtless images and click on his followers.

Ripley: So that's a no to Carly?

I growl, going back to the texts.

Me: No to Carly.

Ripley: Good choice. <clapping emoji>

I pause.

Me: Was this some kind of test from Dad and Gannon?

Ripley: <laughing emoji>

"Fucker."

I open the app again, and this time, I type Blakely's name into Tate's followers.

No users found.

"Ha," I say, laughing as I drop my phone onto the bed. With more satisfaction than I should have, I head for the shower.

CHAPTER 5

Blakely

"Now *this* is self-care."

I lift my foot out of the water. Bubbles form a chain around my ankle, dripping lazily back into the tub. I close my eyes, resting my head against a bath pillow that doesn't slip no matter how much I move. And, after fiddling around with the buttons on the side, I discovered the glass opens onto a small balcony, essentially allowing you to bathe outside ... but not.

It's incredible.

Citrus and eucalyptus scents fill the room. I searched high and low for bubble bath but came up empty. My shampoo sufficed, and thanks to a candle by the bed, I created a mini in-room spa experience. *Close enough, anyway.*

Hot water caresses my body, causing the stress and tension I've been carrying to leach into the tub.

And, apparently, my emotions.

Tears prickle my eyes as I gaze through the windows and across the Strip. It's a beautiful view from a luxury suite that I'm enjoying while preparing for a night out with three of my closest friends. I'm so lucky, so grateful. *But still ...*

My chest burns from holding back an ugly cry just beneath the surface.

Birthdays are always hard.

Growing up, Mom would treat birthdays with the pageantry of a royal coronation. There would be balloons greeting you in the hallway when you woke up. A cupcake for breakfast. A rendition of "Happy Birthday" that was off-pitch and wonderful. There would be the warmest hugs and multicolored icing—enough sprinkles to drown a small child. And laughter—*so much laughter.*

I've been dreading this day for weeks. I dread Brock's too. With every year that passes, it's more time without Mom—the sound of her voice fading, the warmth of her hugs harder to remember. I'm that much closer to losing Brock, too.

Although I'd never admit it to him, or anyone, I secretly fear the day he gets married. I hate that I feel this way and feel so guilty about it. But he's my only family, and I'll be alone when he starts his own.

Unless I get my shit together and start one myself.

"I'm not alone right now," I whisper, pulling my fingers out of the water and watching droplets form and fall into the bath. "So go enjoy the night, live it up with my friends, and start Operation Get Your Shit Together tomorrow."

I sniffle before taking a deep breath and blowing it out slowly. *Breathe in new beginnings and exhale the old.*

"Hey, Blakely. I need your help," Ella says from the other side of the bathroom door.

I sink lower beneath the bubbles. "Come in."

She nearly trips on her armful of dresses and catches herself on the sink.

I giggle. "If you had packed less, you would have fewer choices to struggle with."

"Don't talk to me like that." She drops a load of colorful fabrics on the counter. "Negative energy isn't welcome here."

"I'm sorry."

She blows a lock of hair out of her face and sits on the edge of a footstool. "I'm glad you're as far behind as I am with getting ready."

"How long has it been?"

"Since I was up here, and we agreed to leave in an hour? Forty-five minutes."

37

"*Shit.*"

She laughs. "It's fine. I think Brock knew better and made the reservations for later to begin with. I don't know what I was thinking, giving us *an hour* to get ready. Did I forget who we are?"

I eye the dresses filling the basin. "So how many have you narrowed it down to?"

"Four."

I snort.

She pulls out an emerald-green garment. "I love this color, and this cut is great on me, but I'm not sure it's *birthday festive*. It might be more *holiday party*." She holds it against her body. "Thoughts? Opinions?"

"That's definitely Christmas with acquaintances."

"That's what I thought." She trades it for a canary-yellow option. "What about this one?"

I hum in thought. "That's more beach vacation, I think."

"Dammit. You're right." She picks up a black dress with a bit of sparkle. "I really like this one."

I run my hands through the water, ensuring the bubbles cover my bits. "Me too. And you are always hot in black. But what else did you bring?"

"This." She holds up a red number that I know from previous outings looks incredible on her. "I love this one too. But I feel super bloated today, and I'm not sure how it really looks. I tried them all on for Brock, but he was no help at all."

"I bet he was absolutely riveted about the dress options with you standing naked in front of him."

Ella shrugs. "You do make a valid point."

"Try on the black and the red ones for me. We'll see which one makes you feel the prettiest."

Relief washes across her face. "You're the greatest."

"I know."

We exchange a smile as she strips off Brock's T-shirt. *Modesty left this friendship months ago.*

"So," she says, grinning. "How was it with Renn?"

I smile, sinking even deeper into the water.

"Go. Put some distance between us. Now."

"Oh, it was fine," I say, hoping I can blame my blush on the water.

"*It was fine*, my ass. Things are never *fine* with the two of you unless that means on the verge of fornication."

I laugh. The movement causes a wave of bath water to roll into my open mouth, choking me.

Ella laughs harder. "See? God knew you were about to lie to me and stopped you."

My palm presses against my chest as if the motion will help expel the liquid from my lungs. I cough and sputter until all that's left is the taste of soap.

"How's this?" Ella does her best model walk across the travertine. "Black is slimming, and the lace peeking out at the tops of my boobs is super sexy, right?"

"You're hot. Try the red, though, to be sure."

She busies herself by swapping dresses.

My mind, however, floats to Renn.

"Remember something," he says, eyes sparkling. "You said no."

"No, I didn't. We said no."

He releases me slowly, smirking. "I didn't say shit."

Even if nothing can come of it, Renn's attention is fun. It boosts my confidence. It makes me feel like Ella looks in the black dress—*sexy*.

I usually avoid being so outright playful with men, lest they get the wrong idea. There aren't many men, maybe zero, that you can tease without them thinking you'll sleep with them later. The line between flirting and fucking muddies too easily. But with Renn, too many reasons exist for us not to blur those lines, and we both know it.

I think.

"What's that face about?" Ella asks, checking herself out in the mirror.

"Nothing. Just thinking."

"About ..."

"Why are you so nosy?" I laugh.

She whips around, hands on her hips. "Because I know the answer. I was just being polite and allowing you to bring him back up."

My laughter fades.

"May I just make one quick point?" she asks.

"You're going to anyway, so sure."

"And you will never tell Brock I said this?"

I look at her warily.

"I'm taking that as a yes," she says, perching on the stool again. "There's a difference between flings, feelings, and forever."

"Wow. Look at you getting deep."

She rolls her eyes. "I'm ignoring that."

"Great."

She doesn't ignore it.

"Look, I haven't seen you and Renn together in a while. But as soon as he walked toward us, it may as well have been the Fourth of July with the fireworks around the two of you."

I force a swallow, wanting to squirm. But if I do, the water will splash, drawing attention to my discomfort with this conversation. *That's the last thing I need.*

"I get why Brock doesn't want you with him, and you know, he might be right," she says.

"Oh, *he's right.*"

She leans forward, her boobs ready to fall out of the cups. "But, Blakely—*he might not be right either.*"

I still. *What's she up to?*

If there's one opinion I trust more than any other, it's Ella's. She's never used me for her own gain, asked me for anything, or given me bad advice. She has the best heart, means well, and would hop on a plane at the last minute to celebrate her friend's birthday without blinking an eye.

We've talked about Renn a thousand times, but she's never said anything quite like this.

"It's not just Brock who thinks I should avoid Renn. *It's me too,*" I say.

"*Uh-huh.*"

"I mean it, Ella. Before you came in here, I was thinking about how done I am with dating and how I'm going to find a nice guy with a nine-to-five who wants a puppy." *Or something like that.* "Renn *is not that guy.* He's the prototype of the same men I've been seeing—just maybe leveled up. *But that would only make him worse.* He would ... swallow my whole existence."

"Sounds like a good time to me."

"*Ella ...*"

She laughs. "Let me put it to you this way. Controlled explosions are better than ones that unravel in the heat of the moment. Trust me. I've been there."

I hold my breath, letting her continue.

"I adore your brother," she says, "but he has ulterior motives. He would be in the middle if you and Renn have a falling out. And that would affect him personally and professionally."

Exactly.

"On the other hand, I have no personal agenda here. I just want what's best for you. And as your friend, and as a bystander, and as a person who has eyeballs—"

I laugh.

"You and Renn are a ticking bomb. And I'm not saying you should get serious with him because I hear your objections and can't argue them. But it's okay just to have a good time with someone."

She folds her hands on her lap.

Glad that's over. "I think the red dress—"

"I haven't made my point yet."

"Well, get to the point then. I'm getting cold."

She reaches over and turns on the hot water. "There. Stop bitching."

I want to glare at her, but I can only laugh.

"If you're going to fall over the ledge, it's better to repel down it carefully with a rope and a pulley and those sticky shoes I saw on—"

"*Ella.*"

She sighs. "Right. Focus." She closes her eyes briefly. "It might be better to accept reality and defuse this thing before it goes off in your face. That's all I'm saying. I'll help you pick up the shrapnel, but I'll say *I told you so* the whole time as you recall what I'm guessing would be the best sexual experience of your life."

I don't know whether to laugh, roll my eyes, or allow that to make sense. Thankfully, she transitions out of it for me—like a real friend.

"Black or red?" She holds her arms out and twirls in a circle. "I know what I think. But I need your expert opinion."

"Black."

She smiles. "Right answer."

I reach up and turn off the tap, keeping one arm glued to my chest.

"What are you wearing tonight?" she asks, getting back into Brock's T-shirt.

I shrug. "I don't know. Want to pick something for me? I only brought two dresses, so don't be disappointed at the lack of options."

"That's okay. I brought backups you can use if you need them."

Of course, you did.

Ella disappears into the cavernous walk-in closet just off the bathroom. She shouts a few things, but none are clear enough to discern, so I ignore her. Instead, I grab a towel and climb out of the water.

Her words echo through my head. *"It's okay just to have a good time with someone."*

That sounds amazing.

"I want to do something big for my birthday. Something fun. Something wild that I'll remember forever."

I smile, pulling my towel tighter.

"This one," Ella says, holding up the silver dress and heels. "You don't even have to try it on. I know this will be fire on you, and it's perfect for your birthday."

The image of my silver heels dangling from Renn's fingers flashes through my mind. *"These are fucking hot."*

I grin, taking them from her. It's kismet. "This is it, then. Thank you."

She scoops up her dresses, blows me a kiss, and closes the door softly behind her.

"There is a difference between flings, feelings, and forever."

I set the heels down and finish drying myself.

Ella's words percolate through my brain. She's right—there is a difference between a good time, loving someone, and committing to another person forever. And if I'm going to start looking for a forever candidate, I better get all the good time out of my system while I can.

I drop my towel next to the sink and look at myself in the mirror. A flush of excitement pinks my cheeks and has the golds popping out in my irises.

"Could I just have a good time with Renn as a one-time thing? Something *explosive,* and then ... we're done? Everything would be fine?"

I stare at my reflection in the foggy glass.

"Stop overthinking this and get dressed," I say, heading into the closet for my lingerie. "I have a birthday to celebrate."

CHAPTER 6

Renn

I adjust my collar in the mirror.

"Did they send black or charcoal?" Astrid, my personal assistant, asks. "I put an emphasis on black, but the salesgirl was distracted the entire phone call. I have a note to call the manager on Monday morning."

"Over clothes?"

"Technically, over customer service. Wouldn't you want someone to tell you if I treated them like crap?"

I step back and check out my handiwork. *Not bad.* "Maybe."

"Maybe?"

"Yeah, *maybe.* I hope they'd consider that you might just be having a bad day."

I hear Brock yell at Blakely to see if she's ready, and then her faint giggle in reply. The sound is bright and happy. Just like her. *Dammit.*

"I mean, we all get distracted sometimes," I say, sighing.

Astrid rambles on about what good customer service means and its importance to business. *I get it.* I like good service as much as anyone. But sometimes Astrid gets too *by the book,* and I have to remind her that real human beings are involved.

She doesn't have this problem with my younger sister, Bianca.

Bianca and I mostly share a personal assistant because I feel pretentious for having one and don't give her enough to do. She worked for me virtually while I was overseas, but now helps me in person. Is it nice having someone available to coordinate the landscape crew, return calls I don't want to deal with ... and send dinner clothes to me when I jump on a plane from Miami to Vegas for a birthday weekend? Absolutely. Is it necessary? Nope.

On the other hand, my sister is much better at doling out tasks. She has no qualms about having Astrid take over her personal life while she sits at Dad's right hand and helps run the family businesses. And I get it —Bianca is probably busier than I am. Smarter than I am. More successful than I am. But I still think she could do some shit herself.

"Did she even send a black outfit?" Astrid asks.

I step away from the mirror and find my cologne. "Yes. Even my underwear is black."

"That's more info than I need."

I chuckle. "How much did you tip the salesgirl?"

"Enough."

"*Astrid* ..." I say, teasing her.

"For fuck's sake, Renn."

She laughs. "Don't forget that you have a charity game at the end of the month. You got a packet in the mail today about it, reminding you to share it on your social media and giving you the details about the charities it supports. I added it to your calendar since you verbally agreed and didn't give me details."

"Hey, look on the bright side. I told you about it, at least."

"That would be a bright side if you had. Except you didn't."

Fuck. I put her on speakerphone and apply a few squirts of cologne. "I'm sorry. Gabe Henderson called me a few months ago and said he was trying to start this foundation and *blah, blah, blah.* What was I supposed to do?"

"You say yes. *And then you tell me about it.*"

"Want me to send you a selfie to make you feel better? That always seems to help irritated females."

"Sure. I'll use it as a dartboard."

"That's mean."

She only laughs.

I dig around the bags from the boutique Astrid sent the clothes from and find my belt.

Her mention of the charity game reminds me that I need to call Gannon and get him to cut a check from Brewer Group as a donation. *Since he's so worried about my image and all—he can put his money where his mouth is.*

"Okay," she says. "I'll let you get back to your night. Any plans?"

"Oh, that wasn't begging, Ren. I can be a lot more persuasive than that."

That line has gone through my head a hundred times already.

If Blakely were anyone else, I'd have her bent over the bed by now. Then again, if she were anyone else, I wouldn't be this messed up about it.

I weighed the risk versus reward for about five seconds earlier. Is there any way I could get away with fucking Blakely and not have Brock rip my throat out? The answer was a resounding *no*. But even when I pretended there was a chance, something was wrong with that picture.

The thought of having Blakely in my bed makes me lose my mind. *Naked. Spread open. Moaning my name as she comes on my cock.* But the idea of seeing what I've seen in other women's eyes when they have to leave makes me ill.

Blakely's not like that. She's a treasure, and for the first time in my life, I don't know if I could actually fuck a woman and not give a shit afterward.

What the hell is wrong with me? When did I grow a conscience?

"Renn? Plans?" Astrid asks again.

"Nope," I say, trying not to imagine Blakely's ass going up the stairs. "Just having dinner with Brock and his sister for her birthday. Keeping it low-key."

"Sounds good. It's just so sad that they lost their mom so young. She was only in her early forties, right?"

I tighten the belt. "Yeah. Something like that."

"Okay. Well, have fun tonight but, for the love of God, *behave*, Renn."

"You're starting to sound like Dad."

"The last time you were in Vegas, you wound up in the emergency room with head trauma, a prostitute refusing to vacate your hotel room, and a public relations nightmare that nearly gave your father a heart attack."

I roll my eyes. "I'm so misunderstood."

"*Right.*"

"That was three years ago. The head trauma was because I got hit over the back of the head in a brawl that had nothing to do with me, in a room that wasn't mine—I was only paying for it—over a prostitute that had nothing to do with me at all." I blow out a breath. "I have a suite here, you know. I'm not as exposed to the elements."

"A suite and a pretty brunette. Am I right?"

I grin.

"That's what I thought," she says, sighing. "If you do something stupid, I quit. I'll give all my energy to Bianca."

I snort. "You wouldn't do that."

"Try me."

I pull open my door. Brock stands beside the table, taking in the view. He glances over his shoulder, sees I'm on the phone, and turns away.

"Is that all you need?" I ask. "I gotta get going."

"Yes. That's it. I'll see you on Monday."

"Hey! Call that poor salesgirl back and double her tip."

She groans.

"Thank you. *Bye, Astrid,*" I say, taunting her.

"Goodbye."

She ends the call with a *click.*

Brock slips a hand in his pocket and looks at me. "Everything all right?"

"Yeah. All good. Astrid just updating me on some shit. I forgot to tell her about Henderson's charity game. So she was super peachy."

"Shit. I forgot about that too."

"You probably have a packet of info waiting on you."

Brock plants his hands on the table and rolls his neck around his shoulders. "Thank you for coming with me, by the way. I don't know if I've said that. You're a good friend."

Guilt riddles me. *No, I'm not. I've imagined turning your sister inside out on my cock for the last three hours. I'm not a good friend.*

"Thanks," I say instead—mostly because I like my face. "I'm going to grab my wallet, and I'll be ready. Have you seen the girls?"

"They should be about done. I'll go check on Ella and hurry her ass along."

Shall I go check on your sister's ass? "Great."

He gives me a sideways look as he leaves.

"I gotta get it together," I mutter, entering my room and closing the door.

I lean against the wall and blow out a long, harried breath.

My heart feels like I'm gearing up for a game. Every cell in my body is on high alert, waiting on ... *nothing*. Nothing is going to happen.

I should've jacked off in the shower. It would've at least taken the edge off things.

Maybe.

My phone buzzes, offering me a reprieve from my thoughts.

> Bianca: If I tell you something and it turns out to be true—and it's illegal—am I considered an accomplice?

> Me: Did you do it?

> Bianca. NO. Not me.

I sit on the edge of the bed.

> Me: Out of all your siblings, you chose the brother playing rugby for legal advice?

> Bianca: No offense, but out of all our siblings, you have the most experience dealing with legal issues.

> Me: Touché. Continue.

> Bianca: Maybe I should call you so it's not written down. Paper trails are a real thing.

> Me: Why? You think I'm going to rat you out?

> Bianca: I'm calling you.

"Thanks for the warning." As promised, the phone buzzes in my hands. "If you didn't know, I promised your father I would be on my best behavior until his purchase goes through. I don't think he'd appreciate you dragging me into the dark side."

"*My* father?"

I shrug. "He likes you best. *And me least.* Anyway, I knew you had illicit behavior in you. I could tell. It's in your eyes. Real recognizes real."

"Renn? Shut up."

"Fine."

She sighs. "I think my new neighbor might be holding someone hostage."

"*What*? Why?"

"I was sitting on my patio, enjoying my tea and doing some paperwork, and all of a sudden, this muted ... *banging* was coming from that direction."

"Maybe he's doing construction."

"Have you seen him? He's not construction-y, and there are no work trucks or anything here."

Huh.

I've seen her new neighbor a couple of times. He seems like a decent guy. We briefly chatted about running and the best place to get burgers.

He didn't seem weird or hostage-holding-y. *But what do I know? People have surprised me before.*

"I think it began last week. Not just banging, but thumps too. And I swear to God I heard screaming the other night," she says. "It's freaking me out."

"Damn. How thin are your walls?"

"I had the window open, Perry Mason."

I laugh. "Look, do you think you might be jumping to conclusions?"

"No, and here's why—*he's hot.*"

The line stills. I wait for her to expound on that brilliant observation, but she doesn't follow her statement with anything more.

"Did he nab you too? It's awfully quiet over there," I say.

"*You are not funny.*"

"*Bianca.* Your reasoning for thinking your neighbor is holding someone hostage is that he's hot. Have you listened to that out loud?"

"He's *extremely* good looking, Renn. *Beautiful.* And attractive people always get away with stuff because no one suspects the gorgeous doctor in the gated community of wrongdoing."

"Call the police then."

"And say what?"

"That your beautiful neighbor is thumping on his walls, I guess. I don't know. Come to think of it, how do you know he's not just fucking his girlfriend?"

The line goes quiet again.

I sigh. "When I get home, I'll come over and do some reconnaissance, if that will make you feel better."

"Not if you're just going to make fun of me."

"I'm not."

"I hear it in your voice, Renn."

"So what do you want me to do? If you seriously think something is weird over there, call the police. I suppose that's the responsible response."

She groans. "Now I don't know. What if you're right?"

"It won't be the first time."

"I won't dignify that with an answer." She takes a deep breath. "Forget it. Calling you was a mistake. I'll call Tate."

My laughter is loud and immediate. "Why? So he can come over and shout mean things over the fence at him?"

She tries not to laugh but fails.

"Set your security system," I say. "And if you hear anything else, call the police. Or Ripley, at the very least."

"Okay. But I can't be held responsible for anything right?"

"No, Bianca, you can't." I roll my eyes. "Anything else? I have reservations."

"Reservations? Where are you?"

"Vegas. It's Blakely Evans's birthday, and I came with Brock for the weekend. I'll be home on Sunday."

She pauses. "So what are your plans while you're there?"

I twist my lips, knowing exactly what she's asking—without asking.

"Oh, not much," I say. "Strip club. Shots. Might get married tonight. That sort of thing."

"Renn Patrick Brewer, don't you even joke about such a thing. You'll lose your contract if you so much as breathe the wrong way, and Dad has hundreds of millions of dollars tied up in this Arrows purchase—"

"I'm aware. *Damn*. Don't any of you have any faith in me?"

"Is that rhetorical?"

"Call someone else the next time you think you're living next to an apex predator."

"I will." She takes a breath and blows it out. "Enjoy your night. *Safely*."

"And *safely* enjoy yours."

"Love you, Renn."

"I love you, Bianca. Goodbye."

"Bye."

Before I put the phone in my pocket, I enter a quick text just to piss her off.

> Me: I can't believe you're helping your neighbor hide bodies! That's wrong!

Sure enough, it buzzes in quick succession as I shove it in my pocket and walk out of the room.

No one is visible, and the suite is quiet. I start to check the kitchen. But just as I pass the staircase, movement catches my attention.

And then it steals the breath right out of my lungs.

Ho-ly. Fucking. Hell.

Blakely stands at the top of the stairs looking like a gift waiting to be unwrapped.

Her dress fits her like a glove that shimmers as she moves. A deep, plunging neckline showcases her breasts. The hem stops just low enough to keep it classy, capping off her toned, tanned legs that look a mile long thanks to those silver heels I found earlier.

Fuck. Me.

"Does this look okay?" she asks, running her hands down her stomach.

"I don't know. Why don't you come closer so I can get a better look?"

She takes her time descending the staircase, taking my hand as she reaches the bottom. It takes every ounce of power I have not to kiss the hell out of her.

My body buzzes as we make contact, skin to skin.

Big hoop earrings. Lipstick the same color as her cheeks when she blushes. She's gathered her hair loosely at the nape of her neck, letting strands hang around her face.

I'm not mature enough for this.

"You are *absolutely beautiful*," I say, holding her hand and encouraging her to twirl. "My God, Blakely. How do you expect me not to get punched tonight?"

She giggles, her eyes twinkling. "I'll take that as a compliment."

"That's how I meant it."

"Then thank you."

We exchange a smile that makes my stomach tighten.

"Are you guys ready?" Brock yells.

Fuck you, Brock.

I pull Blakely closer, spreading my fingers against the dip in her lower back. "Want to ditch them and go out by ourselves tonight?"

"That's funny. I thought you'd want to ditch them and *stay in* by ourselves tonight."

"Say the word." I lean closer. "*Say the fucking word.*"

Thoughts of unwrapping her out of that dress roll through my mind.

She winks, stepping away. As she moves, she brushes her hand against my crotch. "We're ready, Brock," she calls sweetly.

I growl as she walks away.

This will be the longest, *hardest* night of my life.

CHAPTER 7

Blakely

"Would you like anything else?" Gerald asks, glancing around the table.

Renn sits back, rolling up his sleeves. The motion draws attention to his thick, muscled forearms and the tattoos etched into his skin. His smile hints at debauchery.

"Need anything, Blakely?" he asks.

His question is an innuendo, one I think managed to slip by Brock and Ella. But it didn't miss its mark ... *me*.

Renn has made me feel like the center of the universe this evening— giving me all his attention, prioritizing our conversations, and not missing a moment to tell me that I look beautiful.

I sweep the lingering notes of overpriced tequila and toasted almonds from my lips. "I'll have another one of these."

He lifts a brow. "*Really*? You've had two."

"I'm glad you can count."

Renn smirks and turns to Gerald. "She'll have another one of those, and I'll have another scotch and soda."

"Yes, sir. What about your companions?"

Renn takes in Brock and Ella's canoodling and shakes his head. "I think they're good."

"I'll return shortly. Thank you."

The restaurant pulses around us, the air filled with laughter, music, and excitement. Vaulted ceilings and deep wood tones blend with twinkling lights and walls of flowers to create an illusion of being indoors and outdoors at the same time. It's *comfortable luxury*—and I'm here for it.

My skin tingles from the tequila. *It better tingle.* I tried to order a cheaper brand, but Renn insisted I try the most expensive version on the menu. It should've come with its own bartender for what he will pay for it.

"It's still fairly early—for Vegas, anyway," Renn says, glancing at his watch. "What else do you want to do tonight?"

I trail my fingertip around the edge of my glass. "Well, Ella and I did have plans."

"Yeah, about that," Brock says, returning to our conversation. He looks at his girlfriend, then at me. "What *were* you two planning?"

"You wanna tell him, El?" I ask, teasing her. "You said you wanted him to know."

Her face flushes. "I was mad at him then."

Brock's jaw sets. "What's that supposed to mean?"

"I have a feeling you might be revisiting that emotion soon, El," Renn says, then downs the rest of his drink.

"What was it, Ella?" Brock asks, unamused. "Let me know what you planned on doing when you were mad at me."

"You know what? I don't care. *You* went to Miami and did who knows what *with Renn*," Ella says, sitting taller.

Renn gasps. "I'm offended."

"Shut up." Ella gathers herself, setting her attention squarely on my brother. "We had plans to see a bunch of ripped, oily men take their clothes off." She leans closer. "*And I was really looking forward to it.*"

Renn bursts out laughing.

"*Me too,*" I say, taking my drink from Gerald. "Thank you, buddy."

Gerald tries not to laugh. "You're very welcome." He places Renn's drink in front of him. "There you go, sir."

"I won't make this awkward and call you buddy," Renn says, getting a full-bellied laugh from our server. "But thank you. Also, please bring the check to me."

"Of course."

Ella takes a small sip of her drink, looking expectantly at Brock. "If you have something to say, *say it*."

Renn and I hold our drinks and air toast, settling in for the show.

Ella and Brock banter back and forth, their voices sharp yet hushed. It's impossible on a good day to follow along when they're like this. But I don't bother trying after the two tequila drinks I've already consumed —two more than usual. Instead, I swirl my beverage around the glass and watch Renn across the table. *Damn, he's gorgeous.* His black shirt makes his hair appear darker and his eyes more mysterious. *His lips more kissable.*

My heartbeat quickens. A welcome warmth spreads like a full-body blush, eventually pooling the heat between my legs. My shoulders fall, giving up any tension still in them, and I sigh happily. *Maybe I should drink tequila more often.*

Renn sets his glass on the table, his brows pulling together. "You good, Blakely?"

"Yeah. *I'm great.*" I smile from ear to ear. "Nice and relaxed."

We exchange a grin that amplifies the fire in my veins.

"Are you two about ready to head back to the room?" Brock asks, intruding into our moment.

I snort. "I'm not leaving this drink. There's one hundred fifty dollars' worth of alcohol in here. Besides, tonight is supposed to be fun. Remember?"

"Well, your brother put an end to that," Ella says, giggling as Brock grabs her thigh. "Or maybe not."

"You want a show? Let's buy a bottle of oil on the way to the room," Brock tells her. "I'll give you a fucking show."

Ella grins back at him. "Don't threaten me with a good time."

"*What's that gonna do for me?*" I ask, quickly lowering my voice. "It's always *Ella, Ella, Ella.* It's *my* freaking birthday."

Renn smirks. "We'll buy a bottle of oil too. Don't worry."

Count. Me. In.

"The hell you will," Brock says before downing the rest of his drink and setting it down with a thud. "All three of you are giving me a fucking headache."

56

I sigh dramatically. "*Again*, you weren't invited to this party. You're free to leave, and Ella and I can pursue our objective of making this a night to remember."

Renn chuckles, sharing in my amusement. "How about this? Brock, why don't you and Ella go back to the suite. Make up so we can have a fun day tomorrow." He turns his attention on me. "And I'll stay with Blakely. We'll finish our drinks and maybe get some ice cream since we promised her that—"

"That's not due until tomorrow," I say, trying to point at him, but my finger hangs unsteadily in the air. "My birthday is tomorrow. Tonight is my birthday prelationship."

Ella groans, holding her forehead.

"Your *what*?" Renn asks.

"My birthday prelationship. It's the stage ..." My brain is too cloudy to make it make sense—even though I'm sure it does. "It's the lead-up to my birthday where expectations are met. Or not. Or ... something."

I cock my head to the side and try to think that through. *I swear it makes sense.*

Brock looks at me warily. "Why don't you go back with us?"

"Because *I'm* finishing this drink," I say. *Because I don't want to give up this night because you want to go fuck my best friend.*

"Are you sure you'll be okay with Renn?" he asks.

Renn's leg moves beneath the table and brushes against mine. I shift in my seat, pressing my palms against my thighs in an attempt to quell the heaviness building in them.

"I think I can handle it," I say smugly.

"I'll take care of her." Renn's eyes are trained on me. "I promise I'll get her back in one piece."

"See, Brock? We all get what we want this way. Stop being a spoil-sport and get out of here."

Ella slides her hand onto Brock's lap—and that does it. She looks at me and winks.

"I'll get the bill tomorrow night," Brock says, helping Ella out of her chair. They start to leave, but he pauses and turns back to the table. "Don't make me regret this."

"*Oh, come on,*" I say. "Stop it. What do you think we're going to do? Go streaking down the Strip?"

"Hey, I actually haven't done that before," Renn says, impressed. "We could give it a go."

I laugh. "*No,* because *you* signed a *good boy clause,* remember?"

His eyes sparkle. My stomach tightens in a worthless attempt at rebuffing the trouble dancing in them.

Brock lifts a brow, lets it linger on both of us for a long moment as if to seal his point, and then follows Ella through the restaurant.

As soon as he's gone, Renn and I laugh.

"I love him," I say before taking a quick sip of Gerald's concoction. "I really do. But I think I will always be a seventeen-year-old little girl to him."

"That's how old you were when your mother passed, right?"

"Yeah." I set my glass down and release a breath. A heaviness settles on my chest at the reminder. *I need a distraction.* "Tell me about your family. I've gathered the basics over the years, but you never *really* say anything about them. Just superficial, searchable stuff."

"Do you ever look them up?"

I half laugh, half snort. "Um, no. Not taking anything away from you all, but it's never occurred to me to look them up. Should I? I mean, besides Tate, of course."

He lifts a brow. "I'm not talking about Tate again."

"I checked out his Social," I say in a sing-song voice. "He's very ... *shirtless.*"

Renn crosses his arms over his chest. "But you don't follow him."

"How do you know?"

"Because I checked."

What? I laugh, not sure whether to believe him or not. "*No, you did not.*"

"Yes, *I did.* And you know what else?"

I hum, enjoying the playful look on his face.

"*You* follow *me,*" he says, almost beaming.

I try to hide my amusement by taking another drink, but the bottom of the glass appears. *Damn, this stuff goes down too easily.*

Gerald returns and hands Renn a bill. He scribbles something on the paper and thanks Gerald for his help. I don't know what Renn wrote, but Gerald's eyes widen.

"Thank you, Mr. Brewer," Gerald says. "I ... I don't know what to say."

"You don't have to say anything. Thank you for taking care of us this evening."

"Of course, sir. It was my pleasure."

Renn smiles as Gerald walks away with a pep in his step. Once he's out of earshot, Renn holds out a hand.

"Let's get out of here," he says.

I lay my palm in his. The warmth of his hand and the roughness of his scars from rugby send a myriad of sensations through me.

My legs are a little wobbly as we make our way to the exit. He never lets go of my hand, never eases his grip. *And I like it way more than I should.* I expect him to release me once we're out of the restaurant, but he doesn't.

We wander down the long corridors of shops inside the hotel. Name brands I recognize but have never owned hang with authority over large, intricate doors. Storefronts highlight shoes, jewelry, and handbags—anything you want or need can be obtained without leaving the hotel.

"I wouldn't *really* want to live here," I say, relishing how my body and mind are calm. *At the same time.* "But you could. And think about *this*—if you used the walkways over the streets and were really careful, you could manage to live without ever stepping foot on the actual Earth again. Ever. Isn't that nuts?"

Renn chuckles. "I've never thought about that."

"It's the beauty of tequila. It opens your mind."

"That's not all it opens, from what I hear."

I laugh, resting my head against his arm. "I've heard that too, so I don't drink it too often. I'm usually a vodka girl."

"Why tequila tonight, then?"

"Because I'm letting loose. One last hurrah before I buckle down and focus on my life."

"What do you mean?"

He looks down at me, curious.

I shouldn't answer him—I should transition the conversation to something else. Something lighter. *Something less personal.* But maybe it's the tequila talking or the tender curiosity in his big brown eyes, but instead of twisting our discussion elsewhere, I continue.

"I have a great life—don't get me wrong," I say as we stroll through the mostly empty corridors. "I have a great brother, an amazing best friend, and I just got a fancy new job promotion that I'm excited about. But I want ... more for myself, Renn. I know that sounds really unappreciative—"

"No, it doesn't. You're allowed to want and go after whatever your heart desires. You *should* do that." He pauses. "People get stuck in the everyday shit and forget they have choices. That or they think they don't deserve more than they already have."

My head rests against his arm again. "I'm not sure it's either of those things for me."

"Then what is it?"

We walk in silence for a while. Renn doesn't pressure me to talk or dismiss the conversation by bringing up something else. He just holds my hand, softly stroking the back with his thumb.

My body buzzes, basking in the effects of the drinks—and of Renn's sweet touch. I think I'm making more out of it than I should, and he's holding on to me so I don't fall. I should pull away from him. *But I don't want to.*

"I'm kind of afraid, Renn."

He flinches, squeezing my hand. "Of what?"

"Of so many things." *Of so many things I haven't told anyone. They're the sort of admissions—confessions—you tell your mom. God, I miss her.*

We round a corner toward a large fountain. I consider leaving our conversation there, hanging in ambiguity. But it's so nice getting this off my chest, and with Renn at my side ...

"I've spent the past thirteen years *surviving,*" I say. "I survived Mom's cancer, then I made it through having Brock as my guardian for a year and a half. I got through college somehow. I barely left Edward unscathed."

Renn glances at me across his shoulder.

"You know, I look back on that now and can't believe that didn't ruin me," I say. "I was so emotionally vulnerable when we got together. I didn't recognize myself in that relationship. I was stuck and shamed, and ... my existence served to support him and his dreams. And then the breakup that was supposed to make things better. But then it was the accusations, the headlines—the paparazzi used to camp outside my work. I kept waiting for Mason Music to fire me." My heart sinks. "That was really, really hard. No one should have to go through that."

He squeezes my hand again. "No, they shouldn't. And he should never have put you in that position."

"Well, considering he did it on purpose ..." I shake my head. "It's left me with wounds that haven't healed."

"Like what?"

"Like being made a joke of in public. Like having a fear that when I love someone, they'll leave." I pause, gathering my courage to say this aloud. "I think the biggest one, though, is that I'll wind up alone. That no matter what I do, everyone will move on with their lives, as they do, and I'll be left in the dust."

"That won't happen, Blakely."

I smile sadly. "I know—or, I hope so, anyway. But, at this point, I'm fairly certain I sabotage myself out of a fear that it won't work out anyway." I look up at him and laugh softly. "I mean, have you seen the guys I've dated? It would be bad even if you left out Edward and just looked at the ones that followed."

He chuckles. "You do pick winners."

"That I do." I swing our hands between us. "I have to stop doing that. I have to do better for myself. No more dating men who take me for granted. No more one-sided relationships. No more picking out guys who have the potential to ruin me—emotionally or publicly."

"Sounds like a great plan to me."

"Me too." I breathe, feeling lighter than I have in a long time.

A weight has lifted from my shoulders. I'm immediately freer from my admission—one I didn't realize just how badly I needed to make until now. *One I never thought I'd make to Renn, of all people.*

"And *that*, Mr. Brewer, is why tonight was a tequila night. It's a proper goodbye to my twenties."

Renn looks at me and smirks. "And that was being accomplished with tequila and a male strip show?"

"Yup. Ella said it would get my juices flowing." I cringe, giggling. "That sounds just as bad now as it did when she said it."

He laughs.

"I just wanted a good, fun memory so when I look back on this decade, I don't automatically go to the other stuff, you know? Instead of camping in my house for a week to avoid having my photo taken, I could remember tonight."

"Makes sense." He comes to a stop and drops my hand. His brows pinch together. "Can you give me a few minutes? I need to take care of something."

"Sure."

I watch him remove his phone from his pocket. His thumbs fly over the keys.

Renn bites his lip while he takes care of whatever is happening on the other end of the line. I just stand and stare. *He's so stupidly handsome.* His forearms flex as he types, his Adam's apple bobbing as he swallows. A grin slides across his lips.

It sends a shiver down my spine.

He looks up with a glimmer in his eye. "Ready?"

"For what?"

"I have a little surprise for the birthday girl."

His lopsided smile makes me grin.

"What kind of a surprise?" I ask.

"You'll see."

He takes my hand again and leads me outside.

CHAPTER 8

Renn

What the fuck am I doing here?

A bolt of lightning flashes over the stage. Screams fill the venue moments before loud, pulsing music replaces them. The auditorium goes dark and every person in attendance loses their mind ... except me.

Blakely leans against the balcony rail with her back to the five men marching across the stage in trench coats and snaps a selfie.

"You look like you could use a drink," a muscled, shiny man says from behind me. "What can I get you? It's on the house."

I pull the only hat we could find—the one that says *Soduku Champ* on it—as low as I can. "I'll have the biggest, strongest drink you can give me."

"One for me too." Blakely sits beside me, the strobing lights making her dress sparkle. Amusement fills her eyes.

I take a hundred-dollar bill from my wallet and hand it to my slick savior. "And please—hurry."

He laughs and disappears. *I hope that wasn't a scam.*

"I can't believe you brought me here," Blakely says, beaming. Her face is flushed from the mini bottle of tequila we downed from the gift shop when we stopped to get my hat.

"Well, *I* can't believe out of all the things you wanted for your birthday, you wanted this."

She makes no secret out of glancing down at my cock. "Yeah, well, sometimes you can't have what you really want."

Fuck. Me.

We take our drinks, Blakely's splashing on my pants as she tries to turn, cheer, and laugh at the same time.

I sit back in my seat and watch her get into the performance.

I'm going to have a lot of questions to answer with Astrid in the morning.

The seats my assistant was able to score were ridiculously priced but on a private balcony. *"At least you can drink for free while you watch men gyrate on stage," she said. "Please try not to get photographed—for all of our sakes."*

Blakely dances to the music, her round ass shaking back and forth just inches from my knee. Sweat dots her skin. Her hair clings to the back of her neck as she moves.

I spread my legs apart and grip my cock. It's so hard it hurts. It aches. It fucking throbs.

I don't know what I was thinking bringing her here, other than I wanted her to have a memory of the two of us tonight. *Of me, tonight.* One fun, unforgettable experience that when she looks back on her thirtieth birthday weekend, she can't help but think of me.

The dancers open their trench coats to piercing screams as I feel a buzzing in my pocket. I've never been more thankful to have a text in my life.

Dad: I had dinner tonight with Bobby Downing. Remember him? He helped us close the deal when we bought the hockey team, so I brought him on board with this Arrows mess. Hoping he can force the purchase through.

Me: Great.

Dad: He's interested in getting in on the rugby expansion. Thinking about trying to get the pieces together for a team in Cincinnati. Wondered if you were interested in talking about it with him.

Me: I can't own a team and play. Against league ethics. You know that.

Dad: You won't play forever.

I study the words on the screen ... and the ones he meant without typing them.

You won't play forever. You'll probably blow your contract like the fuckup you are, and then what will you do with your life?

Dad's lack of faith in me is never surprising. He's there for every photo opportunity, willing to give statements when pressed by the media. He was too happy to sign the consent form to be videoed for a documentary about my life for an Australian news agency. But behind the scenes, the veneer wears thin fast. Ever the businessman, rarely a dad. *For me, anyway.*

It's always been this way.

He questioned my love for rugby as a child. He second-guessed my ability to play at the collegiate level, despite being scouted by every top school in the country. He insisted that I have a backup plan and was livid when I chose to go pro.

When I signed with my first international contract? It sent a fracture through our family. Dad and Gannon on one side. Mom, Ripley, and me on the other. Tate and Bianca stayed out of it. Our brother Jason tried to mediate, thinking his ability to land airplanes for a living would translate into landing a resolution to our family conflict.

It did not.

Just like Dad's attempt at subtlety doesn't translate tonight.

Rain pours onto the stage, dousing the first few rows with water. The performers stomp and splash, fucking chairs and grinding against poles.

> Me: I'm not retiring for years.

> Dad: You need to be pragmatic.

Blakely leans against the rail again, her dress sliding up the backs of her thighs. I reach up and hook a finger under the fabric, and tug.

My fingers rub along the smooth skin just beneath her ass. Her head whips to mine. A slow, seductive smile slides across her lips as I trail my fingers down her legs.

The contact is dangerous. I'm toeing a line we've worked hard to maintain over the years. *I know it. And she knows it.*

She lifts her drink to her mouth and downs the rest of it. Her lips around the rim of the glass. Her neck bare, exposed. Her eyes looking at me, begging me to touch her again.

There's nowhere to go. No one to interrupt. No one to remind us that *this* isn't supposed to happen.

I glance down.

> Dad: Can we jump on a call right now?

No, we cannot. I turn off my phone.

Blakely grips the rail behind her with both hands. A voice booms through the venue, asking women about their fantasies. The rain shuts off, and a song plays that repeats the question.

Men begin to descend from the ceiling, and others march onto the stage as firemen and construction crews. Blakely doesn't notice.

"So," I ask, smirking. "What's your fantasy?"

I think she's going to laugh or turn around to the show. Instead, she puts one hand on each of my armrests and leans forward.

The front of her dress hangs, giving me a full view of her chest. Her mouth is inches away from mine.

I hold my breath, keeping my hands glued to the chair. "Yeah."

She grins. "Yeah, what?"

"I'm looking at my fantasy too."

She giggles, swaying on her heels.

"If I touch you right now, we'll both be in trouble," I say.

"Yeah, but a little trouble never hurt anyone."

I growl, making her smile.

"Since you won't touch me ..." She cups my cheeks in her hands and lowers her mouth to mine. "I guess I'll have to touch you."

I lean toward her, to cut the small distance between us. *Holy fuck.* But before our lips meet, a hand lightly touches my shoulder.

"Can I get you another drink?"

Blakely laughs, pulling away. "*Oh my God.*"

My teeth grind together as I try to breathe while not exploding on the server.

"We're good," Blakely says, resting her hand on my knee. "But thank you."

"Not helping," I mutter.

She laughs again, watching our intruder leave. "You know something?"

"I know a lot of damn things."

"I was only kidding about coming here."

"Now you tell me," I say, shifting in my seat, desperate to find some sort of relief.

Everything on me, around me, and inside me is too much. Too loud. Too pressurized. Too sweet, too intense ... *too beautiful.*

"Wanna go somewhere else?" she asks.

"Thought you'd never ask."

She fixes the top of her dress. "I don't want to go back to the suite yet. I'm having fun with you."

This time, I think it's my heart that does something funny.

"We've already been drinking," she says. "We might as well finish off the night right. Go all-in."

I get to my feet. "Who am I to turn down the birthday girl?"

She takes my hand and leads me to the exit.

CHAPTER 9

Blakely

"*top*," I mumble into the pillow.

Instead of stopping, the phone begins ringing again. The sound pierces the air ... and my skull.

My eyes are too heavy to open. A massive headache splits my head as I attempt to wake up—a headache so intense and painful that a shot of puke comes up my throat.

My mouth tastes awful. The air leaving my lungs is hot, and I smell ... *tequila?*

The ringing starts all over again.

I pull the pillow over my ears, desperate for the sound to stop.

It takes more effort than I've ever used to open my eyes, but somehow I pry the lids apart. I peek into the dark, cool room. *What a relief. It must still be night. I'll just go back to sleep.*

My weight shifts as I curl one leg toward me. A warm, sticky liquid pools around my ass. In the haze of the migraine, and tequila, apparently, I try to make sense of the situation.

The phone begins to chirp. And again. And again. And again. Then it starts to ring. *Again.*

But this time, the pillow helps.

I'll deal with all of this in the morning. It's probably just some fuck-

head from work thinking it's cute to tell me happy birthday before anyone else.

I drift off into a sweet, comfortable slumber. But I can't be asleep for more than a minute when the door flies open and slams into the wall. I jump, my heart going too quickly from *sleep mode* to *speed mode*, and I gag.

I'm never drinking tequila again.

"Get up!" Brock's voice booms through the room. "Now!"

Lights turn on. Despite my closed eyes, they're still too bright. The curtains are yanked apart, and the button is pushed that opens the space to the atrium. Bright sunlight floods the bedroom.

"Stop yelling," I mumble, rolling over. "Turn the lights off."

"Um, Blakely? You probably need to get up right now, friend." Ella's voice is soft and at head level.

I squint open one eye and see her pretty face. "No. I'm good." I close it again.

"Blake ..." Ella takes my hand and pats it with hers. "Come on. You need to wake up."

I whine, straightening my legs. The warm stickiness sloshes around me. *Fuck. What is that?*

The phone starts ringing *again*. This time, it's followed by another one.

"Oh my gosh," I say, wincing with pain. "Turn that thing off."

"They're going to keep ringing until you two wake the fuck up and deal with this," Brock says, his voice ten decibels too loud.

I groan, reaching behind me and pushing Ella away. My hand touches her. *Wait.*

I still. The fog begins to roll away, and reality starts to float in.

Ella is right in front of me. I squint again. This time, I see the knowing concern on her face. *And Ella doesn't have a dick.*

Slowly, I withdraw my hand from what has to be a morning hard-on. Even more carefully, I open both eyes.

Ella stands. Her hair is a mess and she's in Brock's T-shirt.

My brother stands in a pair of boxers by the foot of the bed, looking like he's ready to rip someone apart limb by limb.

So if they're there, then ...

Oh no.

I struggle to sit up. Ella loops an arm under my shoulder and helps me upright. The room ripples like we're on a boat, but I distinctly remember we're in Vegas.

With Renn.

My gaze drops to the bed beside me.

What. The. Actual. Hell. Happened. Here?

Renn lies beside me, completely oblivious to the situation unfolding.

"B—" Brock starts.

I hold up one finger. "I need a minute. Please."

Ella whispers something to my brother. I, on the other hand, try to piece together what happened.

A bandage covers the skin above Renn's left nipple. My shirt is draped over the lamp on Renn's side of the bed. Clothes are strewn everywhere.

A trucker hat with *Sudoku Champ* written on the front sits on top of a giant stuffed llama smoking a cigar in the corner.

The chair by the bathroom door is turned on its side. But what's most curious, and concerning, is what appears to be the imprint of two palms and two breasts against the window. *In chocolate.*

My stomach sloshes, the contents burning my insides. *I'm going to throw up.*

I nudge Renn as the phones begin again. "Hey." I shove him again —this time, with both hands.

He moves, groaning like he's in the same pain as I am.

My brain scrambles to put the pieces of last night together. *What the hell happened*? I glance down at Renn's body and spot the waistband of his briefs. *Did that happen?*

At the mere suggestion that Renn and I had sex last night, my body fires off a set of internal explosions. *Are they in celebration? Is it some kind of foreshadowing of what my life will be like now? Is it cueing the police lights that might appear once Brock gets his hands on Renn?*

"I think you need to get up," I say, noting a container full of melted ice cream and two spoons between us. *Well, that's one thing explained.*

"You might want to put your whole boob back in your bra," Ella says, pointing at me.

I look down and find half of my chest poking out the side. It's no more than would be visible in a bikini, but I suspect we aren't about to have a lighthearted, poolside-worthy conversation.

Renn runs his hands over his face. "What the fuck is happening?"

He sits up, pissed. But the anger quickly melts into confusion, *and maybe a little fear*, as the situation surrounding him sinks in.

"*Dammit*," he says, swiping his phone off the bedside table. "Who keeps calling? My head is killing me."

He pushes the red button ... and then freezes. His jaw hangs open as he squints at the screen.

"*Yeah, motherfucker*," Brock says, practically trembling in anger.

Ella grabs his arm and steadies me with a slight nod.

I cover my mouth as the taste of alcohol creeps up my throat again.

"Oh shit," Renn hisses. "*Oh. Shit.*"

"What?" I drop my hand, irritation getting the best of me. "What did you do now?"

He looks at me in disbelief. Slowly, his head turns to our friends. "Just ... I need you to hang on."

"Too fucking bad," Brock says through clenched teeth.

"Oh, for heaven's sake." I rip the blankets off me. At the sight of my naked bottom half, I cover right back up. *Oof.* "Um ... Well, that's a ... shocker."

"Do you think this is funny, Blakely?" Brock asks, making it super clear he's not amused. "Because if you do, I'll let you deal with the fallout."

"What the hell are you talking about?"

Ella disappears into the bathroom and comes back with my satin pink robe. "Here." She helps me get out of bed and into the robe without showing everyone my ass.

Renn clears his throat. "Well, this is one hell of a way to wake up."

I take a deep breath, holding my forehead and squeezing.

Nothing makes sense.

Brock's anger. The repeated phone calls. The ice cream in bed.

The fact that Renn is in my bed. Practically naked.

How did that *happen*?

"Look," I say, tying the robe around my waist. My face flushes. "I don't know what happened last night, but I feel like absolute shit. I need to go back to sleep."

"You have to be kidding me," Brock says.

I throw my hands in the air. "Listen, I'm as surprised as you are that I apparently, maybe ..." I glance at a startled Renn over my shoulder. "Had sex with Renn last night." *I can't believe those words just came out of my mouth.* I pivot back toward my brother. "But if I chose to do that, it's really none of your business, and I'd appreciate you returning to your room so I can go to the bathroom and puke my guts out alone."

"Blakely ..." Ella says.

"*You* can stay."

Renn rips the blankets off him. His hair is wild, like it's been pulled and twisted all night. He has the same melted ice cream covering his side, groin, and shoulder as I do. Aside from the bandage on his chest, there's a red streak down his abdomen.

I glance down at my nails.

"It can't be real," Renn says, eyeing my brother. "Let's all just calm down."

"Oh, it's real," Ella says. "The media got a copy of the papers this morning."

Renn's eyes shoot open. "*What?*"

I sigh as a shot of pain flames behind my temples. "Can someone tell me what the hell is going on?"

"*Blakely*—" Ella begins.

"Do you have any idea what you've done?" Brock yells at me, a vein in his throat popping out. "Do you have any fucking clue what you've just gotten yourself into?"

"Don't yell at my wife like that!" Renn shouts back at him.

What?

"Too soon?" Renn asks, the words leaving his lips just as Brock launches himself at Renn.

Ella grabs my arm, pulling me toward the bathroom door.

Renn sidesteps Brock as he comes hurling over the corner of the bed. Brock gets an arm hooked around Renn's head, bringing him down with him on top of the bedside table.

Wood splits. The lamp breaks. My shirt flies across the room like a frisbee, landing on the back of the llama.

The guys fall to the floor.

I press a palm between my eyes. "*Will you knock it off?*"

Renn has one knee in the middle of Brock's chest. The other is on the floor. They both pant while watching each other like they're about to commit murder.

"I'm going to let you up, and you're going to calm the fuck down. Got it?" Renn asks before slowly lifting himself off my brother.

Brock isn't on his feet before he swings at Renn. Renn sees it coming and leans into it, taking the punch to the side of the head. As they collide, Renn's face smashes against Brock's. Blood trickles down my brother's face.

Renn grinds his face against Brock's. "Stop it. Do you hear me? *Stop it.*" With a final shove, Renn steps back.

"Do you think they'll stop?" Ella asks.

I start to shake my head, but it hurts too much. "Nope."

Brock's chest heaves as he glares at Renn. Blood pours from his nose. He brings a hand to his face and then pulls it back, looking at his crimson-stained fingers.

He lifts his eyes to Renn again, letting the drips fall to the floor. "You know what?"

"What?" Renn asks, his phone ringing from somewhere behind Brock.

"*Fuck you.*"

Brock tackles Renn again, knocking them both to the bed. They're too close to punch each other, *thank God*, and too evenly matched to do too much damage. Renn almost has Brock mounted when he throws him off. They land side by side in the middle of the bed—Brock wiping the blood off his face—and then ice cream from his chest—and Renn coughing. The entire scene is hilarious ... or it would be if it made sense.

"That could've been hot," Ella says, assessing the two of them.

"Really, El?"

Pillows are everywhere. The blankets are on the floor and the sheet is ripped off. The lamp on the other side of the bed, the one not broken, sits perilously close to the table's edge.

"Are you two done?" I ask.

"I'm done if he's done," Renn says, gasping for breath. He turns his head toward Brock.

Brock's chest heaves as he struggles to breathe.

They sit up. Blood and melted ice cream coat them both. A spoon is stuck to the side of Brock's head. It falls to the mattress with a thud.

They look at one another, taking in the mess, and burst out laughing.

"Can someone please, for the love of God, explain to me what's going on?" I ask as they get to their feet. "Why are we fighting first thing in the morning?"

Brock looks at Renn. He looks at Ella. Ella glares at them both before turning to me.

"You married Renn last night," she says flatly.

I what?

The smile slides off Brock's face.

I half laugh. "What? *I married Renn?*" My heart pounds. "No, I didn't. What are you talking about?"

Ella hands me her phone. An article from Exposé, a tabloid that has almost transformed its image into a real news source, is on the screen.

My stomach drops.

I take the phone in my shaky hands.

A photo of Renn and me from last night—me in my silver dress and him in the *Sudoku Champ* hat—appears under a big, bold headline.

Breaking News: Rugby's bad boy marries his best friend's little sister

My gaze snaps to Renn's.

"Blakely, I don't know ..." he says.

75

I go back to the article.

File this under—we didn't see this coming.

Our sources confirm that the Tennessee Royals own Renn Brewer married friend and teammate Brock Evans's sister last night in a surprise Vegas wedding. Witnesses say the rugby phenom and his fiancée stood in line with other couples eager to get their marriage licenses. Afterward, they made their way to King and Bling Chapel and said their *I do's*. This is a developing story. We will keep you posted.

"Oh my God," I say, almost dropping the phone. My hand shakes as I hand it back to Ella. "That ... can't be right. We didn't ..." I look at a half-naked Renn. "I wouldn't ..."

I mean, *I would,* but not *marriage.* Marriage? *Marriage?*

There's no way.

I shuffle to the bed and sit on the edge.

"There are pictures," Ella says. "If it helps, you look beautiful."

"No, that doesn't help." I look up at her. "Who lets two inebriated individuals get married?"

"The State of Nevada." Brock comes out of the bathroom with a towel. He throws one to Renn a little harder than necessary. "You are legally married. I had my lawyer check to be sure before I came up."

Renn's phone rings again. He plucks it out of the heap of sheets and cracked wood, sighing as he looks at the caller.

"Why don't you take that? I need a few minutes alone," I say, finding it hard to breathe.

He wipes the towel down the side of his face. "Okay. I'll be back, and we'll figure this out."

I nod.

He walks by me, pausing to grab my shoulder for a moment. The look he gives me—like he's as bamboozled by this news as me—helps.

I look at Ella. "Could you get me something for this headache? And could you," I say to Brock, "leave me alone for a little while? I need to ... think."

Brock doesn't look pleased but appears slightly less angry than before. *I'll take it.*

They form a line and leave the room, Ella shutting the door softly behind her.

I head to the bathroom to throw up.

CHAPTER 10

Blakely

I rinse my toothbrush and look at my reflection.

My hair is ratty, matted in places by what I'm hoping is ice cream. Eye makeup is smeared across my face. The evidence of red lipstick is hidden on an earlobe.

I can't decide if it looks like I've had a good night or if I was mauled by a bear. A very large, muscled, handsome bear. *Ugh.*

"How do you run off and get married after dinner, Blakely?" I shut off the tap. "Marriage isn't an after-dinner snack." I set the toothbrush in the travel case. "Renn might be a snack, but marriage is not."

I groan, mentally lambasting myself for making light of the situation. *Because light, it is not.*

There must be something no one has caught—a lie, a misstep in the paperwork, *some freaking reason two people can't just accidentally get married.* This is Vegas, for Pete's sake. *Doesn't this happen all the time?*

Ella comes in, offering me a pain reliever and a sports drink. "Here. This will help."

"Thanks." I toss the pill in my mouth. The drink makes me want to hurl when it splashes into my stomach.

Ella runs a bath, adding a squirt of shampoo for bubbles. "Okay, this feels like a rough start to the day, I'm sure. But this isn't the end of the world."

"Easy for you to say. Your name isn't on the front page of Exposé. *Again*."

Memories of the first time my name was in bold lettering online have me gripping the tub's edge to steady myself.

"I agree—this isn't a best-case scenario," she says. "But this isn't Edward we're dealing with. Renn isn't feeding the tabloids stories to distract them from his bullshit. It's not the same thing."

I exhale a shaking breath. "It doesn't matter. The magazines don't care about the truth. They blamed me for crashing Edward's car, trashing his house, and trying to blackmail him for cash." Bile creeps up my throat. "Do you think there's a chance they aren't going to call me a gold digger again? If so, you're being naive."

"Get in the bath. Everything is better in the bath." She turns her back to give me some privacy. "Besides, you stink."

"Gee, thanks."

"How much did you drink last night?"

I shed the robe and what's left of my bra. Then I sink into the tub. "Enough to get married."

Ella pulls the footstool across the room and sits.

The heat of the water soothes my stomach and helps clear some of the funk from my head. I take my loofah and clean the melted ice cream from my skin.

"You're *sure* it's a real marriage?" I ask, still in shock.

"I'm sure, friend. Here." She clicks around on her phone and then hands it to me. "There are pictures. Maybe if you look at them, it'll help trigger your memory."

I take the device warily after drying my hands on a towel.

Resting my pulsing head against the bath pillow, I look at the images from last night. In the first picture, we're standing in a line.

"Hey, I remember this. There was a couple in front of us—Oliver and Izzy." My jaw drops, and I look at Ella. "How do I remember two strangers' names and not my wedding?"

She shrugs.

"Oliver kept taking selfies. He was adorable. And I think they took a picture of us? Maybe? I can't remember." I swipe to another image. "Don't remember that. Or that," I say, swiping again.

I stop on a picture of Renn and me in front of a black-haired, lip-curled man holding a book—a Bible, to be exact.

Renn has his arms around my waist, his hands locked at the small of my back. I have no idea what he's saying, but my face is scrunched in a laugh that makes me smile. The way he's looking at me makes my chest tighten.

His eyes are bright and pinched at the corners. His smile stretches across his face. There's a gentleness in his hard exterior, happiness—a carefree vibe in his features. *Oh, Renn. What did we do?*

"Do you remember that?" Ella asks softly.

I shake my head. *I wish I did.*

I give her phone back to her. "So how pissed is Brock?"

"Oh, he's livid. He was ready to tear Renn's limbs off and beat him with them."

Yikes.

"But don't worry about him, Blakely. You need to worry about yourself and what you need to do. Brock's a big boy. He'll deal with this —you know that. He's always on your side."

I shift my gaze away from her.

That's easy for her to say—to not worry about my brother. But she wasn't there when the fallout of dating Edward landed partially on Brock. She didn't watch him feel handcuffed by the situation, wanting desperately to help me but feeling the pressure from his team and managers not to get too publicly involved. It was almost as hard on him as it was for me. *And I still feel terrible about that.*

"I don't want this to affect him," I say.

She smiles. "I think that's the last thing he's worried about this morning."

I press my fingertips against my eyelids and blow out a breath.

"What do you want to do?" Ella asks. "We need a game plan. I'm here to ride this out with you, but I need to know what way we're rolling with it so I can prepare for battle."

My lips quiver. *This sucks so bad. But at least Ella is here.*

"Nope. Don't start crying," she says. "I swear to all that's holy that if you make me get emotional about this, I'll never forgive you."

I laugh, choking back the sob that wants to escape. *Thanks, tequila.*

"Do you think you need an attorney?" she asks. "I can call my dad and see if he can help us find one. He usually knows someone who knows someone."

"I don't need an attorney ... right?" *Do I?* "I just want to get this thing annulled as quickly and quietly as possible. It's not like we're *really* married."

Ella nods as if she's just going along with me.

"Look up annulments—or hell, canceling a marriage license," I say. "There has to be a way for people who wake up married in Vegas to end it. This has to happen all the time."

"Uh-huh." She types into her phone. "I hope you're right."

I lay my head back and close my eyes.

Thankfully, my stomach has settled. The ache in my head isn't as sharp as when I woke up. But the stress in my neck that I managed to shed last night is back—with a vengeance.

I'm married. I snort. *This is not the birthday memory I wanted to make.*

"All right," Ella says. "There are two types of marriages you can annul in Vegas. One is *void marriages* and the other is *voidable marriages.*"

"Gimme. How do I void this?"

"You don't have a *void marriage* because neither of you were already married, and you aren't closely related."

I make a face. "Nope. We're not. What's the other kind?"

"*Voidable marriages* are those without consent if under age, lack of understanding, mental incompetence, and the existence of fraud."

I sit up and turn off the tap. Water sloshes around me. "*That's it.* Lack of understanding. Clearly, we didn't know what we were doing."

Relief floods through me. My shoulders slump. *Thank God for the internet.*

"Not so fast," Ella says, grimacing. "Keep in mind that I'm on a random lawyer's website, okay? So I could be wrong. *He* could be wrong for all I know. But I think this says that if you have a spur-of-the-moment wedding and regret it, that's hard to prove in court."

"*In court*? I don't want this going to court."

She sets the phone on her lap and winces. "It looks like the fastest you can get this taken care of is one to three weeks—*if* you can get it annulled."

"And what if we can't?"

"Then you have to get a divorce."

I stare at my friend as if she will suddenly spit out the answers I want to hear—that this will be quick, easy, and quiet. But she fails me.

No, I failed me.

This is no one's fault but my own. And as bad as this will suck for me, I know it will suck for Renn even more. *There goes his good boy clause.*

The only way out of this is to get to the courthouse. The sooner we start the dissolution of our accidental marriage, the sooner it's over. Because if I know one thing, I know this—I don't want to be Mrs. Brewer.

I can't be Mrs. Brewer.

Tears fill my eyes once again.

There's no way to escape this. Things will get progressively worse as the hours, and days, go on. And I have no idea what it will do to Renn or his family's business deal, but I'm sure it's not good for them, either.

Oh, Blakely. How do you get into these things?

I promised I'd do better. For me. Yet *here we are.*

I married a proverbial bachelor, one of a few men more popular than Edward DiNozzo. It doesn't matter that Renn is a good friend or that he's been nothing but kind to me. Too much is on the line. He'll have no choice but to save himself.

And I can't blame him.

There's little chance we end up anything more than enemies when this is over. *We might as well get it over with as quickly as possible.*

"Fine," I say, lifting my chin. "I guess I get cleaned up, get dressed, and go file the papers because, either way, this has to end."

* * *

Renn

I sit on the bed and hold my head in my hands.

Dammit, Renn.

My lungs fill with air, doing their job and keeping me alive. But, somehow, it doesn't feel like I'm breathing.

I jump back to my feet and pace across the room.

The enormity of the situation hangs over my head—*I married Blakely Evans last night.* The burden of the event sits heavily on my shoulders—*it was my job to protect her.* The responsibility for the fallout lands squarely on me—*and I don't know what the fuck to do.*

And for the first time in my life, *I care.*

I go back and forth across the bedroom, my footsteps falling hard against the floor.

When I usually wake up in some kind of scandal, I take a shower and have breakfast—an omelet, if I can find one. Festering bullshit doesn't bother me. There are always two sides to every story, but I don't often care if my side is told. No one listens, anyway.

My suspensions are always a spectacle. But things happens when you get a group of aggressive, competitive men on a field and hand them a ball—and I get paid to win games. Sometimes, when I do what I'm told, the powers that be decide it was the wrong move. Someone must publicly pay for that—and it's not going to be team management. It's interesting to get punished by the same people who requested the behavior, but there are NDAs to keep players from talking about that.

And the outcry against my social media snafu was amusing. Sure, I inadvertently posted a picture not meant for public consumption. My dick should not have been in my Social Stories for six minutes. *Got it.* But the same people chastising me only do it to be on the right side of the conversation. If it were socially acceptable to post dick pics, they'd be all for that, too. Yeah, me accidentally sharing a picture of my own body is *so* awful. *Please.*

The night I was carted away from a bar in handcuffs? That made a terrific headline. I bet the tabloid downloads the following morning were off the charts. But the part of the story that got left out, and the one I didn't mention to anyone but the police, was the guy I sent to the hospital had just physically assaulted a woman in the bathroom. He wanted to fight—maybe not me. But when you swing at a woman, you lose the right to be selective about who swings back. So, yeah, I'm the bad guy. Fine.

But this time, it's not just about me. It involves Blakely, too. While I might not care what is said about me, I care—*a lot*—about what is said about her.

My hand clutches my stomach. *Don't get sick. There's no time for that.*

I stop next to the bed and rest my head against the wall. So many thoughts, ideas, and possibilities swirl inside me. I don't know which to grab. There are so many moving parts ... but only one that really matters.

Her.

I glance at the door. *Should I check on her? Should I see if she's okay?*

"*I need a few minutes alone.*"

"Dammit, Renn," I mutter, smacking the wall as I shove off it. "Think, asshole. How do you manage this?"

"*But then it was the accusations, the headlines—the paparazzi used to camp outside my work ... That was really, really hard ... It's left me with wounds that haven't healed ... Like being made a joke of in public. Like having a fear that when I love someone, they'll leave.*"

I run my hands through my hair and tug hard.

I haven't looked at anything besides what Astrid sent me this morning, and that was bad enough. If Blakely thinks it was bad with DiNozzo, she has no idea what's about to come her way.

A shot of vomit races up my throat. I dart into the bathroom and spit it in the toilet.

I rack my brain for a list of contacts, searching for the right person to handle this public relations disaster. My PR team is the logical solution, but I know what will happen. They will spin the situation to benefit *me*. That's what I pay them to do—especially when I have so much on the line. So much to potentially lose.

But not this time.

I won't allow them to put Blakely in a bad light, no matter what it costs me.

My heart pulls in my chest as I think of her. *I've got you, cutie. I promise.*

I pick up my phone and ignore the missed calls, voicemails, and text messages. I scroll until I find Frances's direct number. She answers in two rings.

"Renn, you're making me work for my money this morning," she says, her tone edged in annoyance. "We've been inundated with requests for a statement. I've put together a response for you to approve. It's in your email."

"I'm having a terrific morning, thanks. How are you?"

"Cut the shit. We don't have time for that today."

Her abruptness eats away at my already frayed nerves.

"Have you checked your email?" Frances asks.

"No. As you might imagine, I've been pretty busy since I got up."

"I'll break it down for you. The only solution is to try to get ahead of the story and admit it was a mistake—"

"I'm not saying that." I stop in my tracks. *This is exactly why I'm calling you.* "I'm not throwing the door open for Blakely to get smeared by those fucking snakes that call themselves journalists."

"I understand that. But I'm paid to protect *your* image. Your father has already called this morning—"

"Who pays you, Frances?" I ask, my voice shaking with anger. "Me or my father?"

"*You*. But sometimes, in these situations, *you* forget the value of your image. Of your family's image."

I laugh angrily. "And what about Blakely's? She's disposable—why? Because her last name isn't worth as much financially as mine?"

She sighs. "Renn ..."

I start pacing again. "I'm not issuing anything that puts Blakely in the crosshairs. Period. *It's out of the question.* Don't frame this as a mistake that'll have everyone speculating that she coerced me into it, tried to trap me, or is looking for a payout. I won't sign off on it."

"You realize that short of this being a real marriage because you're in love, the only way to *possibly* save Blakely's image, your contract, and your father's purchase is to nip this in the bud, right? Make it a nonissue. We need to frame it ourselves—and we have a very small window to do that. The media will have their day with it; we can't help that now. Our best option is to own it, sit back, and let it burn itself out. You can make a sizable donation to a charity next week for a good photo op, then move on."

I clench my jaw, hissing a breath through the phone.

She's right and I know it. We've done it before. Frances can whip something together, phrased just so, to explain this off, while putting the least amount of blame on me as we can. I'll probably keep my contract. Dad will figure his shit out; he always does. *But what happens to Blakely?*

"An annulment takes time," Frances says, her voice lower. *Calmer.* "We need your attorneys on this now—if you haven't called them already." She takes a deep breath. "We need to stay on top of this, Renn. The longer we go, the less control we'll have over the narrative. So what do you want to do?"

I close my eyes. *"You realize that short of this being a real marriage because you're in love, the only way to possibly save Blakely's image, your contract, and your father's purchase is to nip this in the bud, right?"*

"I'll call you later, Frances. Just hold off for a little while."

She sighs in frustration. "Make it quick, Renn."

The call ends.

I look at the ceiling and groan, sliding a hand down my face.

My right eye is sore from one of Brock's shitty punches. There's a small knot on my jawline. And ... *what's that on my chest?*

I glance down and spot a bandage. "Huh?"

I pull it off to uncover a tattoo ... of Blakely's name. Over my heart.

My laughter shakes my whole body as vague memories of lying on a chair with Blakely standing over me with a marker trickle through my mind. I can hear her giggle as she drew on my skin. The playful sweetness in her eyes as she watched the artist imprint her design onto me.

The memory doesn't bother me. It doesn't make me mad or embarrassed. In fact, it makes me smile.

She makes me smile.

If the paparazzi weren't involved, this whole thing would be hilarious. *I married Blakely Evans.* For once, I made a great choice.

And I'm the only person in the world who will get on board with that.

My spirits sink.

I wander around the bedroom, wishing my life was simpler. That I could run upstairs, laugh about this with Blakely, and then go to brunch with her, Brock, and Ella. I wish I didn't have to worry about headlines, publicists, and contracts.

But I do.

Anger floods me again as my conversation with Frances hits me again. *"I'm paid to protect your image. Your father has already called this morning..."*

Fuck this.

I'll be damned if this is handled like Blakely is a nonissue—if my father tries to get involved to save his own skin and act as if Blakely is inconsequential. He might treat me like that, but I'll be damned if he does it to her.

What does she even think about this? I'm sure she's as gobsmacked as I am. *And what is Brock's reaction going to be once he's settled down?* I'll be lucky if he doesn't try to fight me again.

I don't know whether to smash something or vomit.

My phone rings, tipping the scales toward vomiting. I know it's Dad without looking. I can feel the judgment, the wrath about to come my way.

I take a long, deep breath before looking at the screen.

I might as well get it over with.

"Hello?" I say.

"Renn, *what the fucking hell is this shit*? I wake up this morning to calls that you *got married* last night? Are you out of your damn mind?"

I wince. "Ah, you heard ..."

"How about for once in your damn life you listen—and you listen good. This little stunt of yours could cost me a deal worth three-quarters of a billion dollars that I've been working on for two years—not to mention your contract. *My God, Renn.* Do you realize how badly you've fucked up this time?"

"You know, it's really not that big of a deal."

I regret the words as soon as I say them. I pull the phone away from my ear just in time.

"*Not that big of a deal?*" His laughter—loud and obnoxious—is at my expense. "Son, getting married and filing for an annulment less than twenty-four hours later is a *big* fucking deal. That's especially true when your employer just made you sign a fucking waiver that you won't embarrass the team or become a media distraction!"

"You realize that short of this being a real marriage because you're in love, the only way to possibly save Blakely's image, your contract, and your father's purchase is to nip this in the bud, right?"

I tune out my father's rant and do my best to sort through the alcohol still in my system and think that last thought through. *Short of this being a real marriage because you're in love ...*

My heart pounds.

What if we didn't get an annulment? What if Blakely and I stayed married? Would it really hurt anything?

I pace back and forth across the bedroom.

It wouldn't hurt anything for me. I'd have a beautiful wife who's respectable and classy. *But would it hurt anything for her?*

I'm kind of scared to answer that. But I can answer what staying married could help ... lots of things.

Maybe everything.

"This is a ridiculous question because I know you didn't think this through. But on the off chance that you had any thoughts at all—did you think about a prenuptial agreement?" Dad asks. "Or a postnuptial one? Tell me you took some precautions."

His insinuation cuts through me like a hot knife, and I stop in my tracks. *"Excuse me?"*

"You have to think about this shit. I'm sure the pussy is great, but—"

"Watch your mouth."

"Oh, Renn."

My blood boils as I stare out the window. "Believe it or not, there are other people in this world besides you. And all of them aren't bad."

"What has she done to you?" he asks, chuckling.

I ball my hand at my side. *Fuck this.* "I'll call you later."

"Renn!"

I end the call before I say things I can't take back.

My anger grows as I replay our conversation. *Prenuptial agreement. Postnuptial agreement. "I'm sure the pussy is great ... "*

"This is what they'll do to her—what *my own father* will do to her," I say to the empty room. "And I can't let that happen."

I toss my phone on the bed and head for the shower.

I need to wash some sense into myself before I do something really stupid—like propose a fake marriage.

CHAPTER 11

Blakely

"I don't even want to know what this is going to cost," I say, taking in the ice cream-stained mattress.

After my bath, I gathered the sheets and pillowcases. I wasn't sure what to do with them, so I filled the tub with hot water and body wash and added the bedding. I read somewhere that soaking stuff after it's freshly stained helps. *But the mattress?* I don't know how to clean chocolate and blood out of that.

I grab the trash can from the bathroom and start picking up the pieces of the broken lamp.

"You married Renn last night."

Now that the shock has worn off—and some of the alcohol, thanks to the Gatorade and a breakfast sandwich Ella got somewhere—the sentence doesn't make me quite as ill.

Memories have slowly come back to me over the last hour. We went to a show on the Strip. There's a fuzzy recollection of roulette, a limo, maybe, and visions of a small room draped in white with a man smelling of too much cheap cologne.

Apparently, that's where we pledged to love one another until death do us part.

I can't help it. I grin.

It's almost funny. It might *be* funny if it didn't have the potential to bring so much negativity on me, Renn—probably even his dad.

My stomach twists and pulls, wondering what Renn is doing. *How is he sorting this out on his end?*

I pluck a few wood fragments off the floor and deposit them in the trash can.

"Hey."

I look over my shoulder and find Renn standing in the doorway. He's fresh out of the shower. A pair of jeans hang low on his hips, and a plain black T-shirt is stretched over his frame.

I could've done worse in the husband department. The thought has me choking back a laugh. *Yup. I'm still in shock.*

"You and Brock did some damage," I say, getting to my feet. "I'm soaking the sheets, but I don't know what to do with the mattress. And this end table is busted. The lamp is toast."

Renn looks around the room, his gaze falling on the imprint on the glass. He fights a smile. "Is that ... what it looks like?"

I look at the silhouette. "Palms and boobs? Maybe."

"What the hell did we do last night?" he asks, chuckling softly.

The sound washes over me. It undoes some of my anxiety since the marriage thing was dropped in my lap.

"Renn, I don't know," I say. "I'm getting pieces of it coming back to me here and there. I think we rented a limo, played roulette, and I keep having this recurring image of riding a mechanical bull."

He grins. "Sounds like a good night."

"I wish I could remember it."

He leans against the doorframe, looking at me curiously. "Do you happen to have any tattoos this morning?"

My eyes grow wide. "No. Why? Should I?"

He walks to me, his eyes glued to mine. "Check this out." He lifts his shirt over his chest and his stacked abs. The bandage from this morning is gone.

I cover my mouth. "*No.*"

"I guess we did this instead of rings."

"Renn. *Oh my God.*" I suck in a breath, laughing in disbelief. "You got a tattoo? *Of my name?*"

He drops his shirt. "Complete with a heart. And I think you wrote it there. I have these flashbacks of you with a marker."

"Yeah, well, it does look like my handwriting."

We stare at each other for a few long seconds. Finally, we begin to laugh. *Loudly.*

It's such a relief to laugh with him— to know his life didn't spiral completely out of control downstairs and that I managed to keep mine together up here. And that we're still ... friends.

For now.

"Ella and I looked up what we're supposed to do," I say, picking up another piece of the lamp. "I think we can get an annulment based on lack of understanding because we were obviously drunk." I drop the shard in the trash. "But it can take one to three weeks."

Renn watches me warily.

"Our amateurish investigation did say that we might run into problems, though." I search the floor for anything else I can pick up— anything to avoid his gaze. "Apparently, proving a lack of understanding can be tricky. If that doesn't work, our only option seems to be an actual divorce. We both want to avoid that and get this done as quickly and quietly as possible."

He runs a hand down his face.

"Look, I know this is really bad for you," I say, my heart hurting for him. "This really fucks up your good boy clause, I'm sure."

He drops his hand, a crooked grin on his lips. "A little bit."

"And your dad's business deal?"

His smile falters. "Don't worry about him."

"Okay ..."

He roams through the room like he owns the place. Casually confident—like a man gearing up for a war he knows he'll win. I would swoon if I wasn't a combatant in this battle ... and worried that I might end up being his opponent.

"Blakely, do you have any clue what the media is going to say about you?"

I still, my insides reminding me that tequila or not—puke is still a possibility.

Renn stops moving and faces me. There's a somberness, a seriousness in his eyes that scares me.

Yeah. I might need a toilet.

"They're going to say you're after my money—"

"*I don't want your money.*"

He takes a step toward me. "*I* know that. But they're going to say it
anyway. And they're going to speculate if you're pregnant. They're
going to wonder if you tricked me somehow and a million other terrible
things just to spin a story."

I move backward until my legs hit the edge of the mattress. Then I
sit. Although I knew all that, hearing it from Renn makes it much more
real.

"I told my PR person not to make a statement until we—*you and I*
—talk," he says.

"You probably have a nightmare on your hands, huh?"

He looks me in the eye. "I'm less concerned about that right now
and more worried about *you*."

You are?

It takes a few moments for that to register.

I knew, or hoped, that Renn would realize we're on the same side of
this disaster. But the thought that his needs would swamp mine has
lingered in the back of my mind. I've experienced enough to know that
big-dollar deals sometimes outweigh other things—like truth and people.

My heart swells. The man who has so much to lose is worried
about *me*.

He sent me flowers for Valentine's Day during the DiNozzo disaster.
Of course, he wrote a sarcastic card that wasn't exactly sweet, but I read
through the lines. He was just showing his support—and it was very
appreciated.

Renn returned to the US one year when Brock had to have surgery
because he knew it would just be my brother and me. One summer, he
hooked us up with a place to stay when Ella and I went to Europe for a
week. And when a coworker's son got osteosarcoma, and she mentioned
Renn was his favorite athlete, Renn didn't hesitate to jump on a video
call with him ... for an hour.

He can be a good friend. A great human. *Just not a good husband.*

"What is happening with your contract?" I ask. "Have they said anything?"

He shrugs. "I don't know yet. I haven't gotten that far."

"What about your dad's deal? I know you said not to worry about him, but I can't help it."

His jaw pulses. "*Don't worry about it.*"

"But Renn, *he's your dad.*"

"And you're my wife."

We face one another, feeling each other out.

I'm relieved that being with him feels the same as always—that *our marriage* didn't make things tense or hostile. We can smile and be play-ful, despite the impending disaster swirling around us. That I'm not labeled the bad guy.

And I can't ignore that it's the second time he's claimed me so fiercely. That's kind of hot.

He's not really your husband, Blakely. Back out of this thought process.

"How are things going?" Brock marches into the room unan-nounced, flashing a look at Renn that would kill a weaker man.

Ella is at his heels, looking apologetic.

"We're going to get an annulment or a divorce—preferably an annulment. That way, it's like the marriage never happened," I say brightly, trying to avoid another fistfight.

My brother looks at Renn. "What's going on with your contract?"

"Let's talk about that later."

"Did you talk to your dad?"

Renn runs a hand through his hair. "Yeah, and he's about as pissed as you'd imagine."

"What did he say?" Brock asks, unflinching.

"Oh, that I'm a little punk," Renn says, dropping his hand to his side. "That I probably just cost myself my job and him two years and a deal worth three-quarters of a billion dollars. I'm careless and selfish. You know, the usual."

My jaw drops. "Your father said that to you?"

Renn chuckles angrily.

"Reid Brewer can be a real gem," Brock says, returning his attention to his friend. "What was your response?"

"I told him I'd call him later. Besides, we have bigger fish to fry."

The two of them exchange a look I don't understand.

"How are you feeling, Blakely?" Ella asks.

"Hungover." I tear my attention away from the guys and kick the end of the broken table. "Do you know if there are any big trash bags in the kitchen? Maybe we could load this thing—"

"Forget the furniture," Renn says, irritation thick in his tone.

I put a hand on my hip. "I'm trying to minimize the charges you get for destroying a hotel suite. Or do you want to say *fuck it* and add that to the things you have to deal with?"

"*Blakely* ..." Renn looks at the ceiling and sighs. "No one is getting charged for anything."

"Have you looked around?"

"Yeah, a few times. I own this suite."

I still, the room shifting beneath me. "What do you mean that *you own it*?"

"I mean, it's mine. I own it. I bought it. I wrote a check—or made a wire transfer, actually. Then they sent me a deed."

"*You're joking.*"

"Hey, it's half yours now, too, technically," Ella says, shrugging.

Brock fires her a dirty look. "*Don't.*"

She returns his glare with just as much passion. Even though she stands up to Brock—a lot—it's moments like these when I wonder if they'll survive.

But even that's too much to deal with right now. As Renn said, we have bigger fish to fry.

I move to the glass and stand by the body print. But, as soon as I do, I realize the boobs line up with the height of mine. With a flushed face, I stand by the llama instead. *This isn't how I imagined Renn seeing my boobs.*

I gulp.

What more did he see?

What more did we do?

My eyes find his. The corner of his lip twitches.

Nope. Move on.

"So what now, Renn?" I ask, forcing a swallow. "What's the best way to handle this? How do we minimize the drama?"

"It's a little late for that," Brock says.

I turn to my brother, my head starting to hurt again. "Brock, I love you, but shut the hell up."

"Excuse me?"

I don't want to fight with him. I don't want him to fight with Renn, either. But I simply don't have the bandwidth to deal with his unreasonableness. My wits are already frayed to the point that they're about to snap.

Ella tugs on his arm. "Let's give them some privacy to work this out."

"The last time we gave them privacy, they got married."

That does it.

"You know what?" I ask, charging forward. "You're not helping."

"Someone needs to help you. *You married Renn, Blakely.*"

"Easy ..." Renn warns.

"Or what?" Brock asks, looking at his friend. "You married her twelve hours ago, and now you're her protector? Give me a fucking break."

I can't take it. I can't do this again. "Brock ... leave."

"You're out of your mind if you think I'm leaving you. You're about to be embroiled in another fucking scandal that will make the last one look like a piece of cake. The two of you dragged me into this when you strolled into a *wedding chapel* and *got married.*"

"*Lower your voice,*" Ella says.

He turns to her and lifts a brow.

"*Lower. Your. Voice.*" Ella glares at him. "I know you're unhappy right now, but this isn't about you."

"This affects me as much as it does them," Brock says. "They're both selfish—"

"Do *not* talk about your sister like that," Ella says, gasping.

"Ella, don't ..." I say.

"I'll be here to help you any way I can, Blakely." She glares at Brock. "But you and I are done."

"Ella …" he says, watching her storm out of the room. "Dammit. Come back."

I cover my face with my hands. "Someone, anyone—how do we fix this before we all fall apart?"

Renn takes a deep breath. "We have two options."

"Name them."

He exhales. "One, we try to get the annulment. If that fails, we get a divorce. Pros … it's straightforward. Cons … we'll both get annihilated in different ways."

Yay. "And two?"

He looks at me, then at Brock, and back at me. His gaze is wobbly. "We stay married."

"*What*?" I yelp.

"It's just an option. You asked for the options."

My mouth hangs open. "I'm not staying married to you. *Have you lost your mind*?"

"I don't mean for real. I just mean …" He groans. "I don't know what I mean."

I snort. "I hope you can back that statement up with a reason, considering you had the guts to say it."

He takes a step away from my brother. "Look, this sounds … Well, I know how it sounds, okay? But one option we have is to stay married for a little while. We take the steam out of the media. We play it off like we did it on purpose. Like … it's real."

"Oh, come on," Brock says, laughing in disgust. "You can't be serious."

I glare at him. "Leave. Be quiet or leave."

"Or what?"

"Or …" I glance quickly at Renn. "I'll call security and have you removed. This is my suite now."

Renn turns his back to my brother and covers his mouth. His body shakes as he suppresses a laugh.

Brock's eyes widen.

"I'm kidding," I say. "But I'm also not. I understand you're worried and not vocalizing that in the best way. Considering the situation, I'm willing to overlook it. But I'm a grown woman, Brock. I appreciate you. But either be helpful or leave."

"What's gotten into you?" he asks.

"I'm wasting a perfectly good birthday on this bullshit. It's irritating me a little," I say.

"*Oh fuck.* Blakely, your birthday ..." Brock says, frowning.

"Yep. Happy birthday to me."

"Happy birthday, Mrs. Brewer," Renn says, testing the waters.

"Renn—" Brock starts.

I hold up a hand—which he never likes—and pray he stops talking.

Walking back and forth across the room—from Brock to the llama with a cigar—I weigh my options.

If we get an annulment, our lives go up in flames. We'll survive it, but it'll be a nightmare for a while. *I'm not looking forward to all the trash that will be spewed my way. But I survived that once before, so I can again.*

If we stay married, there might be some smoke, but we could avoid an inferno. *Maybe. It also might drag out the whole thing and waste more of my life with a man who isn't for me.*

Renn's eyes are clear and concerned. Even though the answer is obvious, he's not pressuring me to do what's best for him.

"Oh, that I'm a little punk. That I probably just cost myself my job and him two years and a deal worth three-quarters of a billion dollars. I'm careless and selfish. You know, the usual."

I don't know Reid Brewer, but I hate him. *Fuck that guy. Who says that to their own son?*

My hand shakes as I run it over my head. "Renn?"

"Yeah?"

"What happens if we stay married?" I ask. "What does that look like? I'm not saying I want to do that, because I really don't, but theoretically ..."

"I'll be honest—I don't know. We'd have to play it off and look convincing. Otherwise, it would bite us in the ass even worse."

Play it off. Look convincing.

How the heck do we do that?

And how do I ensure I don't get my ass handed to me in the end?

Brock clears his throat. "It's obvious I think you two just fucked all the way up, and I'm pissed about it." He swallows. "But I'm going to back away and let you figure it out."

"Thank you," I say.

He turns to Renn. "I want to say one thing."

"Go for it," Renn says.

"Blakely is more important to me than anyone else on this planet," Brock says. "She trusts too easily and sees the good in people. It gets her in trouble."

My heart lodges in my chest.

"I expect you to protect her," Brock says. "I don't want to see her go through this all over again. You got her into this; you get her out of it. But if you do anything to hurt her, Renn, so help me God—"

"*I won't.*" Renn squares his shoulders to Brock. "You have my word. Whatever happens, I'll do everything I can to ensure she's as unaffected as possible. I love you, man."

Tears cloud my vision.

Brock's jaw tenses as he pulls Renn into a hug. I don't breathe until they part without throwing punches.

My brother steps back. "Okay. Let me know if I can help."

"I love you, Brock," I say, my voice wobbling.

He crosses the room and wraps his arms around me. "I love you, B. No matter how many times you fuck up—"

I laugh through the tears falling down my cheeks.

"I'll always be here." He pulls away. "*Always.*"

"Thank you."

He rubs the top of my head before giving Renn a final stare. Then he heads for the door.

Reality fills the room again. It's just me and my now husband—and a million unanswered questions.

If we file to end this mess, we're handing ammunition to the tabloids. But if we play it out, will the injuries be less? *Or worse?*

"I feel like we need to talk this through—you and me," I say. "There's a lot to consider and my head is scrambled."

Renn nods. "Agreed."

"I don't want to stay here. We'll be held captive in this room since everyone in the world knows we're here. And I really want to get away from my brother and Ella."

"If I really married you, I'd take you on a honeymoon. If we went away somewhere for a few days, that would give us some time to work it out without confirming or denying anything. And the optics would be good *if* we decide to play this out."

Makes sense. "Can you get away from here for a few days?"

"I don't have anything I can't move around until late next week. You?"

"I have next week off. My new boss is gone, so they told me to enjoy the break."

"Nice."

I laugh softly, remembering how excited I was to lie around and do nothing. *I didn't expect to be negotiating a divorce.*

The more I sit with the options, the more it's obvious that we really have only one viable choice on the table. But we can't make a spur-of-the-moment decision. That's what got us in this mess.

"Renn?"

"Yeah?"

"Can you find us a place with an ocean?"

"Absolutely."

I take a deep breath. "Then do it. Let's go somewhere and ... figure this out."

Renn's shoulders fall as he crosses the room. He holds his arms out, and I collapse into them. I fist his T-shirt in my hands and press my cheek against his chest.

"Are you sure about this?" he asks.

"No, I'm not. Not even a little. But I'm as sure as I'm going to be."

He chuckles, pressing a soft kiss to my forehead. "We'll sort this out, cutie. Trust me."

I dip my chin and pull back from him. *I hope I can trust you, Renn. I really do.*

At that, he walks out of the room, and I'm left alone. Finally.

What the hell have I gotten myself into?

CHAPTER 12
Blakely

Aren't electronics supposed to crash the plane or something equally catastrophic?

Renn paces the center of the aircraft, his phone glued to his ear like it has been for a good part of the past hour.

Maybe the rules are different on private jets.

Music plays softly through the cabin. A tray of snacks—fruit, crackers, and the most delicious sugar cookies I've ever eaten—is beside me on one of two plush sofas facing each other. A bedroom, lavatory, and a small storage compartment are through the archway on my right. On my other side is a dining area, where our sweet flight attendant, Kimbra, said a meal will be served shortly. Beyond that is a small space dubbed "the entertainment area" with oversized chairs and a large screen. It's open to a full galley that greets visitors as they board the aircraft.

If I weren't already bamboozled from my surprise marriage, *this* would render me speechless. But this isn't the most impressive part. The wildest part of the whole experience is the understated Brewer Air logo embossed on the head rests, linens, and the side of the plane.

My. Head. Is. Spinning.

"Everything okay?" Renn asks, disrupting me from my thoughts.

The weight of the day is etched on his face. I'm certain it is on mine as well.

"Everything is the same as it was when we boarded the plane this afternoon," I say.

He squeezes his temples. "I'm sorry I've been on the phone—"

"No, don't apologize. I didn't mean it like that. I just meant ..." *I don't know what I meant.*

I pull my legs beneath me, and gaze past his shoulder into the clouds.

The day feels like it's taken both the blink of an eye and a calendar year. By the time Renn dealt with his publicist, fielded a small selection of the incoming calls and texts blowing up his phone, and arranged for our travel to a *place with a beach*, it was after four in the afternoon. I intentionally did not check my phone, sent Ella out for travel essentials —despite Brock and Renn melting down over it after the fact—and attempted to manage the panic attack sneaking up on me.

What neither Renn nor I have done over the past almost ten hours is discuss anything relating to our newly formed union. And while I know we bought ourselves a few days to figure that out ... I still want—*need*— a resolution. *Soon.*

Renn shuts off his phone and tosses it on the sofa. As it drops, so do his shoulders. "I should've turned that off a long time ago. I hate people."

I grin. "No, you don't."

"Oh, I do. I really, *really* do." He blows out a breath. "My publicist put out the statement we approved before we left Vegas."

"Which one did we end up going with? I forgot. There were so many renditions."

"She copied you on the final email. It basically said we are enjoying a few days away and asked the world to respect our privacy."

"Which it won't."

He rolls his head around his neck. "Probably not. But I'm taking you to the one place we have a shot at it."

"Are you going to tell me where that place might be?"

"Nope. It's a surprise."

His smile, boyish and proud, eases the lines around his eyes. Coupled with his messy hair and the way the collar of his shirt is crooked, Renn is adorable.

I want to prod him about our destination. I'm *so* curious about the Brewer Air logo. And I really want to curl up on this sofa and get some much-needed sleep, but I can't. I can't do any of *that* until we get to the bottom of *this*.

"I have a call with the Royals general manager tomorrow," he says, falling back against the sofa.

"What are you going to tell them?"

He shrugs. "That's the multimillion-dollar question."

Yes, it is ... "I think now is as good a time as any to talk this out. Don't you think?"

"We're going to be on this plane for a while, so we might as well."

We are? "Define *a while*."

He smiles. "A while."

I roll my eyes.

"So let's do this. Let's get to the bottom of it," he says. "Where is your head right now?"

I fiddle with the hem of my sweatshirt. "I'm waffling between what's best for you, what's best for me, and what's best for us." My eyes lift to his. "Where is *your* head right now?"

"Honestly?"

"Honestly."

His Adam's apple bobs. "I think the best thing for us is to stay married."

My head falls into my hands. *Of course, you do.*

"Just think about it," he says, leaning forward. His voice is calm and careful. "It puts out the fire. No one can say shit if they really think we're married."

"No offense, but I don't really want to be married to you."

He gasps. "And why not?"

I stare at him. I know he's trying to take the edge off the situation— to keep things light and fun. And I appreciate that ... but it doesn't help.

"Answer that, please," he says. "I'm a catch."

"*Because.*" I stand and pace the small area as he watches from his seat. "This is just so ... wrong. I don't even remember marrying you."

"I don't remember marrying you either, but here we are."

"On that note," I say, facing him. "You realize that the only thing worse than the world finding out that we got married while inebriated is the world watching us pretend to be in love and then watching you screw around on me."

His jaw clenches. "That's awfully presumptuous of you."

My hands go to my hips. "An accidental wedding isn't going to change who you are. Let's not pretend that it will. And it won't change who I am, either, and I'm not someone who wants the stress of being married to a rugby player—real or not." I stare at his handsome face and watch as his features soften. *Dammit.* "Look, I understand why you want to stay married. But that scenario really only serves you."

"Blakely, I'm not trying to force you into anything. And I have no interest in doing anything that only serves me. Okay?"

I sit again, the edge of my frustration duller than before.

"We're on the same team here, cutie."

My lips twitch into a smile. "I know. I'm sorry." *I'm just used to having to protect myself.*

"Don't apologize. I get it. Trust me. Ripley had to remind me of the same thing today."

We watch each other for a long, quiet moment. As the seconds tick by, the more settled I become ... and the clearer this situation becomes.

"Look, Renn, I understand that staying married *could* benefit me." I scoot to the edge of the sofa. "But that could backfire worse than just pulling the plug now. Why is it worth the risk for me to pretend to be married to you when we'll end up getting divorced anyway and I'm at the mercy of the media? I like you, buddy, but not that much."

He nods. "Okay. Fair. Tell me what you want."

"What do I want? I want to be focused on myself. I want to grow, to be excited about appliances and understand how life insurance works. I want to find a nice man, get married, and have a family. Basically, the opposite of what we have going on and the longer we draw that out, the longer I'm just treading water—and I *need* to move forward. I need it, Renn. I promised myself that I would do it."

"Define *nice man.*"

"What? That's what you took from that?"

"I want to know what a nice man is to you. Go."

I sigh.

What does it matter to him? Explaining the characteristics of the man of my dreams to Renn Brewer feels pointless. But as I begin to tell him to stay focused on the task at hand, I realize that humoring him—describing what a good man is to me—will help him understand that this is a waste of time. For me, anyway.

"He's responsible," I say. "A nice man has a job and is passionate about something—anything. He's kind. Has protector vibes. Likes to have sex. I wouldn't mind being choked a little." I grin at the fire that flashes through his eyes. "And he wants to start having babies with me before I'm too old because he's not a commitment-phobe and values monogamy." I shrug. "He knows a damn good thing when he sees it. And ... he loves me."

Renn starts to speak but stops. He cocks his head to the side and begins again. "So what I'm hearing is that you don't want to stay married because you think I'll embarrass you—"

"I think there's a chance I wind up looking like a fool. Yes."

"And there's nothing in it for you. The risk and reward balance is skewed."

Finally. He sees the light. "Yeah. Basically. I promised myself that I would take care of me this year, Renn—not waste more time by continuing my *bad choices with bad boys* era."

He gets to his feet, combing his hands through his hair. The lines around his eyes are back. So is the tension in his shoulders.

He walks to the dining room. Muffled voices slip through the cabin, ending moments before he reappears.

"Hear me out," he says, his pupils wide as he sits again. "I have a compromise—a proposal, if you will."

This should be fun. "Propose away ... especially since I don't know if you did before we got hitched. You owe me one, anyway."

His grin is wobbly. "Stay married to me for ninety days—tops."

What? My brows pinch together. "Stay married for ninety days? That's *three months*."

"I know." He clears his throat, steadying his gaze on mine. "In exchange for you not ending it, I'll give you a baby."

Suddenly, the Brewer Air logo isn't the wildest part of the evening.

105

Did he just say he'll give me a baby?

"I'm sorry, Renn. Repeat that."

His eyes stay glued to mine. "I said that I'll give you a baby."

"*What?* How are you going to do that? Steal one?"

"No, I was thinking I'd put it there."

"*Renn.*"

He leans forward, resting his elbows on his knees. "I know this sounds crazy, and hot, but—"

"*Renn.* Stop." I gulp as fire streaks through my veins. "You just asked me to ... *My God.*"

"Will you just think about it?"

My mouth hangs open. "No, I won't just think about it. I'm not having a baby with you!"

"Why?"

The question is a full-on sentence, a challenge for me to explain why having a baby with my brother's best friend is a terrible idea. While I know that's true and that there are a million reasons for it, the only thing I can focus on is the heat in his eyes ... and the heat building in my core.

"This is the perfect answer," he says. "You'll realize it if you think about it."

"This is ... ridiculous! That's what this is."

"Ridiculous? I'm asking for a ninety-day commitment and I'm offering you eighteen years. I think it sounds pretty damn generous."

I roll my eyes. "You've lost your mind."

"Do you not want a baby?"

"Yes."

"I can give you that. I'll pay child support. You'll have a whole family waiting to embrace you and the baby. Hell, I'll play by your rules. I'll sign a contract—whatever you want. It wouldn't want for a thing."

Except the love of a father. "I can't believe we're discussing this right now. Yesterday, I was in a bikini in Vegas wanting to see a male strip show and today I'm married and discussing having *your* baby."

"So you're considering it?"

"*No.*"

He smirks. "You have to admit, our baby would hit the genetic lottery."

I lean forward to smack him, but he catches my hand in the air. The feeling of his fingers wrapped around my wrist is electric. He releases me slowly, one digit at a time.

Once I'm free, I fall back onto the sofa cushions and drag in a shaky breath.

"To be perfectly honest with you, I want a kid too," he says, flexing his fingers as if they're buzzing from the contact like mine. "But I've never met someone I'd trust enough to have a child with ... until now."

"You're just saying that to get what you want."

"If you know me as well as you say you do, then you know the one thing I won't do is lie."

As much as I don't want to admit it, he's right. Renn Brewer isn't a liar. That's what gets him in trouble most of the time—his failure to pass the blame. Sure, he might skirt it and try to minimize the damage. But he never lies.

"Somehow, you just complicated the hell out of an already overcomplicated situation," I say.

"Mr. Brewer," Kimbra says. "May I please see you for a moment?"

He turns to me. I motion for him to go, thankful for the interruption.

"In exchange for you not ending it, I'll give you a baby."

I hold my forehead. *What the hell is happening*? I chuckle quietly, in disbelief with myself. *Could I still be drunk?*

Although I want a baby with a man I love, I'm not sure I'll ever find him. People are weird. They have secrets. Having a child with someone means you're bonded with them in one way or another for the rest of your life—or not. But which is worse? Falling out of love with someone or having your child's father not being in their life?

Renn's voice drifts through the room and a warmth flows over me.

He has his flaws, sure, but he is a good person. I trust him—mostly. If he says he'll play by my rules and sign a contract, I believe him. And he seems to have a strong family. *Besides his father. Fuck that guy.*

I *was* considering a sperm bank. Would having a child with Renn be that much worse? At least I know him, and he could be a part of our child's life, maybe. Our child could have more than just me and Brock ... *Am I really considering this?*

If he could stay out of the spotlight and not make a mockery of me —which, as Renn suggests, would be counterintuitive to this whole process—maybe this could work. It's only a ninety-day investment, after all. *Right?*

Why does this kind of make sense?

"At least you look less shocked now," he says, sitting again.

Less shocked? How am I looking less shocked? This is the most bizarre day I've ever had.

I shift in my seat. "*If* I agreed, and I can't believe I'm even entertaining this—*what is wrong with me?*—I'm on birth control. I don't know if I can get pregnant in ninety days."

"If not, I'll give you my DNA in a little cup or however they do it."

"You realize you're talking about a child like a business transaction, right?"

"Is it that much worse that getting pregnant accidentally with some guy you don't even know? *You know me.* Hell, we're married." He bites back a laugh. "Look, you want a child, and I'm more than willing to give you one. I'll take care of it. I'll be a part of its life. I'm kind of excited about it. I get a kid, and I don't have to deal with a woman I don't like. And it'll even be conceived during our marriage, Blakely. I don't see why this is a terrible plan."

Fucking hell. "What if you're in another relationship? Your new woman won't like you giving me your DNA."

"I'll give it to you before we get divorced, and she'll have to deal with it."

"Can you even do that?"

He shrugs. "We'll figure it out." He leans against his knees again. "Look, I'm serious about this. It'd be pretty great to be the father of your child. But if you don't want to do this, I respect that, and we'll file for annulment as soon as we land. I'll protect you as much as I can from the media. You have my word."

Kimbra returns, handing me a glass of red wine. She says something about moving to the dining room, but it sounds like gibberish.

Today has been too much in every sense of the word. But as I sip my drink and take in Renn—who is calmer than I would expect under the circumstances—the chaos in my head begins to settle.

The baby aside, because I'm not sure I can actually do that, if he can promise he'll play the part of the doting husband for ninety days, would it be *that* terrible to pretend to be a loving wife? It's just three months. Surely, I can use that time to benefit me somehow.

I set the wine down and find my purse. The receipt from the strip show is at the bottom; it's the only piece of paper I can find. I pull out a lip liner and face a curious Renn.

"Ninety days," I say sternly. "And if I'm to play the role of wife, you're to play the role of husband. That means no wandering eye, no pictures with other women, no dates."

He smiles. "Deal."

"You agreed to that so easily. What about sex? Can you go that long without it?"

He smirks. "I said *deal*."

Fine. I scribble the agreed-upon length of commitment on the back of the receipt.

"And *you're* filing for divorce," I say. "Not me. And if anyone says I was after your money or whatever, you have to defend me."

"That's a guarantee."

How is it this easy? I add that to the receipt.

"You have to accompany me to events," he says. "You have to live with me."

"*Live with you?*"

"Live with me." His eyes sparkle. "We have to sell it, baby."

"Ugh."

"No ice cream in the bed," he says.

"I'm signing a prenup."

"No prenup."

"Renn ..."

"*No prenup.* It would be a postnup now anyway."

I start to argue the point, but the look on his face stops me. "No co-mingling of money or assets."

"Sure."

Something about the glimmer in his eye concerns me.

"You have to let me treat you like my wife," he says. "For ninety days, you *are* Mrs. Brewer."

"Fine. But I don't think you understand that I'm not the domestic type."

"I didn't marry you for your domestic abilities."

"You married me because of an alcohol made from agave," I say.

"We should name our first son that."

I sigh as the whole baby thing hits me again. "I'm on the fence about the baby part of this, Renn. I'm not sure I want to do that."

He narrows his eyes. "Can I choke you during sex?"

My insides burn so hot that I shift in my seat. "You said you could go ninety days without sex."

"But you won't be able to." His smirk is so deep, so delicious, that I shiver. "And you also have to change your name."

"That's a little unnecessary for three months, don't you think?"

"I want my wife to have my name," he says with a casual shrug like we're discussing the weather.

"You're getting a little demanding for a man who needs this more than I do."

He holds his hands in the air. "Fair. But that's my last demand."

"It better be," I mumble, listing the rest of the agreements on the receipt. But as I lift the lip pencil, I think of one more thing. Maybe the most important of them all. I take a deep breath. "One more thing ..."

"What?"

Our gazes lock in the middle of the walkway.

His features are free from the stress he's carried all day. The playfulness he's known for dances through his eyes.

My stomach clenches at the thought of doing this with Renn. But it sours just as quickly at the idea of getting too close to him.

Yup. Gotta add this.

I refuse to grow feelings for a man who will never reciprocate them. Who isn't interested in love—especially mine.

"If either of us develops real feelings for the other," I say, my voice quiet, "then we walk away immediately. No questions asked."

He studies me for a long time, the playfulness turning somber.

My heart skips a beat, then two, as I hold my breath and wait on his response. Just as I'm about to tell him to forget the whole thing—that we're both out of our heads, he stands.

"I agree," he says, offering me a hand.

I set the receipt and pencil beside the snacks and tentatively place my hand in his.

He jerks me to my feet faster than I anticipate, and I'm hauled into his chest. My body crashes into his, his hardness to my softness. And just like that, I melt into him.

His smile is wicked.

"What?" I ask, nearly panting at the way he's looking at me.

"I'm just deciding whether I should kiss you here or wait until we land."

I lick my lips. He follows the trail of my tongue with his eyes.

"You might want to do it here," I say, my heart thumping. "Our first kiss shouldn't be in front of people, you know, in case it's awkward."

He locks his hands on the small of my back. "You're right."

I lift on my tiptoes, my hands on his shoulders. "I'm always right."

"Kimbra is watching, so we better wait."

He winks and lets me go.

What the hell?

"We're about to have our first marital fight," I say, my body screaming for him to come back.

His laughter fills the air. "Wait until we get to where we're going before we fight. Because you're going to look so hot on your knees, begging me to forgive you."

With a lingering look, he walks away.

CHAPTER 13

Blakely

I gasp.

"If you would've waited, I would've carried you over the threshold," Renn says, shutting the door behind us.

"This is unbelievable." I cover my mouth with my hand and slip through the bright living area. "Renn—*oh my God.*"

The late morning Australian sunlight floods the home. From the outside, the structure is beautiful but fairly unassuming. It's tucked into the back of a neighborhood, nestled behind a group of trees. White siding peeks out from the foliage. A wooden porch that looks handmade and intentionally crafted to look rustic wraps around the side of the home, disappearing into the trees.

I had no idea, none at all, that the inside would be this stunning ... and the beach would only be steps away.

The interior is bright. White walls, transoms over every window. Natural materials everywhere you turn, from the timber pillars to the hemp curtains and rattan lighting fixtures. Gold accents bring a luxurious element to the place.

A wall of glass separates the living quarters from the outside, providing a jaw-dropping view of the bay. The water is crystal clear, the vegetation is bright green, and the beach is so perfect, so immaculate, that it doesn't even look real.

"*Look at this.*" I tug on a brass handle. The entire glass wall moves—sliding to the side, seamlessly connecting the inside with a huge deck overlooking the sea. "I can't form words. Holy crap."

"This is my buddy, Quade Kellaway's place. We played together for a few years and used to sneak up here on our days off." He leans against the doorframe as I venture onto the deck. "It's quiet, and the folks around here really don't pay much attention to anyone but themselves."

"They're probably too busy looking at this view."

I sit on the arm of a wicker loveseat and take in the surf crashing against the sand. Despite my exhaustion from Las Vegas, plus the eighteen-hour flight, I'm invigorated by the salty air.

"I can see why," he says, his voice entirely too sexy for eleven in the morning.

Looking over my shoulder, I take in his long, lean body standing upright. He moves effortlessly across the deck. Confident. Casual. Cool. Not at all like a man who's dealing with a scenario that includes massive contracts, fuming parents, and publicists that have threatened to quit. *I know because I eavesdropped.*

"Are you flirting with me?" I ask, pretending to be surprised.

"Hell yeah, I am. I won't be one of those men who take my wife for granted." He stops inches before me, hovering over me as I sit. "I'm going to make sure you know how hot I think you are daily."

"Well, I suppose there are worse ways to spend the next three months."

He grins. "Just wait until you realize how I plan on spending the next three months with you."

My stomach flutters as our old dynamic returns. The teasing. The flirting. The teetering on the edge of trouble. Only now, it's not trouble. We're married.

"What did you say to me on the plane?" I ask. "That something was very presumptuous of me? It's presumptuous to insinuate that I'll sleep with you, too."

He lifts the hem of his shirt up and over his stacked abs.

I've seen Renn shirtless several times and been speechless each time. But to have him this close, *alone*, with nothing—no fabric, no person, *no reason*—to stop me from touching him, I'm more than speechless. I can barely breathe.

His body is a work of art. Crafted. *Sculpted*. Each muscle has been built with an artist's care; no fiber has gone unnoticed. His shoulders are wide, and his lats are thick. His waist is trim, highlighted by a deep-set Adonis belt running diagonally from his hips to his pelvis.

He smiles with his shirt wadded in one hand. His heavily veined forearm flexes, and debauchery swims in his eyes. "*Okay.*"

This man is so frustrating.

"But do me one favor, though," he says, smirking.

"What's that?"

He leans down like he's going to kiss me. I hold my breath, my heart pounding so hard I think it's audible.

"It's not polite to stare," he whispers before standing again.

I exhale, making him laugh.

"Asshole." I get to my feet and move away from him. "What time is it in the US?"

He glances at his watch. "It's about eight o'clock at night in Nashville."

"And what time is it here?"

"Eleven in the morning. I ..."

Our attention is redirected to movement inside the house. *Foxx.* Renn's security detail.

Why do gorgeous men only show up when I'm unavailable?

I was introduced to Foxx Carmichael in Vegas, shortly before we left for the airport. He's tall, with dark blond hair, bright blue eyes, and a jawline cut from granite. He's not rude, nor is he kind. I can't tell if he's pissed off or quietly entertained. I think Foxx has been with us since we left Vegas, but this is only the second time I've seen him.

He's a mystery.

"The driver left your luggage in the foyer, and the llama is on top of your suitcases," Foxx says. "I've secured the premises. Mr. Landry advised me that you prefer me to stay off-site. Is that correct?"

"Well, I mean, this *is* my honeymoon, Foxx," Renn says jokingly.

Foxx's lips twitch.

"I know this area well," Renn says. "We'll be good on our own for the most part. But if Blakely wants to do something alone, I want you to go with her."

"Excuse me?" I ask, my head whipping to my husband. "I don't need a bodyguard."

He taps my nose. "Well, you're getting one, anyway."

I huff. "We're going to talk about this."

"Looking forward to it," he says, grinning before turning back to Foxx. "I'll call you if I need you."

Foxx nods.

"Thank you, buddy," Renn says, moving across the patio. "I appreciate you coming at the last minute."

Foxx shakes Renn's hand. "It's my pleasure. I was afraid I would get sent with Brynne Abbott to Cabo."

"You don't like Mexico?" I ask.

"Mexico is fine. I take instructions from her husband. She, on the other hand, does not."

I laugh.

Foxx nods again and slips out the front door.

"He's an interesting individual," I say, following Renn inside the house.

"He has an interesting background."

"Oh, *do tell.*"

"Can't, cutie. That's not my story to share."

"*Come on,*" I say, hopping on the gray and white stone counter. My feet swing back and forth. "I wanna know."

He plants a hand on either side of me. "*No.*"

I grin. "It sounds way more interesting than Tate."

Renn growls, making me laugh.

The sound of my laughter catches me off guard. It's breezy and easy. I sound ... happy.

I don't really know what to make of that.

"You going to speak to Brock?" he asks.

My shoulders slump, and my forehead falls to his shoulder.

Renn chuckles. "I'm taking that as a not yet."

My brother has been on my mind since we left him in Las Vegas. I hate that we left things so strained between us—between him and me, and him and Renn, too. But despite that, I'm also irritated that he didn't offer more support during the meltdown. And that he hasn't called to offer it by now.

"He hasn't called or texted me, and I haven't contacted him either." I raise my head off Renn. "I don't know what to say. I mean, how do I tell him about our agreement?"

"That you're having my baby?"

I laugh, ignoring the way my belly tightens. "*No*. That I'm ... *Mrs. Brewer* for the next ninety days."

"Damn, I love the sound of that coming from your mouth."

I gently push him away and jump off the counter.

My body tingles from his proximity and the gravel buried in his voice. Even though a nice breeze floats through the house from the ocean, I'm suddenly hot.

Renn's eyes find mine. *And bothered*.

The muffled sound of a ringing phone in my pocket breaks the silence. I blow out a breath, thankful for the reprieve.

"That's my ringtone for Ella," I say.

He wipes his face with his shirt. "I need to make a few calls. We need food and toiletries because I'm sure Kellaway doesn't have shit here. He never does."

"What can I do to help?"

"What can you do?" He smiles. "*Relax*. That's what you can do. Let me have Astrid figure out the logistics. She'll be happy I need her for something."

A bolt of jealousy fires through me. "Who is Astrid?"

"My assistant—*our assistant* now."

"I don't need an assistant."

"Well, I don't either, but I have one. I'll give you her number. Anything you need, you can ask her. She's a magician. Sometimes I think of random shit to see if she can do it. And she always does."

I giggle. "That poor woman."

"Ah, she loves it." He heads for the foyer. "I'll take our stuff to our bedroom."

My heart skips a beat. "*Our bedroom?*"

"Didn't I mention that?" He spins around, grinning like the cat that ate the canary. "There's only one bedroom here."

"How convenient." *And probably utter bullshit, given the size of this place.* But I'm not exactly mad about it. I'll get to sleep next to this Adonis. I'm sure I'll survive.

He shrugs like the innocent man he is not. "I'll make some calls and then hop in the shower. Feel free to join me."

With a wink, he walks away.

"Damn you," I mutter, taking out my phone.

I dial Ella while I head back to the patio. She answers on the first ring.

"Hey, how are you?" she asks, concern thick in her tone.

I lift my face to the sky. "I'm good. In Australia, of all places. Right on the beach."

"Lucky you."

"Something like that," I say, stretching out on the loveseat and shoving a pillow under my head. "What's happening back there?"

"Oh, the usual. I'm doing laundry from our trip and ignoring your brother's phone calls."

I laugh. "So you two didn't make up?"

"No, we didn't. I have no interest in making up with him unless he gets his head out of his ass."

"What did he do?"

She sighs. "I just don't think we're going to work out, Blakely. We moved from fling to feelings, but we're not inching any closer to forever."

I frown.

This revelation does not shock me; I often wonder if they've met their end. But I also know they both really do care about one another, and I hate it that they can't work out their problems.

My eyes fall closed, and I yawn. "Well, I'll always be his sister, but I'll always be your friend, too."

"I know, and that's why I'm not involving you in any of it."

"You're the best."

"I know that too." She laughs. "So what are you and Renn doing at the beach all by yourselves for a few days?"

"Well, we're on our honeymoon."

"Is that the official story?"

I take a deep breath and prepare to tell the first person I'm married —even though she knows the truth. It's good practice saying it.

"I'm changing my name to Blakely Brewer as soon as we're home."

She gasps. "What?"

That was fun.

"What do you mean you're changing your name?" she asks.

"We're going to stay married for three months."

She pauses. "You're good with that?"

"Yeah. I mean, he offered to give me a baby in exchange for—"

"*What?*"

My whole body shakes as I laugh.

"He offered to, what? Impregnate you? *Blakely.*" She stutters. "*That's hot.*"

My laughter gets louder.

"Did you say yes?" she asks. "Wow. I think I have a breeding kink."

I put a hand on my stomach to try to steady myself. "Well, good for you. But I don't."

"Well, if your marriage doesn't work out, and he wants to—"

"That's my husband you're talking about."

She laughs, unable to keep her amusement to herself. "I'm kidding, I'm kidding. But, seriously—he suggested that?"

"He did. I didn't take him up on it, exactly." *Although* ... "But I did agree to do the whole wife thing until this blows over and he makes nice with the Royals."

"Three months?"

"Yup. Ninety days."

"Wow. Okay. I wasn't expecting this turn of events, but I can't say I don't like it."

Yeah, well, me either. "I expected to be a little more ... I don't know ... nervous about it. Weirded out, maybe. Unsure. But so far ... so good."

She sighs. The sound of the chair in her living room squeaks. "I expected to be a little more unsure about this too. But it makes sense in an odd sort of way."

"Right? I mean, this isn't what I had planned, but what's three months? It could be fun."

"Oh, Blakely. It could be *a lot* of fun."

I yawn again. "Right now, I don't have enough energy to be fun. I can barely keep my eyes open. I've lay down on the patio, and I'm not sure I can get back up."

"Okay. Go. Get some sleep so you can have all the fun and report back to me."

I chuckle. "Sure."

"Call me if you need anything."

I nod. I want to tell her about the house and Foxx, and I want to tell her to let Brock know I'm okay. But she says goodbye, and the line goes dead before I can.

And then sweet, sweet sleep covers me in its warm embrace.

CHAPTER 14

Renn

"Here you go," Foxx says, slipping me a small pink box. "Need anything else?"

"Nothing you can give me."

Foxx gives me a look—a warning not to waste his time. It's always funny when he acts this way since I'm paying for his time. *Shouldn't I be able to waste it?* Maybe on mere mortals. Foxx Carmichael is one tough motherfucker, and when you're that much of a badass, you make your own damn rules.

"Thanks, Foxx."

He nods and closes the door behind him.

Blakely is still in the bedroom, finishing her manicure and pedicure. Bianca suggested a little pampering for my new wife, and Astrid arranged for a nail technician to arrive after Blakely's nap. It took everything I had not to bother her while she slept. Lucky for her, I had a lot to get done ... including *this*.

I open the box with the *Siggy* logo drawn in a delicate white script. Inside is a light pink diamond ring with two baguettes on either side. Surrounding the stones is a ring of smaller diamonds that trails down the platinum band. A tiny emerald is embedded on the side, a trademark of the high-end jewelry boutique that my mom and sister love.

I haven't seen the ring in person until now. The plane left the hangar in Tennessee, made a quick stop in Savannah to pick up the ring and Foxx, and then jetted to Las Vegas. Foxx locked it in a safe, and I didn't get a chance to look at the most expensive piece of jewelry I've ever, and probably will ever, purchase.

It's worth it, though. Or, it will be if she loves it.

My stomach flips at the thought of giving Blakely Evans a wedding ring. It should scare the hell out of me. I go out of my way to ensure that no woman ever reads too much into our relationship, lest they get the wrong idea and think it'll become something permanent. But I'm not nervous. Hell, I might be a little excited to watch her reaction.

That's what scares me.

"Hey, Mom," I say after picking up my ringing phone on the table in the foyer.

"Hi, kiddo. How are you?"

Her voice, calm and kind, makes me smile. "I'm on my honeymoon, you know. It's kind of rude for you to call."

"I can't help it. I'm excited. I can't wait to meet your wife and take her shopping and invite her over for dinner and—"

"Whoa, lady. Chill out a little, will you?" I chuckle. "You can't come at her with all that at once. You gotta ease into it. Maybe start with hello and work from there."

"So I shouldn't mention that I've been going through her social media, right?"

I shake my head. "Why would you do that?"

"I have to know what my daughter-in-law likes, Renn. Will she want coffee or tea? Does she like dogs, or should I put Willard and Winifred in the kennel when she visits? And it helps to know what she looks like …"

Sighing, I lean against the wall and stare across the ocean.

Unlike my father, my mother has been all-in from the start. It's unsurprising, being that this is her dream. But what is a little curious is that she's never once asked me if it was real. And I wonder why.

"Mom?"

"What, sweetie?"

"Why have you never asked me about the Vegas wedding to a

woman you've never met? I mean, I appreciate the support, but I do find it a little odd."

She laughs softly. "I figured you got enough of that from your father. Besides, you are an intelligent, capable man, Renn. You've known Blakely for years, so I knew there was a solid friendship there." She breathes through the phone. "You seem happy. At the end of the day, that's all I really care about."

A smile slips across my lips.

"Are you happy?" she asks.

Voices whisper through the house just before a door shuts. I glance over my shoulder as Blakely enters the room.

My God.

"Renn?" Mom asks.

I clear my throat. "Hang on." I drop the phone to my side and turn to my wife.

Her face is bright and beautiful—*refreshed.* A blue tank top with thin straps accentuating her dainty shoulders hangs close to her body. Every curve, every bend and dip, is on full display.

"That was the most relaxing thing I've experienced in a long time," she says, padding barefoot across the floor. "You didn't have to do that for me."

"So you enjoyed it?"

She laughs. "Yeah. Of course, I did."

"Then I had to do that."

"Renn! What's going on?" Mom says, her voice growing louder.

Shit. I chuckle, bringing the phone back to my ear. "Sorry, Mom. Blakely just came in."

"Oh, may I please say hello?"

"I don't know," I say, teasing her. "I'm afraid of what you might say."

She scoffs. "Renn Patrick, you underestimate me if you think there's no chance of me having Jason fly me to Australia to meet your wife."

I laugh, my eyes trained on Blakely. "You wouldn't dare."

"*Try me.*"

"My mom wants to say hello," I say, tilting my mouth away from the phone. "You don't have to humor her."

122

"*Renn* ..." she warns from the other side of the world.

Blakely holds a hand with sheer pink nails. "Gimme."

I give her the phone. "Is the phone all you want? Because you, my lady, are smoking hot."

"Behave. Your mother can hear you." She blushes and lifts the device to her ear. "Hi, Mrs. Brewer."

I can't hear what my mother says. I only know it makes Blakely laugh.

She moseys around the room, totally at ease. She chats with my mom about our wedding, filling in details, which I'm pretty sure she fabricates, and what led to our decision.

"Oh, you know—tequila," Blakely says, lifting her gaze to mine. A playful smile kisses her lips as she laughs at my mom's reply. "That whole night is such a blur. But that's how it's supposed to be, right? When you're in love and marrying the man of your dreams, you get lost in the bliss."

I raise my brows approvingly. "The man of your dreams?" I whisper.

She rolls her eyes. "Yes, Mrs. Brewer, that sounds lovely. Let's have lunch when we get back to Tennessee." Blakely's eyes widen. "Absolutely. Here's Renn."

I take the phone from a flustered Blakely.

"Okay, Mom," I say, my heart beating fast. "I need to go take care of my wife."

"I love this for you, Renn. I really do. She sounds like a delight."

"I'll see you in a couple of days."

"Renn?" Mom asks.

"Yeah?"

"Coffee, dogs, and she's absolutely stunning."

Will she want coffee or tea? Does she like dogs, or should I put Willard and Winifred in the kennel when she comes to visit? And it helps to know what she looks like ..."

I grin.

"Are you happy?" I ponder the question for a few moments, taking stock of how I feel. *Am I happy?*

I shouldn't be. I should be afraid of losing my contract, fucking up Dad's deal, and dealing with my father when we return to the States. *Of being married*. But the longer I think about it, the more evident it becomes that the only thing that makes me unhappy is the idea of going back home.

Is it the excitement of something new that's giving me a shot of adrenaline? Maybe. *Is it being back in Australia, a place that feels a lot like home?* Could be. *Or am I truly enjoying being around a woman who has fascinated me from the moment I met her but has been off-limits from day one?*

My stomach knots. "Mom?"

"Yes, son?"

I watch Blakely inspect her manicure and feel a deep sense of satisfaction from knowing I did something to make her feel good.

"I am," I say. "I really think I might be."

She sighs happily. "We'll talk soon. Enjoy your honeymoon."

"Love you. Goodbye."

"Goodbye, sweet boy."

I exhale and turn off my phone, tossing it onto the sofa.

Blakely shrugs. "Is it weird that I just met my mother-in-law for the first time on a phone call?"

"Nah. Everything I do has a bit of irregularity involved. It's to be expected."

She laughs.

"Are you hungry?" I ask.

"Starving."

"Great. Follow me."

We enter the kitchen to a spread of food delivered just before Foxx came by with the ring.

"I didn't know what you like," I say, a rush of frustration over that simple fact filling me again. "So I ordered a few things."

"A few things?" She leans over the table and inspects the dishes. "There are three, four—five main courses here." Her head twists to me. "You could've just asked what I wanted and saved yourself a hefty sum of cash."

I chuckle, opening a bottle of wine and pouring us each a glass. "Yes, but you were supposed to be enjoying yourself. I didn't want to put the burden of what's for dinner on your shoulders."

She slumps before shoving off the table. "That's the sweetest thing."

"*Wow*. Don't set your expectations too high."

She laughs, accepting a glass from me. "What are my options?"

"We have Jerusalem artichokes with local mushrooms, scotch fillet, a mussel dish with leeks and saffron, and beef tartare with karkalla seaweed. And a chocolate cake for dessert."

"You got a chocolate cake?"

"I promised you one for your birthday and then kind of married you instead."

She hums and takes a seat at the table. "Look at me now, getting the best of both worlds."

"I'd hold off on saying that."

"Why?" She watches me sit across from her, smug. "Do you have plans to show me something better?"

My cock twitches to life. I want to answer her, to tell her exactly what I plan on showing her. But if I do, it'll only embolden her. It'll drive her much crazier if I ignore it.

"What do you usually have for dinner?" I ask, taking artichokes from the dish.

She blinks, momentarily confused. Her recovery is quick and rather impressive. "It depends if I'm alone or with someone."

I spear a piece of vegetable a bit harder than necessary.

"If I'm alone, I'll do a simple pasta or takeout," she says. "But if I'm with someone, I'll make chicken or a steak—whatever they like that I have on hand."

"It's good you won't have that problem anymore."

She scoops a mussel onto her plate. "Oh really? Why?"

"Because I'll always have what you like at home."

I chew slowly, watching her attempt to be coy.

"Oh, I see," she says. "You're insinuating that I won't have to worry about having a man over any time soon."

Ever. I flinch. *Easy, Brewer.*

The unexpected blast of jealousy catches me off guard. I wipe my mouth with a linen napkin, keeping my eyes on my plate.

"What about you?" she asks, switching gears. "What do you have for dinner?"

"Depends on where we are in the season. A protein, sometimes fish, green vegetables. I like sweet potatoes, pasta."

"Do you cook?"

I chuckle. "Nope. I order out. It's my specialty."

"Well, I love to cook. It's the only domestic gene I possess. It reminds me of being with my grandmother and my mom, breaking green beans in the summer. Canning tomatoes. Sunday dinners with fried chicken, mashed potatoes, and too many salads to keep track of." She smiles sadly. "I can't smell fried food without thinking about my childhood."

I reach across the table without thinking about it and lay my hand on hers. She looks up at me, her eyes wide and full of appreciation.

Blakely has told me that she misses her mom and wants a family of her own so she's not alone. I've heard what she's said. But this moment, this look on her face, tells me more about what she wants and needs than any story she's ever shared.

My throat squeezes as I pull my hand away.

"Well, guess what?" I say. "I have a massive kitchen with every gadget in the world. You can cook anything you want, and I promise to eat it."

She bites her lip and returns her attention to her plate. "What about you? Did your mom cook for you when you were little?"

"Hell no." I laugh. "She had six kids with six schedules and six sets of friends—and a husband that might come home at four in the afternoon or four in the morning. Unless it was a holiday, we were probably ordering food. She gave up trying to wrangle us while I was still in elementary."

"Your mom was super sweet today."

I take a sip of my wine. "Yeah, well, she's having the best day of her life—I assure you."

"Can I ask you why she's so lovely and your dad ... isn't?" She sets her fork on her plate. "I don't know what I'm allowed to ask, so I apologize if it's too personal."

I sit back in my chair and study her. *What an impressive, unique woman.*

I've never been with someone who asks questions to actually get to know me—*the real me.* Someone who seems to care. Blakely isn't pushing or prodding, but she does have an honest curiosity to get to know things about me that aren't superficial. *And I like it. Probably too much.*

"Mom was always around," I say. "She got us off to school, came to the principal's office when Jason and I got suspended—which happened more than I care to admit."

She grins, sipping her wine.

"You know, she was at our practices, games, and science fairs. But Dad ..." I take a drink and let it settle in my stomach. "He was busy. I don't fault him for that. I respect it. But he has this warped sense of reality."

"What do you mean?"

I shrug. "I don't know how to explain it. It's as if the only things that matter to him are the things he can write down. The things that get written down. It's really just a personality conflict between him and me. He gets along fine with my siblings. Well, he and Tate butt heads—*stop looking at me like that.*"

"Sorry. I'm just excited to get more info about Tate."

The energy shifts around us, and I place my glass on the table. There's a challenge on her face, in her words, and whether she's ready for it or not—*I am.*

"You're going to pay for that," I say.

She lifts a brow. "Promise?"

I don't answer her, letting her sit with her question and ponder the answer. Instead, I drink my wine and study her pretty face. *My wife's pretty face.*

This might be the best mistake I've ever made.

"I have something for you," I say finally.

"What's that?"

Her tone tells me what she thinks, or hopes, I mean. She's not wrong. *But not yet.*

"It's a birthday present," I say. "I know nothing can top me as your gift, but I wanted to try."

She laughs.

I slip the pink box from my pocket and hand it to her. Her eyes widen as it sits in her palm.

"What is this?" she asks.

"Open it."

I hold my breath as she lifts the top from the box. When she gasps, I exhale.

"Renn! What the hell did you do?" she asks, a laugh painting her words.

"It's your wedding ring. I mean, if you like it."

She tears her eyes away from the diamonds. "What do you mean, *if I like it*? It's ..." She laughs in disbelief. "Did you actually buy this?"

"What is it with you thinking I'm stealing shit? First, it was babies, and now it's rings."

Her cheeks flush. I can feel the warmth run through my body.

"Look, cutie. This is a real marriage, even if it's only for a short time. And I'm not about to let anyone think I'd marry you and not treat you like a queen."

"You don't think it's over the top? Should I give it back to you when we get divorced? Yeah," she says hurriedly. "I should. Of course, I should."

"Blakely."

She sucks in a breath.

"That's yours. I want you to have it." I start to tell her to do whatever she wants with it once we divorce, but I can't make myself say the words out loud. It would break the moment.

No, it would probably break more than just the moment. *I like this woman.* I may not have ever thought I'd marry her, but now that I have, I want her to have everything she wants ... which seems like such a one-eighty from my usual position. *But this is Blakely.* Everything is different.

"Please keep it," I say. "I bought it for you. I hoped you'd like it."

"In that case, thank you. You've blown my mind a little bit."

Just wait until later ...

I take the box from her and remove the ring. My heart pounds as I slip the delicate band around her left finger.

She lifts her hand in the air. "Now I get it."

"Get what?"

She places her hands on her lap. "That's why you got my nails done. Because you knew you were putting a ring on one of them."

I smile.

"You, Mr. Brewer, are doing extremely well on your first day as a husband."

"Am I?"

"Yes." Her eyes darken. "But you could do better."

I hum, pressing my shoulder blades against the chair to keep from grabbing her and proving her right.

She stands between my knees, bumping one with the side of her thigh to make more room. The contact sends a shock through my system until it pools in my cock.

The heat of her gaze—how it tells me exactly what she wants—is palpable. The parting of her lips, her hair falling to one side, and the slow, sexy smile that slips across her face makes it very hard to resist.

I lift my chin until our eyes lock. *What do you want, Blakely? Tell me.*

"So you're my husband now," she says, gripping the arms of my chair and boxing me in. The top of her dress hangs low and exposes the top of her cleavage. "That means I can kiss you whenever I want, right?"

I smirk.

She holds my gaze and slowly, deliberately lowers her mouth.

Fucking hell.

Her lips are soft, silky—pillowy against my own. She holds my face as she moves her mouth against mine.

My blood burns hot. Every muscle tenses. My fingers itch to touch, feel, and claim every part of her as mine.

Her lips, sweet from the wine, part and allow my tongue to slip inside. She combs her fingers through my hair as I deepen the kiss, scraping her nails across my scalp.

I bite her bottom lip, eliciting a yelp, just as I palm the backs of her thighs and tug her closer. She sags against me. Her mouth opened for my use, her neck falling to the side to offer me access.

Blakely moans into my mouth, sending a shock wave spiraling through me. I chuckle. She wraps my hair in her fists and tugs my head back.

Heat radiates from her pussy, warming my fingers that are gripping her inner thighs. She spreads her legs farther to encourage me to continue their ascent toward her opening.

I want her. *My God, I want her.* I want her so badly that I could crawl out of my skin ... but I don't.

Instead, I sweep my tongue across her lips. Dig my fingertips into her smooth skin. Absorb the weight of her chest pressed into me.

And then release her. I pull away.

Blakely pants, struggling to regain her composure. The taste of her lingering on my mouth does nothing to quell my ache for her. My painful, desperate need to be deep inside her.

"What?" she asks, her eyes wild. "Why did you stop?"

"Because you haven't begged."

CHAPTER 15
Blakely

I stare at him. "What did you say?"

He smirks, picking up his glass of wine and turning toward the kitchen.

My lips tingle from his kisses. The bottom lip burns from the bite he delivered when I scraped my nails against his scalp. A ball of fire sits in my core, spreading warmth through me that's growing hotter with every minute.

"You do know what honeymoons are for, right?" I ask, leaning against the table.

"Yup." He refills his glass, watching me out of the corner of his eye. "*Fucking.*"

The word rolling off the lips that I can still taste on my own is enough to make me want to scream.

"Yes. So why don't you fuck me, Renn?"

He places a stopper in the bottle. "Aren't you all hot and bothered."

"*Don't play with me.*"

He places a stopper in the bottle. "Funny. I thought that's exactly what you wanted me to do."

The fire from my core radiates to the top of my head.

He sips the wine lazily, like he's in no rush. Like I'm not standing here, practically begging him to have his way with me.

"You are gorgeous, Mrs. Brewer," he says, twirling the glass between his fingers. "If only you knew how hard I am right now."

I shift in a futile attempt at relieving some of the pressure between my legs. "Then show me."

"I warned you—I only get turned down once."

This fucking man. "I didn't *turn you down*. I simply reminded you of the reasons we shouldn't fuck. But the circumstances have changed."

"Some of them."

"Like you're my husband now."

His eyes blaze. "That would be one."

We have a standoff, and neither of us is willing to break. It's ridiculous because we both know how this will end—with me screaming his name. But if he wants to make a game of it, I'll play to see who will give in first.

I down the rest of my wine. Where's the tequila when you need it? And then set the glass back on the table with a thud.

He doesn't move. Doesn't blink. He waits for my next move.

I unwind my hair from the top of my head and let it fall to my shoulders. "It's getting hot in here. Don't you think?"

I flick the hair tie in his direction. He snags it out of the air without breaking eye contact with me.

"You know, I don't think I've said *thank you* for bringing me here," I say, slowly lifting the hem of my tank top.

Renn's eyes flicker to my stomach and then to my chest as I expose more skin.

"I've never been to Australia before." I draw the fabric over my head and discard it onto the floor. "It's beautiful here."

He nods appreciatively. "I've never seen it more beautiful than it is right now."

"That's the funny thing about nature." I slide my hands into the front of my shorts, working the button in the same way he sipped his wine—slow enough to drive him wild. "Things can change minute to minute. They can get more beautiful." I pull the zipper down, looking at him through my lashes. "*Hotter.*" I tuck my hands into the band and slide them over my hips. "More savage."

My shorts hit the floor.

His Adam's apple bobs as I stand in front of him in my bra and panties. "That environment makes things *harder*."

I grin. "I bet it does." I turn around, giving him an unbridled shot of my ass. "And you know what happens when things get to the tipping point." I look at him over my shoulder. "Everything gets wetter."

He chuckles, his eyes flashing with a look that has the potential to cause an orgasm. "This is absolutely worth the pain."

"The pain?" I bat my lashes while unclasping my bra. "Oh, baby. I could help you with that."

"I know you can. And you will."

"Will I?" I twirl my bra around my finger before tossing it to the side. "Or will I not?"

My hands tremble as I slide my panties down my legs. I bend over, showing him what he's missing.

"You're only making this worse for yourself," he says, smirking. "But you do you."

I suck in a breath, wishing again that I had a shot of tequila, and face him.

His eyes sear a trail from my mouth, over my clavicle, and down to my beaded nipples. He bites his lip, his hands going to his pants, as he rakes his gaze over my stomach and hips.

Goose bumps ripple in their wake, leaving my skin singing.

"You are, by far, the hottest woman I've ever seen," he says, taking his cock out in his hand. "I could just stand here and stare at you."

I grin. "Why do that when you could be inside me?"

He strokes himself in a long, slow motion. The size of his cock is outstanding, but I would expect nothing less. He's rock hard—the head swollen. A bead of precum sits on the tip.

I clench my thighs together. They're damp and sticky, and the friction of the pressure is just enough on my clit to bring me to the precipice of his demands. *To beg.*

"I wonder what you taste like?" he asks, his eyes hooding. "Will you moan when you're sitting on my face?"

"Fuck you, Renn."

"Say the word. *Please*. Just say the fucking word."

Nope. I gather what self-restraint I have left and push the food to the far end of the table. Then I climb on it, sitting my bare ass against the cool stone, and spread my legs.

"I'm going to part that little pussy with my fingers and lick every inch of you until you plead with me to stop," he says, walking toward me.

My breathing picks up, coming in and out in rapid succession. Anticipation is killing me, right along with the pulsing of my clit.

I need relief. *I need it now.* But I'm too powerful right now to give in. *And he definitely deserves to be teased.*

I lean back, holding myself up with one hand. My nipples point at the ceiling. They're so tight they hurt.

"There's not a scenario in which I see myself asking you not to put your face in my pussy," I say, inserting a finger inside me.

I gasp, holding my breath as he reaches me. He pumps himself, his eyes on me, squeezing the liquid at the tip. In one quick swipe, he cleans the head with his thumb.

My heart pounds as I watch him lift his hand to my mouth.

"I get a taste before you?" I grin, sitting up and wrapping my hand around his wrist. "So generous, Mr. Brewer."

He starts to speak but stops as I suck his thumb into my mouth. His cum is salty and warm and only makes me want more.

I swirl my tongue around it, looking him in the eye, before I release it. He drags the pad across my teeth and over my bottom lip. It sends a chill down my spine.

"You are dirtier than I expected," he says.

"Are you disappointed?"

He laughs. "Hardly." He pulls a chair over and sits at eye level with my pussy. "You are just full of surprises. That's all."

"And, sadly, not full of your cum."

His brows shoot to the ceiling as I lean back again and shove two fingers inside me.

"You have no idea how much you turn me on," he says, stroking himself. "I'm watching you slide in and out of that tight hole, knowing you're imagining it's my cock instead."

"Do you want to guess how many times I've gotten myself off while imagining it was you?"

He groans. "Hopefully, as many times as I've jacked myself off in the shower and pretended it was you wrapped around my cock."

My fingers slide in and out, brushing against my clit just how I like it.

"There's not one thing I don't love about you, Blakely." His voice is gruff. "The way you torment me. The sound of your laugh." He strokes himself faster, mimicking the speed I'm using on myself. "The roundness of your hips and the heaviness of your tits. I love the way they hang like they're waiting to be sucked."

My head falls back as my back arches. Even though it's not him touching me, his words are a match to my libido.

"Are you going to come?" he asks. "Are you going to get yourself off in front of me?"

"Do you want me to?"

"I'm dying to watch you fall apart, beautiful."

"You're lucky." I moan. "I'm about two seconds from it."

The chair squeaks across the floor as he snatches my wrist. I jerk upright as he pulls my hand from between my legs. His eyes sparkle.

"*Renn*," I say, panting. My legs are stuck to the table. "What the hell are you doing?"

"I changed my mind."

"I'm going to come with or without you."

He shrugs, a smirk pressed against his lips, and walks out onto the patio.

He lost his clothes at some point, and I'm sad I missed that. But as I follow him outside into the evening air, I take in his round ass, thick legs, and a back muscled to perfection.

The sun sets low on the horizon. Sounds of laughter on the beach float up on the warm breeze.

Renn sits on the loveseat and rests his arms along the edge. Naked Renn sitting outside, naked, with his cock straight up in the air, is a sight to behold. *If I wasn't borderline pissed at him.*

"Stop playing with me," I say, my body on fire.

"You started this. *You* took your clothes off and started finger fucking yourself."

"Because you wouldn't."

135

He leans forward. "Because you didn't ask."

I'm pretty sure I did. *I think*. Hell if I know because my head is a pit of chaos that can only think about getting fucked.

"Tell me what you want, baby. Ask me for it," he says.

I'm weak, and he knows it. "I want you to fuck me."

"How bad?"

"So bad that I can't think straight, and I know I'm going to be pissed that I gave in and asked for it."

His laughter is low and throaty. "Well, then, do I have your consent?"

"Yes, motherfucker. You have my consent."

This entertains him too much, but I can't do anything about it. I want him. *I need that cock.*

He stands. "How do you want it?"

"I don't care."

"Not good enough."

I growl. "I hate you."

"Good. Hate fucking is usually better, anyway."

I grit my teeth. "Fine. I want you to take me inside, put me on the table, and throw my legs over your shoulders. I want to be hobbling tomorrow. Got it?"

He grips my chin and yanks me to him. I gasp, but he captures the sound with his lips. His tongue dips into my mouth, forcing its way in without apology. The kiss is loud and wet. *Intentional.*

I stumble forward when he lets go.

"Get on your knees for me," he says.

Fuck it. I drop to the decking and look up at him.

He winds my hair in his fist and smiles, closing the distance between us. "Come here."

I lick my lips. "I'd rather you come in here."

His grin turns devious as he guides my face to his cock. I open wide as he parts my lips, leaving a saltiness behind.

"This is the only way I can get you to stop talking," he says, holding my head still. "But I'm not mad about it."

I wrap my lips around him as he slides deep into my mouth. He hisses, his throat stretching as he tilts his head to the sky. I hum against him as he fucks my mouth. He rewards me with a deep, sexy-as-hell growl.

I'm dying for him. I'm beyond begging for him. I'd do anything he asked to get the relief I desperately needed.

"The first night I saw you," he says, palming my breasts, "I couldn't take my eyes off you. I watched you sitting beside that piece of shit, and I wanted to throw you over my shoulder and get you out of there. You were too beautiful, too sweet for him."

The first night? Wow.

As a reward for sharing that bit of honesty, I cup his balls, massaging them as he presses his cock into the back of my throat. Spit drips down his length and out the sides of my mouth. My eyes begin to burn.

"I want you satisfied," he says. "I want to give you every experience you've ever wanted. Promise me that you'll tell me if you want anything, no matter what it is. Okay?"

I nod.

"Good girl."

He tugs my hair gently and stops thrusting. I suck him as he leaves my mouth. *Nooo. Stop fucking teasing me, you bastard.*

He picks me up and carries me to the kitchen table within moments. He presses a long, lingering kiss to my lips before he urges me to lay back.

"*Renn* ...." I hate how desperate I sound, but there's no denying it. And there's not much energy left to fight it, either.

Sliding a finger through my slit, he growls. "You want to be on the table, your legs over my shoulders, and fucked so hard you hobble tomorrow. Right?"

I pant. "Yes."

"How did I get so fucking lucky?"

I cup my breasts, playing with my nipples as he easily tosses my legs over his shoulders. His hands go beneath my ass. He tilts it up and, before I can register what's happening, his tongue spreads me apart.

"*Oh fuck*," I mumble as a burst of flames ignites in my core. "*Fuck*."

He drags his tongue around my opening and then dips into it, watching me react to his touch. My back arches off the table, my legs

137

trembling on either side of his head. I reach for his head and those silky locks of hair and urge him to tongue me.

"I like that," I say, moaning as he traces circles around my clit. "*Ah*! Keep doing that, and I'll come on your face."

He flicks his tongue against the swollen bud and then stands. He wipes the wetness from his face.

"Warning," he says, licking his lips. "I'll need to spend more time doing that later."

"Poor me."

He chuckles. "I hate to say this, but it is a *poor you* situation. I need to grab a condom from the bedroom."

"The hell you do." I rise and look at him like he's lost his mind. "You were going to give me a baby anyway. Why are you worried about a condom now?"

Renn stills. "Don't say that, or I'll blow right here."

"*Oh*. Who has the power now?"

Two fingers slide inside me. "Whether you know it or not, you always have the power, Blakely."

"Good to know. Then I order you to move this along."

He grins. "I just had a physical when I signed my contract. I'm healthy and clean, and I haven't been with anyone since—strange, and sad, but true."

"I'm on the pill. Had my yearly exam two months ago and haven't been touched since tonight."

He lines his cock up to my opening. "So we're good."

"We're about to be."

"You asked for this."

"Yes, I did—*oh my God*!"

Renn slams into me in one long, hard stroke. The force is so strong that it rattles the dishes still sitting uneaten from dinner. My back rubs against the stone, burning my skin with each movement.

It's deliciously rough—almost painful.

"Do you like this, Mrs. Brewer?" he asks through gritted teeth.

"Give it to me. *Hard*." My legs shake. "Make me come."

He holds both legs at the ankle and pulls me to the table's edge. One ankle goes in each hand as he moves my feet toward my head. He spreads them, opening me up for him.

I scream as he drives into me, giving me just what I asked for. The pounding is so deep, so heavy and hard that I can see nothing, think nothing, do nothing but absorb the motion.

"Renn!" My voice pierces the air as tears form in the corners of my eyes. "*Oh, my fuck.*"

The words are disjointed, broken by the sound of our bodies smacking together. A plate falls from the table, breaking when it hits the floor.

I gasp as he drops my legs and grips my shoulders. He uses the leverage to drive into me, pulling me down as he pushes in.

My eyes open, *barely*, and I watch him fight not to fall apart.

"*Now ...*" I whisper moments before one hand finds my throat.

He squeezes just enough to make me light-headed, just hard enough to take the pleasure from a ten to a twenty.

My muscles flutter around his cock, tightening and pulsing in uncontrollable fits of ecstasy. Renn drives into me one last time.

He lets go of my throat, returning his hand to my shoulder, and holds me tight against him as he spills himself inside my body.

I shake. *I burn*. I shiver as the orgasm continues to wash over me in waves.

Renn slowly, carefully pulls out. A drop of cum hits my leg.

I think I'm delirious. I've never been so thoroughly fucked in my life. *There have been years of foreplay leading up to this moment. Damn, it was worth it.*

I blink up at him and smile. "Hi."

He forces a swallow. "Are you good?"

It's the concern in his eyes that gets me. The softness, the kindness that glues my wits and senses back together again.

"What?" I ask, trying to unstick myself from the table. "Where's the *Mrs. Brewer* now?"

He laughs and helps me sit up.

Renn brushes a hand through my hair and gently kisses my lips.

"Mrs. Brewer, how about we get a bath together?" he asks, his forehead resting against mine.

I wrap my arms around his neck. "I think that sounds like a great plan. But you'll have to carry me."

"You don't want to hobble?"

I laugh. "Not until tomorrow."

His laughter joins mine as he swoops me up in his arms and carries me to the bathroom.

CHAPTER 16

Blakely

"Okay, okay," I say, laughing. "I remember that. I remember carrying the llama down the aisle with me and insisting it was my maid of honor."

"You had everyone in the place dying. It's one of the few things I remember clearly. You and that damn llama."

Water splashes against the tub's sides as I poke my toes through the bubbles. Renn sits behind me, my back to his chest, with his arms wrapped around me. It's so strange how ... *easy* this is. Physically. Emotionally. In every way.

Two empty wineglasses, a plate and fork stained with chocolate icing, and one eucalyptus-scented candle rest on the windowsill, the flame flickering in the breeze through the open window. The ocean air mixed with Renn's cologne could be a bestseller if I could figure out how to bottle it.

"Do you think this is what marriage is really like?" he asks. "Or are we just in the honeymoon phase?"

I rest my head against him. "I'm sure the honeymoon phase is always like this—or it should be."

"I think this is what the whole marriage should be like. If you're going to spend your whole life with someone, shouldn't it be sex on the table and chocolate cake in the bath?"

"Sounds great to me." I lift my hand and let the water roll off my fingers. "When I get married for real someday, this is what I want. I want to feel like it's me and him against the world."

He kisses the top of my head.

I hold his arms against me and relax into him. A smile has permanently been on my face since we left the kitchen an hour ago. I know this isn't real, but I can't help but imagine if it was.

"Do you think you'd be into marriage if it were like this?" I ask. "Would it change your mind about it?"

He blows out a breath. The movement of his chest takes me with it.

I don't know why I asked the question, and I regret letting it pass my lips.

"I've never said I'm not into marriage," he says, his voice low and thoughtful. "I said I was keeping my options open."

True. "But I got the impression you were just being polite."

"Okay, I probably was just being polite. But I'm allowed to change my mind, aren't I?" He shifts his weight around me. "I don't know. Maybe I haven't been against it. I've just never found myself in a situation where I thought—*what if*? You know?"

"And I've spent my whole life wondering about it. I watched my mother struggle with being a single mom and the loneliness that came with the title. I remember lying in bed as a child, hearing her up in the middle of the night sweeping the floors or making lunches for the next day because two in the morning was the only time she had to do it."

Renn rests his chin on the top of my head. "That had to be hard."

"It was hard for her, I'm sure. And the older I get, the more I fear being in that same boat. Lonely. I will be a single mother because I never found a guy who I thought was worth building a life with, and I wouldn't settle for less."

His hands run up and down my arms.

I smile softly—not sadly, but not happily, either. I'm in an uncertain space between both emotions. I'm incredibly happy and content at this moment, but I know this bubble of ease is so very temporary.

I sigh.

What is one to do in this situation? Do you lean into the happy and enjoy all life has to offer? Or do you protect yourself from the heartbreak that's inevitably right around the corner?

We're treading carefully between flings and feelings. *"I've just never found myself in a situation where I thought—what if?"* But I know forever is out of the question.

I blow out a breath and study the ink etched into his skin. Each piece is deliberate—an intentional piece of artwork. They're a story that I'd love to know more about.

"Tell me about your tattoos," I say, tracing a line up his arm.

He pulls his left arm away from me and stretches it before us. Water drips off his fingers and into the tub.

"I got most of them when I was younger," he says. "Let's see ... Okay, this one." He points at a patch of skin in the middle of his forearm. "The seven is for my position on the pitch. I'm the openside flanker."

"That's a forward, right?"

"Yeah. Very good."

"I've learned a little over the years."

He chuckles. "The pineapple was a bet that went terribly wrong one New Year's Eve. The B is for Brewer. All my brothers have it somewhere on their body." He twists his wrist. "This is the outline of Australia, obviously, with a ball inside it. This one says *mom*—self-explanatory."

My heart warms at the sight of the small ode to his mother just below the crook of his arm.

"What about you?" he asks, returning his arm around me. "I didn't see any tattoos on your hot little body."

"That's because I don't have any. I've always wanted one. I've even looked at designs to see what I would get, but I haven't gone through with it."

"Why?"

"I'm scared I won't want it forever, and I'll be stuck with it."

"That's how I feel about Brock," he says, chuckling. "I befriended him, but now I don't want him forever, and I'm stuck with him."

I smile, taking a handful of water and dropping it on my chest. "Have you heard from him since we left Vegas?"

"No. Have you had a chance to call him yet?"

I shake my head. "Something is going on with Brock, I think. Ella said they aren't talking either. It's not like him to just shut down like this. I'm starting to get worried."

He hums. I don't know what that means, so I leave it.

We sit quietly. The peace is only broken by the occasional ripple of the water. The room is warm, the moonlight adding a touch of ambiance to the low-lit room. It's lovely and romantic ... and I'm sitting here with Renn.

"There's a difference between flings, feelings, and forever."

Ella's words echo through my mind, reminding me once again to keep a solid perspective on what's transpiring. Things might be amazing and working out better than I ever imagined. But we are in a bubble, isolated from the real world that will be ready to attack us once we return home.

Renn pulls me against him, nestling his head against mine. My chest fills with a warmth that I'm afraid to name.

"When do you think we should go back home?" I ask, hesitation in my voice. I don't want to go back. I want to stay cocooned in our little beach bubble for as long as possible.

He sighs. "I talked to the Royals today while you napped. They want a meeting with me as soon as I get back. They're pushing for midweek."

"Oh?"

"Yeah. They heard the news, obviously, and said they have concerns. I told them I married the only woman I could ever love and was happy, but I don't think they bought it."

I still.

"I told them I'd get back with them tomorrow and let them know if I could return that quickly," he says. "I feel like a dick cutting your honeymoon short."

My spirits fall. *Don't be disappointed. Keep a healthy perspective.* "Yeah, well, this isn't a real honeymoon anyway, remember?"

He clears his throat, shifting his weight again. "Bianca told me that the headlines aren't as bad as we feared. Naturally, there are some nasty ones, but she thinks our statement changed the narrative. She suggested we post something on our Social accounts to bolster our stance. I'm sure Frances would agree with that if I answered her calls."

My brow furrows. "Your publicist?"

"Yeah."

"Why aren't you answering her calls?"

He chuckles. "I don't know."

"Renn, talk to me."

"*I really don't know.* I'm pissed at her for taking my dad's calls. I'm tired of hearing the same shit." He blows out a hasty breath. "I get that I have a reputation for being a troublemaker, and God knows I perpetuate that. But everyone seems to think that means I'm incapable of making my own decisions, and it eats away at me after a while."

There's a vulnerability in his voice, a rawness that eats away at my heart.

"I'd like to tear my father a new asshole," he says. "That's what I'd like to do. The man doesn't care about *me*, anyway. He's only concerned about how I impact his public persona. And Frances—she cares about the paycheck. There's no loyalty to me. Sometimes, that bothers me more than it should."

"I think it *should* bother you," I say carefully. "No one likes to be surrounded by people who don't value them for who they are, Renn. This isn't a *you* problem. You're not wrong."

"It doesn't matter, anyway. I'm stuck in this role of being the bad boy. It sells tickets. It pays bills. Even if the league reprimands me for my behavior, they win. They're in the papers. There are new eyes on the sport."

I squeeze his thighs. *Oh, Renn.* "You feel like everyone uses you."

"Yeah. I guess I do."

My chest constricts at the hollowness of his voice. It's a sound I can't take—not from a man who I know doesn't deserve it.

"Let's post something on Social," I say, hoping he takes my suggestion correctly.

"Like what?"

I hold my hand out and inspect my beyond-beautiful wedding ring. *"Please keep it. I bought it for you. I hoped you'd like it."*

The pride on his face, the tentative hopefulness in his words that I would appreciate his efforts, sweep through my mind. *And I do.*

Let's show the world I'm on your side, Renn Brewer.

I wiggle my fingers. "Well, a picture of this gorgeous ring with the bubbles in the background would be nice."

"True. I wouldn't have bought that if our marriage wasn't real, right?"

A sad smile slips over my lips. "Right."

He leans over the edge of the tub and grabs his phone.

He takes my hand and moves it around until he finds an angle he likes. It has the bubble bath, wineglasses, and the moon in the background. *Click!*

"Let me see," I say, peering at the screen. "Oh, that's a good one. Look at how pretty it is. The light is hitting the ring perfectly."

He holds his phone in front of me and opens his Social app. He clicks the search bar, types my name in, and follows me.

"*Ooh,*" I say, teasing him. "I get a follow and don't even have to pay you."

"I'm taking it out of your ass later."

"Why wait?"

He shakes his head, his chuckle making me smile, as he returns to his profile. The picture is uploaded. His fingers fly across the keyboard. *The biggest win of all time.* He tags me, hits post, and then closes the app.

I nestle against him, pressing a kiss to his chest. "That was a nice caption."

"I've been thinking about it all evening."

A giggle escapes my lips. "You've been thinking about a social media caption all evening?"

"No. I've been thinking about how true that statement really is."

I lean up and turn to look at him. His eyes sparkle.

"If we have to cut this honeymoon short, I only have one request," I say.

"What is it?"

"I want to come in every room of this house."

He palms the back of my head and brings my mouth to his, grinning. "Your request is granted."

And it was ... over and over again.

CHAPTER 17

Renn

Blakely's soft breathing fills the air.

I stopped being able to feel my left arm an hour ago, but I can't force myself to move. Her head is curled in the bend of my arm with her face against my chest. An arm is draped over me and one of her legs is thrown over mine like she's afraid I might get up.

Little does she know that if I could press pause on this night and stay here forever, I would.

My affection for this woman has only grown since we've been here —since we got married. I expected to grow frustrated or bored with her like I typically do after being with someone for more than a day or two. But with Blakely, it's the opposite.

She's kind and sweet. Funny as hell. Every time I'm inside her, it's better than the time before. And that, in and of itself, is unsettling.

It kills me a little to leave Australia early. Here, we're perfect. Once we go home, all hell could break loose, and life has a chance to wedge itself between us.

I quite like where we are. Glancing down, I brush a strand of hair off her cheek. *I like it here a whole hell of a lot.*

"You're setting yourself up for failure," I whisper into the night.

My chest pulls so hard that I wince.

Call it jet lag, but a strange surge of energy bleeds through me. I carefully untangle myself from Blakely, pressing a kiss to her cheek and tucking her back beneath the blanket before I get up. As quietly as I can, I grab my phone and sneak out of the room.

The house is eerily quiet. The only sound comes from the waves through the open door in the living room.

Restless, I find myself on the patio overlooking the water below. The bright moon hangs high in the sky, casting its glow on everything below.

I grip the railing and hang my head—reality hitting me like a player on the pitch.

"If either of us starts to develop real feelings for each other ... Then we walk away immediately. No questions asked."

She said that for a reason.

I get it. I understand why Blakely wouldn't want to be with a guy like me. I'm problematic and unreliable—at least, according to the world. I'm foolish, according to my father. I'm selfish and crave independence, if you listen to me.

So why in the world *would* she be interested in me?

I grit my teeth.

A week ago, I had a best friend, a solid working contract, and a lull in my never-ending war with my father. Tonight, I have none of that. But I have her. And when I think about it, I really only want her.

"You're getting fucked up," I mutter, taking out my phone and checking the time. I do some quick math and realize Brock will be awake.

It rings three times before he answers. "Hey."

"Hey," I say back, leaning against the railing. "We haven't heard from you. Blakely is getting worried."

"Oh, but you're not?"

I laugh. "Well, I've been a little preoccupied."

"Renn? *Don't.* That's my little sister."

I laugh anyway. "All joking aside, are you okay? I know you're still pissed—or I would be, anyway. But that's all it is, right?"

He exhales harshly through the line. "You'd be pissed?"

I shove off the railing and wander aimlessly around the patio.

My admission probably opened a door to a new argument with

Brock, but that doesn't make it any less true. I would be madder than hell if Brock married Bianca in a drunken haze. There's no doubt about it. She deserves better than that ... and so does Blakely.

I suck in a breath. "I'm sorry for all of this. It was careless and irresponsible—and I should've kept my head together that night and taken care of your sister like I said I would. My life is a shit show at all times, and it was shitty of me to put her in a position to be in the middle of it."

He stills and says nothing.

"But, dammit, Brock ..." I run a hand through my hair. "You have to know that I wouldn't hurt her, right? Tell me that you know that I will do everything I can to protect her from any fallout. *I mean that.*"

I stop at the loveseat and stare off into the night. It takes him a long, tense couple of minutes to reply.

"I appreciate the apology," he says. "I know you mean it."

A sigh of relief leaves me.

"You know," he says, "I've been thinking about this—and other things—a lot since I've been home. I was so fucking angry with you both for getting into this situation ... and I was mad that you added another load of stress on me."

My brows pull together. "Another load of stress on you?"

He sighs heavily. "I had my physical a week ago for the upcoming season. The doctor told me that I'm fine, first of all. I'm not dying or anything."

I release a breath. "Fuck you for that."

He chuckles. "You're welcome."

"So what did he say?"

"Doc had me participate in this study about white matter in the brain of athletes. I go in every six months or so and have some testing done. It's supposed to help gather data so they can learn how to identify brain injuries in people with repetitive head impacts—like us."

My stomach drops to the ground.

"And apparently I show signs of neurological damage." His words hang in the air. "He can't say that for sure because this technology isn't perfect. But he highly suggests that I retire."

Oh fuck. I sit on the loveseat.

I try to process what he's telling me without panicking or jumping to conclusions. How long has he known this? Has he told anyone or is he dealing with this on his own? Is there more to the story that he's not telling me?

Damn you, Brock.

"Are you okay?" I ask. "You're all right, though, aren't you?"

"I'm fine. I mean, I feel fine. But now I have to make this decision about whether I want to believe him and walk away from the game, or risk it and play out my contract."

I gulp. "What does your gut say?"

"My gut says to say screw it and keep playing. I only have two more years until my contract runs out. I can play safe and get out of there before I'm thirty-five. I'll be fine."

"Have you talked to your sister about this?"

"No. And you won't either. Hear me?"

I bury my head in my hand.

My brain reels with this information—and an underlying concern that maybe I'm in the same boat. But either way, Brock is facing this decision, and I know what Blakely would say. *It will kill her if she loses her only family member left. She's had enough suffering. Enough pain.*

"Walk away," I say, my voice dead.

"It's two more years—"

"But it could cost you fifty." I stand, adrenaline building in my blood. "You can't risk it, man. Think about it. Think about your health. Your sister. Ella. Fuck, think about *me.*"

He chuckles. "Of course, you would make this about you."

"Well, yeah. You're about the only person in this world I like. You can't get all fucked up. Think about the bigger picture here."

"I'm honored." He sighs. "I've been an asshole to everyone—to you, to Blakely. Ella won't talk to me. I feel like I'm losing everything in my life all at once, and I have a small opening here to try to catch it."

"Good thing you can catch shit, then, isn't it?"

"What do I do, Renn? Do I tell everyone this and scare the shit out of them? Do I ignore it? What happens if this is a sign of what's to come? Would I even want to saddle Ella with that? Do I let her go? Do I walk away from my contract? What do I do with the rest of my life? *I don't fucking know, and I'm stressed out.*"

The call goes quiet as we process the last few minutes.

For the first time since we got here, I wish I was home.

"We leave here tomorrow night. If you want to sit down and go over it, I'll be there—post jet lag. Tell me when."

"Thanks, Renn."

"Of course." I look at the night sky. "You don't have to tell her, but please call your sister. She knows something is wrong and just needs to hear your voice."

"Do me a favor. Don't fuck this up with Blakely," he says.

"Shut up. You're not dying, asshole."

He laughs. "No, I'm not. But I can hear something in your voice that tells me that things between you are probably exactly what I fear."

"Hot?"

"Fuck off."

I laugh, grateful for the change in tone of the conversation.

"The two of you have always had this ... thing," he says. "If you're in the same room, you find one another. No one else exists. You laugh at the same shit. You have this push and pull that's amusing—or it would be if she wasn't my baby sister and you weren't you."

"Gee, thanks."

"You know what I mean." He sucks in a breath. "I've seen this coming for a long time, and I've tried to keep it from happening. I should've known it was a pointless attempt."

I force a swallow. "What are you saying, Brock?"

"I'm saying that you just told me that she needs me to call her. And that's the first time I've ever heard you give a shit about what anyone else needs." He laughs softly. "Just take care of her and don't hurt her. I trust that you will do what's best for her."

"We're doing this for ninety days. That's it."

"Whatever you're telling yourself. I'll see you when you get home."

I nod. "Okay. I'll see you then."

"Bye."

"Goodbye."

I end the call but keep the phone in my hand.

I can't go back to bed now because I'll toss and turn all night. I can't talk to Blakely about it. And I sure as hell can't sit here with my thoughts and wind up looking at online medical sites. *I'll be convinced Brock is dead.*

My fingers scroll through my contacts until I find Bianca's name. Ignoring the plethora of unread messages, I open her chat box.

> Me: Talk to me.

> Bianca: Hi to you, too. How is married life?

> Me: Going exceptionally well, as a matter of fact. I kind of like it.

> Bianca: That's scary.

I laugh.

Me: How are things with your neighbor? Is he still banging all night?

Bianca: No comment.

Me: COMMENT.

Bianca. <laughing emoji> Oh, he's banging all night …

Me: Oh. I see.

Bianca: It's going exceptionally well, as a matter of fact. I really like it. <heart-eye emoji>

Me: I assume you didn't call the police on him.

Bianca: <hiding face emoji>

"What the hell does that mean?" I ask, typing furiously.

Me: Tell me you didn't.

Bianca: How did I know he was just a dom? I was trying to do a public service.

Me: Okay, now I know you're kidding.

Bianca: I AM NOT KIDDING.

Me: There is no way you're any man's sub.

Bianca: Oh, big brother. The things I can't tell you. Now, let's transition out of this uncomfortable conversation and focus on other lighter things ... like Mom is throwing you a party when you get back. I'm supposed to find out when you're returning.

Me: We leave tomorrow.

Bianca: So anticipate an extravaganza this weekend. I heard there's a champagne fountain, caviar, and a string quartet in the works.

My lips twitch.

Me: Sounds good.

Bianca: You're just going to roll with that?

Me: And show off my beautiful wife to the family? Count me in.

Bianca: I'm ... puzzled by all of this. But I'm going to play along and see where this goes.

Me: You do that.

Bianca: Also, before I go, our family chat has about eighty-three million messages for you, and everyone is annoyed you aren't responding. So when you have a couple of free hours, you might want to dig through that.

Me: Or not.

Bianca: <laughing emoji> Okay, I gotta run. There's a meeting about the Arrows purchase in twenty minutes, and Dad asked that I attend.

My stomach tightens.

Me: What's the status of that?

Bianca: I'll let you know. Xo

Me: xo

"Renn?"

I look over my shoulder and listen. Blakely's sleepy voice calls out again.

"Renn?"

I make my way back to the bedroom. She's half awake, propped up in bed.

"Where did you go?"

"Just got a drink," I say, slipping beneath the covers beside her. "I'm back."

"Good." She snuggles up next to me. "Don't leave me again. Okay?"

I couldn't if I tried, especially with Brock's words bouncing around in my brain.

"I've seen this coming for a long time, and I've tried to keep it from happening. I should've known it was a pointless attempt ... I'm saying that you just told me that she needs me to call her. And that's the first time I've ever heard you give a shit about what anyone else needs ... Just take care of her and don't hurt her. I trust that you will do what's best for her."

I kiss the top of her head. *If you only knew ...*

CHAPTER 18

Blakely

"**D**o you really think I can do this?" I ask, shielding my eyes from the sun.

Renn grins. "Well, you probably won't go pro after this session. But, yeah, I think you can get the hang of it."

I gaze across the ocean. The water is a beautiful blue, glistening in the afternoon sunlight. The rays make the surface of Byron Bay shimmer. Wave upon wave rolls onto the beach, delivering surfers and swimmers back to shore.

"Let's practice one more time before we go into the water," Renn says. "Lie on your board."

"It's so sexy when you say that."

He rolls his eyes but laughs anyway. "Okay. Good. Now, paddle, paddle, paddle."

I pretend to paddle against the sand.

"Good. Now up!"

I hop onto the board like he taught me, keeping my back foot close to the tail. "My crouch is low. My arms are balanced." I glance over my shoulder. "My ass looks great."

He smacks it, his hand causing a crack in the air. I yelp, giggling, and pretend to fall off the board.

"You ruined my wave," I say.

He grabs my hand and pulls me into him. He nips my bottom lip with his teeth. "I'm going to ruin more than that when we get back to the house."

"You know what? I changed my mind." I trace my name on his chest. "I don't really want to learn to surf."

He laughs again while pressing a kiss against my lips. "Too bad. You're in Australia. You have to try to surf. It's the law."

"Oh, it is not." I pick up my board. "Besides, you didn't even let me have the real board with the wax. I have the foam one like a child."

"It'll be easier for you to use. Trust me."

I express my displeasure with a whine. My annoyance melts away rather quickly as Renn approaches the water's edge with his board, leaving me with a view that steals my breath.

Screw Mother Nature. This is the view that will never, ever get old.

His back muscles flex as he walks to the water. The silky dark strands of hair that I love to run my fingers through sit wildly atop his head. Sweat kisses his tanned skin, showcasing the tattoos on his arms and the single line of script down his side.

And his legs—*holy fuck, those legs*. If power comes from your thighs, that would explain a lot.

"Come on," he says with faux exasperation.

A couple walks between us, waving as they pass. Their presence keeps me from shouting something dirty back to him—*come on what?* I think he knows I had a retort because he's chuckling when I reach him.

"How long do I have to do this?" I ask.

"*Blakely*. You are the one who asked to surf today."

"Yes, but that's because you sexually satiated me after breakfast. But you just bit my lip and promised to ruin me. And now I can't think about waves and boards. The only *crouching* I want to do is over your face."

A slow smirk spreads across his face. "You're right. Fuck it. Let's go back."

"*Oh no*." I grab his arm and pull him back. "We're surfing. I had to endure the lesson, so I'm getting use of it. I just don't want to do it all day."

"You're going to be the death of me, Mrs. Brewer."

"Let's just hope that doesn't happen by way of shark."

He shakes his head and leads me into the water. "Try to listen and cooperate so you feel like you used your lessons, and we can go back to the house."

I laugh.

"Get on your board and let's paddle out," he says.

I follow his lead, getting situated on the middle of my orange piece of foam. We paddle a short distance, then place our hands on the board and press up to go over the breaking wave.

"Nice," Renn says, smiling proudly beside me.

"I'm a natural."

He snorts. "Keep paddling."

"Yeah, yeah, yeah."

The only good thing about this activity is staring at Renn without fear of running into someone or wrecking a car. And if I get eaten by a shark, at least I'll go down with stars in my eyes.

His arms are cut to perfection. Watching the water droplets slip off his skin, caressing the lines of his muscles is akin to foreplay.

"Okay, babe, here comes a wave," he says.

Babe? My stomach flurries, distracting me from the task at hand.

"Hands on your board," he says. "Pop up, shoulders square —*Blakely*!"

Splash! I topple spectacularly into the water, taking in a mouthful of salt. I'm met with his laughter once I get back to the surface.

"Are you okay?" he asks, offering me a hand.

I spit a few times to rid my mouth of the grit of the sea.

"Try again?"

I blow my hair out of my face. "I really think you're wrong about the hair being down thing." I struggle but manage to get back on my board.

"Your tits in that bikini top are incredible." He wiggles his brows. "I prefer them in my mouth, but this is my second favorite look."

"Glad to know that. Now focus on the waves, pal."

He fights a smile and paddles alongside me.

"Okay ..." I take a deep breath. "Hands on the board. Pop up. Arms out and shoulders square—*gah*!"

I fall into the water again. This time, I keep my mouth closed.

"I'm not even getting to crouch," I say, jutting my bottom lip out. "What am I doing wrong?"

Renn turns on his board to face me. "Nothing. This isn't easy. It just takes practice. You're doing great."

I get back on my board.

We attempt wave after wave, getting pushed back to shore and having to paddle out again. Renn is ridiculously patient and sweet, encouraging me with tips and positive reinforcement.

The interaction swells my heart as I imagine him teaching his child how to surf. The gentleness in his voice, the pride when I manage to finally crouch. The way he cheers for me when I stand all of two seconds of my final ride.

"Look at you," he says, pulling his board next to mine. Our legs dangle in the water. "You don't even seem like a rookie now."

"So I'm a pro?"

He laughs, bending toward me. I meet him in the middle, keeping my weight balanced on my board, and kiss him.

Renn's lips taste like salt, his tongue hot like the sun. His hands are rough against my face as he cups my cheeks with his palms. He kisses me softly and slowly—like he has all the time in the world.

Not like he has less than ninety days to kiss me like this.

Finally, he pulls away. His eyes search mine as he repositions on his board.

"You know," I say, remembering there are sharks and pulling my feet up on my board. "If I could stop time, I would do it right now." My cheeks flush as I realize I said that out loud.

"In the ocean?"

My gaze locks with his. "Here with you."

His pupils widen, but he doesn't say anything. I don't know if I caught him off guard or if he's unsure how to respond. I'm not sure what to say, either.

Did I just blow everything?

I paddle myself in a half-circle. "I'm going to try to go all the way in this time. My last ride."

"Get it."

I swallow hard, emotionally unbalanced from our shared moment, and wait for the next wave. When it comes, I press against the board, pop up, and slide my foot back to the tail. My crouch is low and fairly wide, and my arms are in the position Renn showed me. I think I hear him shouting behind me as I feel the wind in my hair.

"Holy crap," I say, my legs starting to shake. "I'm doing it. I'm—*ah*!"

The water rolls awkwardly and tosses me from the board. By the time I resurface, I'm so close to shore that it only takes a minute to find the sand.

I pull my foam buddy out of the water and turn to find Renn. He waves.

"Let's see what you got, Mr. Brewer," I shout, shivering despite the heat.

Like a professional athlete, he makes quick work out of getting to his feet and riding a wave that would've swamped me all the way to the beach.

I clap for him as he trudges out of the surf. "That was impressive. Very, very nice."

"That was the goal—to impress you."

"I was impressed before we got here."

He grins. "Did you have fun?"

"Yeah. I did. It's so nice here." I look around us—at the people minding their business. The lush vegetation. The relaxed vibe that makes me feel like I'm in a little piece of heaven. "I think this might be my favorite place on earth. How did you leave it?"

He takes my board from me. "Well, I got fired ..."

I laugh. "Oh. Right."

"I always loved it here, though. I missed my family, of course. But I visited home a lot, and they all came here to visit me off and on. So it wasn't that bad."

"Now I'm upset I never got an invitation," I say, walking alongside him.

"Can you imagine what Brock would've done if I would've invited you to Australia?" He laughs. "I only got you here now because I married you." He clears his throat, his face sobering. "Speaking of Brock, I talked to him last night."

"*You did?*"

We walk a little way in silence. With every quiet step we take, my anxiety rises a bit more.

"Is he okay? Is he just mad?" I ask, prompting a response. "What's going on?"

"He's fine. I promise. He's fine. Just under a lot of stress—physicals and paperwork. You know how it can be."

I watch him curiously. I do know how it can be. Getting clearances from the medical staff and passing the physicals can be a giant pain in the ass. But he's never had trouble before.

"Did he say why he hasn't called?" I ask.

"He's been busy with all of that. And, you know, he figured that you and I were honeymooning ..."

"*Right.* I'm sure he was all about leaving us alone to *honeymoon*."

He opens the little gate that separates the beach from the stairs leading to the house. "I think he's settled down a little bit. He wasn't as upset as he was in Vegas."

"Did you tell him we agreed to three months? If you did, that's probably why."

Renn follows me quietly up the incline.

I wonder why Brock didn't call me and if I should reach out to him. I didn't know he was having problems with work, but it makes sense.

Suddenly, I feel bad.

"Are we going home tomorrow?" I ask.

"Jason is flying in tonight our time to pick us up."

I nod, reaching the patio. Renn rests the surfboards against the house.

"I'll wait and talk to my brother when we return," I say, making my way behind Renn to the outside shower. "Maybe absence will make the heart grow fonder."

He turns the handle, and water sprays from overhead. "That sounds like a solid plan. Talk to him face-to-face. He's more likely to be cooperative if you're in front of him."

"What about you?" I say, stepping in front of him. I rest my palm against my name. "Are you more cooperative when I'm in front of you?"

His eyes blaze.

I drop to my knees, resting back on my heels. The shower mists me as I look up at Renn.

This is one of my favorite things about him—something I've never felt with another man. No matter how much we banter, tease, or do, he never makes me feel lesser than. Or inferior. Or embarrassed or shamed or silly for wanting or saying anything at all.

With Renn, I feel beautiful and strong—worthy in every way.

It's the best feeling in the entire world.

My gaze drops to his cock bulging through his shorts.

Well, it's almost the best feeling in the entire world.

"Husband?" I ask demurely.

"Wife?"

His voice is rough. The sound prickles my skin, settling off an ache in my core.

I bat my lashes. "May I please suck your cock?"

"*Dammit, Blakely,*" he groans as I work his shorts down his legs. "I —*shit.*"

I roll my tongue around the head, then lick down the shaft.

"Watching you with my dick in your mouth is one of the hottest things I've ever seen," he says.

I grin, pulling the tip in before letting it pop free.

"What are you feeling this afternoon?" I hold his gaze while I spit on the tip, running my hand over it and down his length. "Do you want to come in my mouth? On my chest? Deep inside me?"

"Are you trying to break me?"

"Maybe." I lean back and make quick work of losing my bikini top. "Or maybe I just really, *really* like to watch you come."

He palms my breasts and guides me back to his dick.

"I want to come in your tight little pussy," he says, sucking in a breath as I take him in my mouth. "I dream of that—feeling your body explode on my cock."

I moan against him, the sound vibrating against his hardness.

He plays with my nipples, groaning as the tip hits the back of my throat.

The sun burns my back—the skin still sensitive from the table yesterday. Sweat dots my skin as I take him in and out. I'm unable to look away from his face. Watching him enjoy my attempt at pleasuring him is nearly as good as orgasming myself.

He faces the sky, his throat bobbing as he swallows.

A bead of precum sits atop his cock. I lay my tongue against it, drawing it away and sucking the tip like I'm taking the top off an ice cream cone.

"I'm so wet," I say before taking him deep again. "My bottoms are soaked."

He scoops me up beneath my arms and drags me to my feet. His mouth takes control of mine, working my lips like he owns them. His kisses are frantic. Desperate. It's all tongue and teeth, groans and moans. Gasps for air as he kisses along my jaw.

We stumble beneath the water until my back hits the wall of the house. *Oof.*

Without missing a beat, he shoves my bottoms over my hips. I kick them away, flinging them into the makeshift shower room's foliage.

He digs his fingers into my hips as he lifts me. I wrap my legs around his waist. The siding scratches into my back. The water sprays into my face. My breath is stolen as Renn pushes inside me with little notice.

"Fuck!" I shout, arching my back—*needing* more contact.

"I love being inside you," he rasps. "Give it to me. Don't hold back."

He holds me up by my ass, pinning me against the wall. I use my shoulders as leverage against the wall in an attempt to meet him stroke for stroke.

My vision blurs. I dig my nails into his chest. My body is a blend of sensations from my head all the way to my feet locked at Renn's back.

"Fuck me harder," I say, my tits bouncing against my chest. "Like that. Just like that. My God. *Ah*!"

The sound of him driving into me is audible through the shower spray.

"Is that what you like?" he asks through gritted teeth. "Will that make you fall apart?"

My legs quiver. I press harder against his chest and brace for the orgasm that's *right there*.

"I feel you shaking," he says. "I can feel your muscles starting to lose control."

"I'm right there, Renn. *So close*."

"Come for me. Come hard on my cock."

"*Fuck*."

I scrape my nails against his pecs as the most intense orgasm I've ever felt floods me. There's no stopping it. There's no controlling it. It's wave after wave of pleasure so big and strong that I can't see or hear—*I can only feel*.

Renn steps forward and shoves me harder against the house. He shoves deep inside me, his cock pulsing against my flesh. His teeth gritted, his jaw flexing—with sweat dripping down his face, he spills into my pussy.

I grind against him, milking out every last ounce of it.

"There you go," I say against his ear. I move my hips in a slow circle. "You feel so good inside me. Your cum is dripping down my legs already."

He growls against my chest. He kisses my sternum before slowly pulling out and helping me to the ground.

My legs wobble. Face flushed. My body tingles with the aftershocks of my orgasm.

He shakes his head and smiles. "I will never be the same man again. You've wrecked me for anyone else."

I try not to beam, but I think I fail.

"Come on, cutie. Let's get rinsed off."

"Renn ..."

He stops and looks down at me.

When he said he loved everything about me yesterday, I knew he wasn't talking about *love* love. But still ... those words from his mouth are enough to fuck me up.

I know this isn't permanent. Renn isn't my forever husband. But moments like these—when I'm cherished and feel adored—it's hard not to think he meant more with his proclamation.

My heart skips a beat as I realize what I was going to say—three words that are absolutely asinine. *I love him as a friend. That's all this is. Well, that and the sex is hot. So there's pheromones, too.*

I paste on a fake smile and step under the water. "Nothing. Let's talk about dinner."

He pulls me against him, and we stand quietly, letting the shower bring us back to our senses.

CHAPTER 19

Blakely

"Renn?" I whisper. The moonlight fills the room with a muted glow. "Are you awake?"

He runs his fingertips along my arm. "Yeah. I haven't been to sleep yet."

"Me either. And I just had a thought. It's too late to do anything about it now, but I'm still curious."

He hums, giving me the green light to ask.

"Foxx couldn't see us today, right?"

Renn chuckles, his chest rumbling beneath my cheek.

I smack him. "*I mean it*. I'll be mortified if I have to look him in the eye and know he saw—or heard—what we were doing."

"I'm sure he fucks, Blakely. He's not a virgin."

"That's not the point."

"He's under an NDA. He won't tell anyone how you sound when you're moaning my name and begging me to fuck you harder."

"*Stop it*."

His chuckle grows louder.

"Looks like I can't go home now," I say, shrugging. "I'm just going to have to stay here and avoid the humiliation."

"Hey." He moves so he can look me in the eye. "There's not a damn thing for you to be humiliated about. You are every man's dream."

"I wish." I press my cheek against him again. "I'm resolved to having fake marriages and negotiating pregnancies like it's currency."

He pulls me to him. "Stop it."

I blow out an exasperated breath. "I don't want to go home, Renn. Don't make me."

"I'm not making you. I'll stay here with you. We can just become beach bums. You might have to go pro with your surfing to feed us."

"Or we can video ourselves having sex and sell it online."

"Excuse me? No one is seeing you naked besides me. *Ever.* Got it?"

I still at the insinuation. *No one is seeing me naked besides him. Ever.* That would mean ...

"I don't think I can promise you that," I say carefully. "Four months from now when I'm replaying this afternoon, I might need to find someone to give me a hand."

"Call me."

I tuck my chin so he can't feel me grin. "Oh, you'll be busy, I'm sure. I don't want to be needy."

"You don't want to be needy now?" He tickles me until I sit up. "You were awfully damn needy today, begging me to fuck you harder. And the night before when you told me exactly how you wanted my cock."

I laugh, straddling him. His cock twitches beneath the blankets.

He takes my hands and laces his fingers through mine. He's so handsome propped up against a set of white pillows with a sleepy smile.

"Well, if that's needy, I'm needy then," I say. "I have a lot more ideas on how I want your cock."

He smirks. "I think I need to add an addendum to our agreement."

"You do?"

"Yeah. I get the first call you make when you want fucked for the rest of your life."

I gasp. "What if I'm married to someone else?"

"I suppose I'll have to be good enough, so you won't want to marry anyone else."

He squeezes my hands.

The energy between us changes—softens. He plays with my fingers, twirling my ring around my finger.

An elephant sits next to the llama in the corner, and neither of us knows how to address it.

"We go home tomorrow," I say simply. "Back to real life."

"Does this mean our honeymoon is over?"

I laugh. "Technically, yeah. I guess it does."

"So I guess there are paparazzi camped out across the street from your house. Foxx told me today. We need to figure out how to get your stuff from your place to mine."

I groan, rolling off him.

"Our security team can do it," he says. "Or Ella, maybe, if you'd rather. I'd probably still want to send someone with her, though."

My head starts to hurt.

This is reality, the thing I've been avoiding. *The thing I've been dreading.*

Just how different will my life be now?

I take a deep breath. "I don't need a ton of stuff. I mean, I can get things as I need them. There's no sense in moving everything out when I'm just going to be moving everything back."

He nods, not looking at me.

"And I don't want security all the time, Renn. Honestly, I don't. I can't live like that."

Slowly, he faces me. "I have to keep you safe. And until I know that you'll be left alone, I can't risk someone doing anything to you."

The tenderness in his eyes slays me. It cuts me right to the core. I wrap my arms around his neck and lay on top of him, burrowing my face between his collar and jaw.

He rubs my back, pressing me against him like he's afraid I might get up.

"How do I make this easier for you, cutie? What can I do to make you happy?"

I smile softly. "Let's not go home. Let's stay in our honeymoon bubble and pretend nothing else matters. I like the beach bum idea."

"Well, we still have to go home and tell everyone goodbye. I need to cancel my contract with the Royals. Tell my dad to fuck off. You know —the usual." He wraps both arms around me. "Do you like it here that much? Would you really want to live here, or are you being dramatic?"

I ponder his question, unsure about what I mean.

Do I like it here because he's here with me? Because there's no stress between us, only stress against us? Would I want to be here alone? Without him?

"If it were like this? I'd stay here in a heartbeat," I say, finally. "All I have at home is Brock and Ella, and I'm sure they'd come to visit. I don't know how I'd make a living or if I could afford it. But if life was like it has been the past couple of days ..." I shrug. "It's been the best days of my life."

He snuggles me closer.

"But this isn't real," I say, for my own benefit as much as his. "It might feel like it ..."

"It does, doesn't it?"

"Yeah."

The word drops into the room and then slowly fades away.

We sit together in silence, both lost in our thoughts.

The idea of leaving in a few hours makes me want to cry. As soon as we're on the jet, the clock will start ticking to the end of our agreement. Although I wanted a contract, so to speak—a time limit on our commitment—now I regret it. I fucked myself.

"Blakely?"

"*Hmm?*"

"You know ... We don't have to end things right at ninety days, right? If we're having fun and things are working out, we could ... stay married."

It's such a confusing predicament.

On the one hand, my hopes rise sky-high at the thought of being with Renn for as long as I'd like. But on the other side of that token is reality—the longer I play pretend with Renn, the longer I go without having a real relationship.

This fits his lifestyle, no doubt. It's fun. It's sex. He's not beholden to me forever.

He'll happily walk away.

But forever—*a forever with someone who loves me with their whole heart*—is what I want. And sadly, he's made it clear he's not interested in forever ... with me, anyway.

"I think what you're wanting is for us to hang out," I say. "To hook up now and then—not be married for real. Maybe we can work that out for a while, you know? But at some point in the near future, I want to find a real relationship and settle down."

"Yeah."

The hoarseness of the word catches my voice in my throat. I roll over, my heart thumping, and look him in the eye.

"But you are my husband right now," I say, grinning.

It takes a moment—a long one—for his features to soften. "Sit up."

I do as he asks, confused.

He rolls to the side, taking his pillows with him.

I laugh. "What are you doing?"

"Grab the headboard and spread your knees."

My belly clenches. "What?"

"Now. Please."

I grin. "Only because you said please."

He smacks my ass as I crawl across the bed. I watch him over my shoulder as I place both hands on the back of the wooden headboard and spread my knees apart.

Renn slides back on the bed, grabbing my thighs and positioning himself between my legs.

Oh God.

Instantly, my pussy gets wet. My core turns into a pit of molten lava. My nipples bead as I look down at Renn's mouth just inches from my opening.

"Sit on my face," he says. "Let me taste that sweet pussy."

"I won't even make you say please this time."

I lower myself until I'm hovering over his mouth. He clenches my thighs, pulling me down harder. *Man, my legs hurt from surfing—and I didn't even really surf.*

"*Oh damn,*" I say, hissing into the air. And that's *not* from pain. His tongue is pure magic. My head falls back as my eyes squeeze closed. "*Wow.*"

Renn worships me—kissing, licking, and sucking my swollen flesh. I grind myself against his tongue, moving my hips like I'm sitting on his cock. He spoils me with attention. Ruins me with his enthusiasm. Destroys me with his dedication to making me come in his mouth.

There is nothing like this. No dirty talking, no foreplay—no sexual act this intimate and personal. This intentional.

"Can you taste me?" I ask, moaning as he sucks my clit into his mouth. "Can you taste your come from this afternoon?"

His fingers bite into my thighs.

"The way you railed me earlier ... So good, Renn. So good."

My wetness coats my legs. I can feel it as I move my hands from the headboard to his hair. I wind my fingers in his silky strands and urge him to lick me harder.

"Just like that," I say, pressing myself against him. "*Yes! Just like that.*"

I start to shake and begin to fall forward. He clamps his hands down on my legs to keep me from moving. I reach for the headboard and try to steady myself against the array of bombs bursting inside me.

"Renn!" I yell, the one-syllable name extended to three. "Stop! I can't take it. *Fuck!*"

He releases his grip and slides out from under me. I sag against the headboard, struggling to catch my breath.

His arm wraps around my front. He moves me around, laying me against the pillows. I'm a lump. Boneless.

"You seemed to like that," he says, smirking. He wipes my juices off his face with the back of his hand. "Am I wrong?"

"Ha." I start to move but wince. "You know I liked it, asshole."

He puts a hand on either side of me and lowers himself until he's hovering over me.

"I want you to remember that when you're considering letting some other man touch you," he says, staring me in the eyes. "There is nothing they can do that I can't do better. Nothing they're willing to do that I can't outperform. They can't make you come as hard or as often as I will. Don't forget it."

I don't know if this is jealousy or a warning. Is it a playful flex at how good he gets me off? Or is it a thinly veiled attempt at staking his claim ... to me?

Whatever it is, it's hot as hell.

I grab his shoulders and lower his face to mine.

"I might forget," I whisper against his lips. "You better show me again."

He slides his tongue and his cock into me, making sure his point is made.

CHAPTER 20

Blakely

Traffic is light. Renn seems to interpret this as a green light for action because he races through the streets of Nashville like it's his personal racetrack.

"My mom used to have this saying that went something like, 'Better to get there late than get to your grave early.' And that was when we had somewhere to be. The last I knew, we didn't have anywhere to be today," I say.

"I'm anxious."

He zooms by an SUV, crosses two lanes, and takes an exit.

"Well, so am I now," I say, yawning. "Do you always drive like this?"

"Only when I'm anxious."

I wedge my elbow against the glass and prop my head on my hand.

As much as I'd love for him to slow down, I can't deny that watching him drive is a major turn-on. It's the command. The confidence. The way his jaw flexes and his hand grips the steering wheel. It's subtly reminiscent of how he moves in the bedroom ... and the kitchen, outdoor shower area, patio, dining area, bathroom, foyer, and on the plane coming home.

And his backward hat doesn't hurt, either.

"Are you going to tell me what sparked this anxiety you speak of?" I ask. "Because you didn't seem nervous until now."

He glances at me out of the corner of his eye. "I'm taking you home. That's a lot of pressure."

I balk.

"It is." He turns his attention back to the road. *Thankfully.* "What if you don't like it?"

I giggle. "I'm sure I'll like it."

"I just want you to be comfortable there. And it's not like I had a lot of time to prepare for this since you whisked me off and married me in the middle of the night."

"Oh, right. *Sure.*"

He grins. The sight of his sweet, simple smile warms my heart.

"If it makes you feel any better, I'm a little nervous, too," I say. "Think about this from my perspective. I'm going to be in your house."

"*Our house.*"

"With your stuff."

"*Our stuff.*"

"And I won't know where anything is, or if I should be in a certain room, or where to put my stuff. Truth be told, I didn't think about the details of this until now. And it's a little too late to do anything about it."

He slips his hand off the gear shifter and takes my hand in his. He laces our fingers together and gives them a gentle squeeze.

"If you don't know where something is, ask," he says. "Or just look for it and put it wherever you want. As far as rooms go—you can go wherever you want. Snoop away."

I laugh.

"Astrid has organized my closet so you can put your clothes and things there with mine," he continues. "I honestly don't have a ton of stuff. She's always on my ass to get this or that, but I never do. I lived a bachelor life in Australia and didn't want to haul what I did have all over the world. It didn't make a lot of sense."

He pulls onto a quiet street lined with trees. The car slows, the engine roaring as it winds down. We're not on the street long when we pull up to a gate. Renn rolls down his window and waves to a man in a security booth.

"Hey, Rodger," Renn says.

"Good day, Mr. Brewer. Welcome home, sir."

"Thank you. I'd like you to meet my wife, Blakely." He looks at me over his shoulder. "Blakely, this is Rodger."

"Hello," I say.

"It's a pleasure to meet you, Mrs. Brewer. And congratulations."

I blush. "Thank you."

"I will have Astrid bring you the information you need to place my wife on the approved entry list," Renn says.

"Very well." The gates swing open. "Have a good day, sir."

"It was nice to meet you, Rodger," I say, waving.

"You also, ma'am."

Renn rolls up his window and creeps into the neighborhood on the other side of the iron fence.

Massive estates are sprinkled to my left and right. Each is more impressive than the next. Fountains and luxury cars, gardeners tending intricate gardens, and maids sweeping steps—a world I've never seen before.

Brock has always lived in fancy communities. I've teased him about it mercilessly. And I don't live in a bad area by any means, thanks to my brother's insistence on housing in well-to-do areas. But well-to-do or not, none of those places are anything like this.

"Bianca and Ripley live in Four Oaks, too." He looks at me. "That's the name of this community."

"I see."

"It's a little uptight for me. But I needed a place to stay, and I liked the house, and it was close to my family. In retrospect, might've been a bad plan. It makes them feel like they have the right to be nosy."

I smile at him.

"This is it," he says, pulling into a long brick driveway.

"*Wow*. Renn." I gulp. "This is your house?"

The front of the traditional-style home has wood siding and lots of stonework. There are ample windows that let in a lot of light. A cedar shake roof caps off the place with an upscale, beautiful touch.

"Do you like it?" He pulls the car around the side of the house. Three garage doors line the length of the building. "I have three acres here, which I love. It has a little more privacy than most homes in the area."

One of the doors rolls open, and he pulls inside.

"I don't even have words for this," I say, dumbfounded. "This is ... incredible."

His face lights up. "Come on. Let me show you the rest."

I unfasten my belt and climb out of the sportscar. Renn meets me at the front.

"There's too much space here to be practical," he says, opening a tall white door. "But it has a vibe I really love. It reminds me of Australia a little."

We enter a long hallway with light wooden floors, the lightest gray cabinets, and white stone countertops.

"This becomes a catch-all," he says, tossing his keys on the counter. "It's a bad habit."

"If that's your worst habit, I think you're doing just fine."

He reaches back for my hand. I give it to him without thinking.

"Okay, this is the kitchen," he says, bringing me into a gorgeous area.

The gray and white color scheme extends to this room. As predicted, the windows are black-framed, allowing the room to be flooded with light. The stainless appliances include an ice maker, wine chiller, and a built-in double-door refrigerator.

"I usually eat at the bar," he says, pointing at a sitting area around the island. "But there's a table by the windows and a proper dining room around the corner."

"This is ... unbelievable," I say, taking it all in. "It's beautiful, Renn."

His smile softens. "I'm so glad you like it."

"Show me the rest. Please."

He leads me through a sunroom with plush chairs, a small table, a cozy family area, and a larger living space. We tour a den, a bonus room he's yet to use, and an office full of trophies and plaques.

We pass three bedrooms with en suites and giant walk-in closets, and a powder room on each side of the house.

Renn stops to point out features like button-activated window coverings, natural materials, and light fixtures he had custom-made in Mexico. His attention to detail is exquisite.

"And now, to the room you've been waiting for," he says as we walk down a long corridor and through a set of double doors. "This is our bedroom."

Our bedroom.

My stomach somersaults as I step into the grandest, most luxurious bedroom I've ever seen.

Everything is oversized but still warm and homey.

The massive bed has dark wood and white bedding. Pillows are piled against the wooden headboard. The nightstands don't match; both look like antiques. They're a deep walnut color with intricate designs etched into the wood.

A sitting area is set up at the far end of the room with a sofa and lamp—and a fireplace with stone framing it. I move to the windows and peer across the property. A pool and hot tub have been built next to an outdoor grilling area. Beyond that is a lush, green lawn that ends at a tree line. I can imagine forest animals grazing in the backyard in the evenings. *Now it's going to be even harder to leave.*

"I don't know what to say, Renn, except your home is stunning."

"Come see this." He grins. "This is my favorite part."

We pass through a doorway and into an expansive bathroom. All white stone and bright, I see what he means by it giving Australian vibes. It reminds me of the bathroom in the honeymoon house.

There is a closet the same size as the bathroom with a doorway on the other side of the makeup table.

Renn comes up behind me and pulls me into him. He rests his chin on the top of my head. I wrap my arms around his waist and nuzzle into his chest.

"I can imagine it's hard for you to have me here with you," I say softly. "You don't trust easily—and I understand that. You couldn't."

He kisses my forehead, making me smile.

"It means a lot to me that you invited me here," I say. "I know I said on the plane headed to Australia that you were being self-serving with this, but I didn't really mean it. I know you're trying to protect me, too."

"I am."

"Thank you for that."

He holds me tighter.

We stand together quietly, both exhausted from approximately twenty-four hours of traveling. I lost count somewhere over California.

"Renn! Where are you?" A woman's voice carries through the house.

He kisses me again before releasing me. "That's Astrid."

"*Oh.*"

I hold my breath as he calls to her, and her footsteps sound against the floors. They stop inside Renn's bedroom.

"Are you decent?" she asks. "And can I come in?"

"Yeah. Come in," Renn says. He slips his arm around my waist.

A cheery-faced redhead bounds around the corner. Her hair is in a high ponytail, showing off her face full of freckles. I'd guess her to be in her mid-to-late twenties.

"You must be Blakely," she says, smiling brightly. "It's so nice to meet you."

"And you must be Astrid. It's nice to meet you too."

She turns her attention to Renn. "She's gorgeous. Don't fuck it up."

I snort, covering my mouth with my hand.

"What are you doing here?" Renn asks, feigning annoyance with her.

"Making sure you made it. Hoping to get a look at Foxx Carmichael." She whistles between her teeth. "If you get security, demand Foxx or Troy. Trust me."

I giggle at the look on Renn's face.

"What?" Astrid asks, shrugging. "I'm being helpful. Showing her the ropes."

"I'm going to cut your rope and set you free," he says.

"I couldn't be so lucky," she says, wrinkling her nose at him. "Anyway, Blakely. I'm here to help out however I can. I'm usually not here physically. I'm often running errands or helping Bianca. But I can be here if you need me."

What kind of life is this? "Oh, okay. Thanks."

179

"My number is in a little notebook on the desk in the kitchen. I left a bunch of notes for you, too."

Renn makes a face. "What kind of notes are you leaving my wife?"

"Your favorite takeout places. A copy of your schedule. My number. Bianca's. Ripley's."

"Tate's?" I ask.

Renn looks at the ceiling, making Astrid laugh.

She points at me. "*Oh, I like you*. A lot. We're going to be friends."

"I'm kidding," I say, tucking myself into Renn's side. "Come on. Don't be a grump."

"I've never actually disliked Tate, but I'm getting there," he says, sighing.

I smack his shoulder. "Quit it."

Astrid laughs again. "Okay, you two look tired as hell. I'm going to go. If you want me to send dinner over later, let me know. Brock brought some of your things by today, Blakely. There isn't much. It's all in two boxes on the table in your closet."

"Thank you. I ... I'm not used to this. So please excuse what I'm guessing is a look of bewilderment on my face."

She winks at me. "You'll get used to it." She walks backward. "Okay, kids. I'm out of here. I'll lock up behind me. Get some rest, lovebirds."

"It was nice to meet you, Astrid," I say.

"I enjoyed this interaction more than you. Trust me." She laughs. "Bye, Renn."

"Get out of here."

Her laughter trails behind her as she leaves.

I spin around and face my husband. *Astrid was right. He does look tired.*

I'd like to see what Brock brought over. I want to call him, too. Ella doesn't know we're back in town, and I promised her I'd let her know as soon as we landed. But as I read Renn and realize what he needs—sleep, and I know he won't do it if I don't lie down too—I make a decision.

Yawning, I unfasten the buttons on his shirt. "Let's get our clothes off and crawl into bed."

"You don't have to tell me twice."

I smile up at him. "I have a good feeling about this. We'll figure this out and be the best husband and wife team this city has ever seen." I push his shirt over his shoulders.

He cups my face in his hands and stares into my eyes. "Thank you, cutie."

My heart flutters. "For what?"

"For being you." He grins shyly. "For being mine."

I dip my chin, body flooded with warmth, and remove the rest of our clothes. Renn then takes my hand and leads me to his—*our*—bed.

Because this is home.

It feels like it, anyway. *And I already know it won't just be hard to leave.*

It'll be heartbreaking.

CHAPTER 21

Blakely

Everything hurts.

Groaning, I roll over and squint against the muted sunlight. The softest mattress in the universe dips as I move onto my side. The bedding smells faintly of Renn and fabric softener, making me smile from ear to ear.

I know he's gone, but I tap against his side of the bed anyway. My fingers curl against the empty sheets.

"Ugh."

My brain is foggy. I have no clue what time it is and even less of an idea about the day of the week. Time changes and jet lag, surfing, and three rounds of sex yesterday have left me clueless.

It takes a few minutes to fully awaken and convince myself I can stand without dying.

I get to my feet, slipping on a Tennessee Royals shirt that Renn let me borrow to walk to the kitchen last night. It hangs like a dress. But there's something wonderful about being encompassed by something of his.

My toiletries are in a bag on the counter in the bathroom. I'm not sure how they got there, but when we woke in the middle of the night, still wonky from our traveling, and hopped in the shower, there they were.

I quickly brush my teeth, wash my face, and comb my hair. Then I venture into the closet.

Just as Astrid promised, a box of my things is on the square table in the center of the room. The llama propped up beside it makes me smile.

Brock packed a random assortment of shirts, shorts, shoes, and dresses. *Thank God he didn't get into my lingerie drawer. That would've been awkward.* He added my computer and planner—because I refuse to go fully digital, and every item sitting on my vanity. At the bottom of the box is a note on top of a framed picture of me, him, and our mother from my living room.

Tears fill my eyes.

B,

You have twenty-six lip balms. Did you know that? WHY?

Renn asked me to grab you some things. I did my best. I locked everything when I left and set the security system. You had food in the fridge, and I'm sure you're not returning to get it. So I took it. You know I love hummus.

I know I've been an asshole, and I'd like to apologize to you in person. You're my favorite person in the world (don't tell Ella that). You deserve a face-to-face conversation. Please call me when you get back.

Brock

I place the note on the counter and dress. *Oh, Brock.*

It's felt so wrong to be at odds with my brother. He's been my person for so long, so for him to write this note means he's struggled with the past few days as much as I have. *I could use one of your hugs right now, brother.*

I blink back a tear.

My emotions are all over the place. I'm sure it's the culmination of the past week, topped with Brock remembering to send a picture of us with our mother that's the cause. Still ... *I hate being overly emotional.*

I trace my fingers over the glass—something I've done a million times. The three of us are so happy in the image. I remember Mom asking a stranger to stop and snap a picture that day, slinging her arms around our waists. Brock is bent, whispering something that I'm sure was wholly inappropriate. Her face is mid-laugh. My head is on Mom's shoulder while I *cheese* for the camera.

Sniffling, I stand the picture under the llama. "Keep this safe, okay?"

My cheeks are damp. I wipe them with the hem of my shirt as I journey through Renn's house.

The ceilings look higher, the molding more detailed. The rooms are more magical today. Ceiling fans cause the extra-long curtains to flutter against the beautiful floor.

I find my phone next to the sink. Leaning against the cabinet, I open the screen and see a list of texts—but my interest goes to the one on top. *Renn's.*

> Renn: Good morning, cutie. It was so hard, pun intended, to get out of bed with you still in it this morning. Why aren't we still in Australia again? I have a physical and a meeting with the Royals today. Their facility is close to Bianca's office, so I might swing by before coming home. Mom has already "suggested" we have a family dinner tomorrow night so everyone can meet you. If that's too much pressure, say the word. I'll never argue about getting to keep you all to myself.

I smile.

> Me: Good morning, handsome. You'll have to wake up a little earlier so it's not so hard when you get out of bed. Pun intended. I will check my email, try to figure out what I still need, and grab it from my house. Family dinner sounds fun. Will I get to meet Tate? I hope you have a great day. I'll be home when you get here. <heart emoji>

This. I hold my phone to my chest and close my eyes. *This feeling is what I've always been after.*

The device buzzes against me.

> Renn: Tate isn't invited. You can be mad at me, but Foxx is there with you. I asked him to accompany you if you leave. Please don't fight me on this. We can talk about it tonight, but I need to focus today, and I can't do that if I'm worried about you. <praying hands emoji>

I want to be annoyed at him. If it were any other person or situation, I would be. I'd probably leave to prove a point. But ... I'm not. And I won't.

His words make me feel safe. Protected. Valued. He's not trying to take over my life or control my movement. He genuinely cares about me.

> Me: I promise I won't go anywhere without Foxx.

> Renn: Thank you.

> Me: It's going to cost you ...

> Renn: I was hoping you were going to say that. <devil emoji>

> Me: <kissing emoji>

I send quick texts to Ella and Brock, letting them know I'm back. They reply to tell me they're coming over—separately.

"Let's hope they've figured their stuff out," I say, making a cup of coffee. "Because I don't want them ruining my vibe."

I find some milk and add it to my mug. As I put it back, I spot the notebook Astrid was telling me about yesterday. Sipping the liquid caffeine, I open the bright yellow cover. Sure enough, there are phone numbers, notes, dates, and times listed across three pages. Each item is categorized—the house, Renn, food, staff, family, emergency contacts, schedules, and miscellaneous. The top of the first page in bold letters reads I'M HERE TO HELP.

There's a quality about Astrid that I love; I liked her as soon as I met her. I think we could be friends, and the thought makes me smile.

Maybe I can fit into Renn's world.

I save her number on my phone before getting up. My mug warms my hands as I mosey my way through the house.

Renn's home is a balance of understated and grand. There's no way to look at it and not know it costs millions. Yet there's not one singular thing that screams pretentiousness. I can imagine the rooms filled with friends at Thanksgiving and presents at Christmas. A party by the pool with the grill going and music playing. And babies scooting across the floor in walkers, babbling their first words.

I pause in the sunroom doorway with my chest on fire. I stare across the expansive lawn at the back of the house.

This house was built for a family. It was designed for memories and holidays—for birthday parties and backyard rugby games. But he's never said he wants any of that with me.

I try to swallow around the lump in my throat.

Things between us have been heavenly. Almost too good to be true.

Maybe they *are* too good to be true.

Yet having had days with Renn—having him open himself up to me in ways I didn't expect—it's hard not to feel blissful. He's a good man. I knew this, but I had written him off, possibly much like his father, and I feel terrible for that. I hadn't realized how lonely it must truly be for someone at the top. He trusts some of his family, he trusts Astrid and Brock, but he doesn't really have many people in his corner. He doesn't feel like it, at least. And if there's one thing I'm convinced of, *I want to be one of those people he can count on.*

And I can't see that stopping in ninety days.

I fight against my inclination to hope for the best—to put what I want into the universe. I fight even harder to keep from admitting what I *really* want for myself ... *Renn.*

The way he makes me feel is incredible. Who would've thought the bad boy of rugby would be so ... everything. He's passionate and kind. He has major protector vibes. The sex is incredible, and he makes me feel like I'm the only person who matters to him. Hell, he even volunteered to give me a baby.

I'm mid-drink when the realization hits me. *He's a nice man.*

Slowly, I lower the mug and get the mouthful of coffee swallowed.

The room begins to spin.

I'm in love with Renn Brewer.

"No. No, no, no," I say, carrying my drink back to the kitchen. "This can't be happening. I'm just in a sex haze. That's all."

Despite saying the words out loud, I know I'm lying. I really do love him.

A hundred thoughts race through my mind. Everything from *how did this happen?* to *what do I do now?*

I set my coffee next to the sink and breathe deeply.

We promised to abort this mission if either of us had real feelings for the other. I made the damn rule. But the thought of walking away from him makes me want to vomit.

Quickly, my thoughts turn to rationalization.

What will it hurt to ride this out? It's just three months. We're having fun. If I keep my mouth shut and don't make this weird, I can slowly detach myself from him over the next few months so it hurts less when it's over.

I nod as my plan coalesces in my brain. "Yes. Just admit reality, and you'll be fine. Like Ella said in Vegas—manage the explosion so you don't implode." My brows pull together. "Or whatever."

I need to do something to distract myself from this rabbit hole. Renn's mention of dinner at his mother's house jumps to my mind as if my declaration of love somehow puts pressure on meeting his family.

"I'm a fool," I say, reaching for my phone anyway.

> Me: Hi, Astrid! It's Blakely. I promise I'm not needy. But can you give me some advice on what to wear to Renn's parents' house for dinner? I'm trying not to freak out.

Her response is immediate.

> Astrid: No panicking. It's not allowed. <winking emoji> They are very casual, in a rich people way, when they're together. I'd suggest a maxi dress or maybe dark denim jeans with a nice white button-down—chic but not overdone. Honestly, they aren't going to judge you for what you wear.

> Me: A white button-down? It's obvious you don't know me at all.

> Astrid: <laughing emoji> Would you like me to send you a few options this afternoon? Whatever you don't want, we'll send back.

Is she kidding?

> Me: That's unnecessary.

> Astrid: This is my job, Blakely. And I'm under your husband's exact orders to ensure you are happy and comfortable. If he finds out you're worried about what to wear, and I know it … I like my job. Let's keep it at that.

> Me: We could not tell him.

> Astrid: I'm sure it's an adjustment, but this is your life now. I'm here to help. I get paid to help you. And, if I'm being honest, shopping for you will be much more fun than what I'm currently doing.

I pace the kitchen, nibbling my bottom lip.

> Me: I feel very awkward about this.

> Astrid: I'll have a few things delivered this afternoon. I'll let Foxx know to expect them. Let me know how they work. We'll stay on it until we get it right.

> Me: How do I pay for them?

> Astrid: You're funny. I'm off to shop!

"Dammit," I say, setting my phone down and blowing out an exasperated breath.

A door shuts in the distance. I watch the doorway, hoping it's Renn. But Foxx appears.

"Mrs. Brewer, Ella St. James is here to see you," he says.

I plant my hands on the counter, grateful he can't see that I don't have on pants.

189

"He's under an NDA. He won't tell anyone how you sound when you're moaning my name and begging me to fuck you harder."

My cheeks flush. "Can you call me Blakely, please?"

"If you'd like."

I stare at him, dazzled by his blue eyes.

"Blakely?" he asks again.

"What? Oh. Yeah." I stand. "She's my best friend."

"Should I send her in?"

"Yes, Foxx. Please."

He gives me a side-eye that makes me think he's irritated with me. I hate to tell him, but he fails if he's trying to get me to change my behavior. He's hot as hell when he's grumpy.

A few moments later, Ella rounds the corner. "Jealousy is a very ugly shade on my skin tone. But, dammit, Blakely—your life is unfair."

I laugh, pulling her into a hug. "I missed you."

"You did not." She swats my shoulder. "And if you did, then Renn isn't nearly as good in bed as I've imagined."

I gasp. "Don't imagine my husband in bed."

She giggles. "Sorry. What's done is done."

We move into the living room and plop down on the sofa.

"Tell me about your honeymoon. I hope the length of time was the only thing that was fast," she says, winking at me.

I laugh. *Oh, how I missed her.*

"It was beautiful, Ella. The pictures I sent didn't do it justice. The vibe of the place was so chill. Maybe it was just where we were, but the sun seemed brighter, the pace slower, and I just felt so ..." I search for the right word, but only one will suffice. "Happy."

"That makes me happy."

"That's why you're the best."

She smiles. "I'm sorry we didn't get to really celebrate your birthday, though. I felt like you got shortchanged."

I shove my hand in her face. "How can you say that with a straight face?"

"*Holy crap.*" She jerks my finger at a weird angle for better inspection. "Blakely. *My lord.*"

"I know. It's perfect. I can't say I would've picked it because I wouldn't have even looked at rocks this size ..."

Ella laughs, letting my hand go. "Us mortals can't afford things like that. But I guess you aren't one of us anymore." She surveys the space. "This is quite the pad you have here. Renn's taste is more sophisticated and less bachelor. I'm impressed."

"Ella, you have no idea how impressive he really is."

"Saturday night. Me and you. *Not here.* I want every dirty, nasty detail you're willing to share."

I grin. "Deal. Now, what's up with you and Brock?"

The levity melts off her face. She smiles, but I see through it. *What's wrong?*

"El?"

"We're good. Honestly. Probably better than ever, really."

My stomach knots. "Why don't I believe you?"

"He came over, and we had a long talk ... about a lot of things. And I think ..." She gazes through the window. "I think we're on the same page in a way we've never been before."

I watch her work through something in her head.

"I love him, Blakely."

My eyes widen. "Really?"

She turns to me. "I do. We'll talk about it this weekend, okay? I don't want to get into it right now."

Don't want to get into what? What a weird thing to say. Since when has Miss Shameless held anything back? She's not telling me something. *Hmm ...*

A voice clears behind us. "Blakely?"

I look over my shoulder. "Are you a genie or something, Foxx? You show up out of nowhere."

"Doubtful," Ella mutters, loud enough so only I can hear. "Otherwise, women would be rubbing all kinds of things, hoping he shows up."

I shake my head, fighting a laugh.

"Your brother is here to see you," Foxx says, clearly unamused.

"We're going to have to work on this," I say. "I don't want to waste your time by announcing every visitor. You keep scaring the shit out of me."

He lifts a brow. "I'll wear bells on my shoes."

I burst out laughing. The corner of his lip quirks, but he refuses to smile.

"Send him in, please," I say. "Thank you."

He nods, and I'm pretty sure he rolls his eyes once his back is to me.

Ella stands. "I need to get going. I have a massage in an hour, and traffic will be miserable. I just had to see you before you got caught up in life and put me on the back burner."

I laugh. "Right. Like you ever stay on the back burner."

She laughs. "Call me later, and we'll plan our dirty dinner discussion."

"Okay."

She heads for the door but stops when Brock walks in. Her arms go to his neck, and they embrace. Whispers are exchanged, and my brother gives her a single, sweet kiss. He waits until she's out of the room before he makes his way to me.

"Hey," I say, getting to my feet to hug him. "Are you okay? You have bags bigger than mine under your eyes."

He wraps me up into a giant bear hug. "I'm fine. Glad you're back."

I squeeze him tight before releasing him. We sit down on opposite ends of the sofa.

"Thanks for bringing me clothes and my twenty-five lip balms," I say, joking.

"*Twenty-six*, and you're welcome. How was your honeymoon?"

I pause, studying him—trying to get a hint as to the direction of this conversation. *Is he asking because he's curious? Or because he's ready to pick a fight?*

He must read my apprehension because he sighs. "Renn said you had a great time. He said you tried to surf."

"I was catching waves left and right."

He lifts a brow.

"Kidding. I was awful." I laugh. "But it was a lot of fun, though. You'd be good at it."

"I'm glad you had fun, B." He runs a hand over his head. "Look, I want to say I'm sorry for being a dick in Vegas and for not calling you the past few days. I should've been more supportive, and I feel like a piece of shit for letting you down."

I don't know how to respond to that. But something tells me that this talking point isn't over.

A knot forms in my stomach, pulling tighter with every second it takes him to continue.

Finally, his hand drops to his side, and he raises his gaze to mine. "Has Renn said anything to you about my physical?"

I bolt upright. "No. *Why*? What's wrong?"

He blows out a breath. "I'm fine. Okay. Let's get that out of the way. *I'm fine.*"

"You're reiterating that a lot for someone who is fine."

My heart pounds so hard that I feel dizzy. I search his face for any indication that he's lying and try really, *really* hard not to shake him until he explains wherever he's going with this.

He shifts in his seat. "To make a long story short, I've been told I should retire."

"What? Why?"

"There is a study I joined a couple of years ago to learn more about head impacts on athletes. It's a data-gathering project. But when I had my scans as a part of my physical, I showed signs of neurological damage."

My hand flies to my mouth. Tears fill my eyes.

"I'm fine, B." He touches my knee. "I'd tell you if I wasn't. Remember, this is a study. They don't know anything for sure."

"But enough that someone thinks you should quit rugby?"

He nods slowly.

"And you quit, right?" I blink back tears, my mind racing. "Tell me you put in your resignation."

"Blakely ..."

I scoot to the edge of the sofa and twist to face him. Adrenaline spikes through my veins. It's matched only by the hysteria building inside me. "*You're quitting.*"

"I wanted to talk to you about it—"

"*You're quitting.*" Tears break the dam and spill down my cheeks.

They're hot and salty as they cross my lips. My voice cracks. "You're all I have, Brock. You can't risk it. *Please*. Don't do that to me."

I fight the sob as it climbs up my throat. But it's no use.

He pulls me into a hug, rocking me back and forth like our mother used to do when we were little.

Memories of our life with her roll through my mind, duller than they used to be. Less vivid. Mom's voice less distinct.

Making homemade ice cream on hot summer days. Building forts in the living room, using every blanket in the house. Watching her sitting proudly as she watched Brock graduate from high school.

The hole in my heart from the loss of our mother is as gaping as it was the day she passed. Imagining adding Brock to that wound is unbearable.

I pull away, wiping my hands down my face.

His eyes are watery—something I've only seen on him once before. It breaks my heart.

"I'll quit," he says softly.

I take his hand.

He smiles sadly. "I've tried to talk myself out of it, telling myself I only have two years left on my contract. That it's a lot of money to turn down. That the odds I'd get hurt are pretty low ..." He sighs. "But I can't do that to you. I know I can't anyway." He sniffles, the sound transforming into a laugh. "Ella is pregnant."

"*What*?" My voice is a shriek, and I spring to my feet. "What did you say?"

"I'm gonna be a daddy, B."

"*Oh. My. God*!" I bounce on the tips of my toes, laughing. "Brock! When is she due? How long have you known? Why did no one tell me?"

He chuckles. "She found out the day she got home from Vegas. I found out yesterday."

"What are you going to do?"

"Marry the fuck out of her."

I smile so big it hurts. Then reality hits me. I smack him in the arm. "And Renn knew all of this, and I didn't?"

"He didn't know about the baby. Just the physical part."

"Why did he not tell me? Why am I just finding out?"

"I asked him not to," he says, standing. "I wanted to tell you in person so I could assure you I was okay." He hugs me again. "You're kind of my little sister but kind of my kid, too. I want to protect you as much as I can."

"I know you do. And I appreciate you more than I can ever tell you."

He rubs the top of my head. I swat his hand away.

"Okay. I have to go file some paperwork with my attorneys," he says.

"And I need to call my best friend and yell at her for not telling me she's having my niece or nephew."

He gives me a wide, genuine smile. "We're going to be okay. You know that right? Somehow, we made it."

I give him his smile back.

I hope you're right, Brock. I really freaking do.

CHAPTER 22

Renn

"There you are," Bill Galecki says, offering me his hand as I enter his office. "I hear congratulations are in order."

Here we go ... I shake his hand. "Yes. Thanks."

He smiles smugly as he tucks his tie to his chest and sits in his over-sized, pompous leather chair. I take my seat across from him. It's a decidedly smaller, harder, more uncomfortable furniture selection that I would bet my left nut is intentional.

Galecki likes to keep his opposition on edge. And right now, I'm the opponent.

I clear my throat and take in the awards and articles hanging on the wall behind the Royals general manager. It's impressive and would be intimidating if I was open to that kind of thing.

I'm not. And Galecki knows it.

"Let's cut to the chase," he says, his features hardening. "We've had quite a week in public relations."

"Well, marriages are big news. People like to see other people happy."

He strokes his chin. "Is that what this is, though?"

"Sir, with all due respect, my personal life is none of anyone's business."

"Oh, Brewer ..." He chuckles, sitting up and planting his arms on his desk. "That's where you're wrong."

My insides tremble with anticipation of this conversation going downhill. I had mediocre hopes when I pulled into the facility this morning. They've downgraded as the day has gone on.

Surprise from the medical staff when I showed up for my physical. An offhanded comment from a teammate when I stopped for a coffee at the fuel bar in the cafeteria. The cool response from Galecki's secretary when I arrived for our meeting.

I wouldn't be as on edge if I had a plan and knew how to handle what was coming my way. But I don't. I know there are limits to what I will accept ... and I pray we don't touch them.

I pray my instincts are wrong.

"There have been several articles over the past few days questioning the seriousness of our franchise," he says. "Many people are second-guessing our decision to sign you."

"I'm sorry to hear that."

"You should be. It's your fault."

I flinch. "Because I got married? Give me a fucking break."

"Because a middle-of-the-night wedding to a woman no one knew you were even seeing—in Las Vegas, of all places—looks a little suspect. And with your history, a lot of people are wondering if this is where Renn Brewer goes off the deep end. Again."

Stay calm. I force myself to breathe. "What can I say? I'm sorry clair-voyants are moonlighting as journalists."

"May I remind you that you signed a clause guaranteeing this fran-chise your cooperation in protecting our image?"

I stare at him, willing myself to stay quiet.

"Don't think that concerns haven't been raised that you married a woman who caused waves in this industry a few years ago," he says.

Nope. "We can talk about me all day long. But my wife is off-limits."

"If only it were that easy."

"*Make it that easy.*"

He holds my gaze. "Let's also note, for the sake of it, that not only did you marry a problematic—"

"Watch your fucking mouth."

"Woman in Vegas, but that woman was also your teammate's sister.

197

Don't you see the problem with that? Do you not expect tension in the locker room?"

I stare him down. "Not any more than is in this room right now."

He looks away.

He stands, slipping off his jacket and hanging it on the back of his chair. He pours a drink from a sideboard beneath the window that overlooks Nashville. "Would you like one? Water? Gin and tonic?"

"I'm good."

"Here's the thing, Renn. It's my job as the GM of this organization to ensure we are best positioned to make money. A part of that equation is securing the best players." He looks at me over the rim of his glass. "And another part is maintaining a good image."

He takes a long slug of whatever he's drinking like he's giving me time to squirm.

It's not the words he's saying. None of this is news to me. *It's the tone he's using that's grating my nerves.*

I expected him to try to use this as leverage. Honestly, I didn't care that much. Getting fucked by businesses is routine for me; I bring my own lube.

But what surprises me, what crawls under my skin and makes me uncomfortable, is the angle he's taking. And if it's the path I think he's going down, there will be fireworks.

I sit back. "I thought we were cutting to the chase."

He sets the glass down with a thud. "Okay. Let's cut to the chase. We would like to incorporate you and your wife into a marketing campaign for—"

"*What*?" I hold up a hand. *He did not just go there.* "Back up. What did you just say?"

"Marketing has a series of commercials they'll be rolling out this fall, angled at bringing more families into the stadium. We're trying to expand our fan base, and we feel that if you and Miss Evans—"

"*Mrs. Brewer.*"

He smirks. "My mistake. If *you and Mrs. Brewer* would take part, we could launch a promo with the two of you leading into the series. The optics would be great. She's very marketable, and everyone loves a rags-to-riches story. Additionally, we could shut down a lot of this chatter and twist the narrative to fit our needs."

I think my eyes might bulge out of my head. *He has to be kidding.*

"Nothing major," he says, sitting again. "Just something to show—"

"No."

He lifts a brow.

"This is absolutely not happening."

"I'd like you to reconsider."

I run my palms down my pants. "I really don't give a fuck."

My brain imagines what Blakely would say if I even suggested such a thing—not that I would ever bring it up. There's no way I'm exploiting what we have for anything, least of all the Royals.

The last thing she wants is her name in print. The whole reason she married me was to stop that from happening. And now Galecki wants to *intentionally* put her name into the world? To put her up for discussion—us up for evaluation?

No way.

"I'm not saying I know a thing about marketing," I say. "But if your issue with my marriage is people talking, why would you want to give them something to talk about? Why draw attention to it? Doesn't make much sense to me."

"This is bad for business the way it stands. It can be good for business with some ... slight modifications."

"Not my problem."

"Oh, *but it is your problem.* Your contract says it's your problem."

My blood boils. "My contract says that I won't cause you problems. It doesn't say I have to jump through whatever hoop you put before me to make you a little extra cash."

"Let me be blunt. *We own you.*"

"*No one owns me.*"

He licks his lips. "You'll do it, or we'll sue you for breach of contract."

My teeth grind together as I stare at Galecki and his self-satisfied grin. *Fuck you.*

"Do it," I say. "Sue me for refusing to have my wife exploited. That's going to look real good in the papers."

His laugh is haughty. "This is where we are. Either you sign on to this marketing campaign, or we sign legal proceedings. And before you run your mouth without doing your due diligence—go home. Think about it. There's not another team on any continent capable of winning the championship that would be willing to take you on after this."

"You say that like you think I give a fuck."

"Oh, I think you do."

"You're wrong. You *do not* have the right to talk about my wife." I stand. "I'm leaving because, if I don't, I'm going to remind you of who you are when you're not behind that desk."

He flinches. "Are you threatening me?"

I wink at him and head to the door before making a mess of this situation.

"We'll need an answer in the next few days."

"Fuck you, Galecki."

The door slams behind me.

* * *

"Make yourself at home," Bianca says, setting down her pen as I barge into her office. "I take it something's wrong."

"You know what?"

"Well, I know many things, but none are probably what you'll say. We don't really operate on the same wavelength most of the time."

I narrow my eyes as I sit across from her. "Fuck the Royals."

She brushes a lock of her long dark hair out of her face. "I was right. That wasn't what I would say. But, then again, it's not surprising. I'm always right."

"Bianca ..."

"Sorry. Continue. Explain to me why we hate the Royals."

Her grin eases some of my anger.

"Look, I love you, Renny, but I have a meeting in twenty minutes. Start talking."

"Get this. I just got an ultimatum. I can either let the team pimp out my marriage in a marketing campaign, or they'll sue me for breach."

She settles back in her chair, surprised. "Wow. I didn't see that coming. What did you say?"

I don't know what I said.

It took the whole ride to the Brewer offices to stop my heart from pumping so much blood through my veins that I thought the top of my head would blow off.

Who the fuck does Galecki think he is?

"We own you."

No one owns me, motherfucker. And no one owns Blakely Brewer.

"I'm not an attorney," Bianca says, "but I would say that would be hard to prove in court."

"I think that's what I said. Sort of." I groan. "Do you know what pisses me off the most about it?"

"What's that?"

"That they are so damn money-centered that they would take the sliver of an opening that maybe my marriage was a mistake and try to exploit it—try to exploit Blakely. She has nothing to do with them and there they are, not giving a damn about that. She's just a chess piece to move toward checkmate."

Bianca smiles.

"What?" I look at her. "What are you smiling at?"

"Nothing."

"I'm not in the mood, Bianca."

"Fine. I think you went to Australia and fell in love. That's what I think. I think that marriage probably was an accident, but it happened to be with a girl you've held out for, hoping you'd get a chance with for years."

I gulp. "Why would you think that?"

"Come on, Renny. I was at your birthday party eight, nine years ago. And I watched you chase that woman around like a puppy."

My lips twitch. "I did no such thing."

"And then there was the time you had me help you send her flowers for Valentine's Day. That's the only time that's happened. Have you ever sent another woman flowers?"

I chuckle.

"Oh, what about the time you wanted me to friend request her on

Social because she changed her account to private? And you wanted to know if she was with some guy ... I can't remember his name." She laughs. "You called me from Australia to ask how to give her a ring. Come on, brother. Everyone else might not see it, but I do."

I blow out a breath and use Bianca's smile to steady myself.

A slideshow of every interaction I've had with Blakely rolls through my mind—every holiday, party, and barbecue at Brock's. The texts we've exchanged through the years. The way I wanted to throttle Edward DiNozzo.

I'd go alone if I knew Blakely would be at an event. I'd wrangle my way into sitting beside her at dinner or hanging out with her—or close to her—so I could hear her voice. I've canceled dates because an opportunity to spend time with her arose even though it was in a group. Because I just wanted to be with her.

"It happened to be with a girl you've held out for, hoping you'd get a chance with for years."

Is that true? Is Bianca right? Have I waited for a chance to be with Blakely for the past ten years?

"Renn ..."

The room shrinks, my body heating as I think about my wife.

Everything in my world is now framed around her.

When I think about having the afternoon free, I want to make a beeline home to her. The idea that she's home—that my home is her home —feels like the greatest victory in the world. I've spent all morning planning our next trip to Australia because she loved it so much and checking the tabloids to see if there's anything I need to have Frances shut down.

But ... there wasn't. Not like I expected there to be. Sure, there are a few things here and there, most of them from the checkout-line magazines with a picture of us next to an image of a historical figure living in South America.

This life with Blakely could work. I want it to work. It feels like a knife slicing through my stomach when I think about it ending.

But what would she want? Would she want ... *me*?

"What do I want? I want to be focused on myself. I want to grow, to be excited about appliances and understand how life insurance works. I want

to find a nice man, get married, and have a family. Basically, the opposite of what we have going on and the longer we draw that out, the longer I'm just treading water—and I need to move forward. I need it, Renn. I promised myself that I would do it."

I pass a swallow down my throat.

This doesn't have to be her treading water. This can be *us* moving forward. I want to stay married to Blakely. I'm the man she needs ... or I can become him.

"Yeah, Bianca. I love her."

"I know." She smiles. "So what does this mean for the Royals contract?"

"It means I tell them to fuck off and lawyer up, I guess."

"And we are telling our wife we love her, right?"

"*Our wife?*" I chuckle. "Yes, but I want to make it special. Maybe I'll wait until after dinner at Mom's tomorrow night. Get a few things in place. I don't know if she'll feel the same way. I need to wine and dine her to be sure."

Bianca snorts, gathering her things on her desk. "You're adorable when you're goofy."

"I knew Renn was here when I heard you say goofy." Gannon walks in and stands by Bianca's desk. "How was Australia?"

"Good."

"Good." He turns to our sister. "Change of plans. You meet with McCallister. I'm heading to the conference room with Dad. He's signing the Arrows deal."

"He is?" I ask.

Gannon looks at me. "Bobby Downing came on board and pulled some strings. He helped Dad get it expedited."

I sigh. Even though I think Dad's a dick, I'm still glad he closed his deal.

"Anyway, don't forget to come in strong with the numbers from the last quarter," Gannon says to Bianca. "Text me when you're out."

"Will do."

"Later, goofy," Gannon says.

"Bye, fucker."

"Renn, I gotta go," Bianca says. "Call me tonight if you want. I'll be home around eight."

"Thanks for letting me barge in here."

"Anytime. Let yourself out."

She pats me on the shoulder as she leaves.

I exhale a shaky breath and look at the tray ceiling. There's so much to do, so much to work out ... and all I want to do is go home to my wife.

Grinning, I get to my feet and leave.

CHAPTER 23

Blakely

"That smells so good," I say, taking the cake out of the oven and setting it on a rack to cool.

I feel like a character in a movie, bustling around the kitchen in the early evening. The ambiance is perfection. Enough sun hits the room to make it warm and cozy, but just shadowy enough to ease you from afternoon to dinner. The layout had to have been designed by someone who frequented kitchens because everywhere I turn to look for something—there it is.

And the appliances. *I can be excited about appliances, after all.*

The thought makes me laugh.

I sway to a honeyed voice coming from my phone, singing about flying them to the moon. The saxophones, trumpets, and piano fill the air with a soothing, sexy beat.

The day has been exactly what I needed. After Brock's bombshell about the baby, I called Ella and named myself godmother before yelling at her for not telling me. Then I promptly started planning a baby shower. Is it too early? Yes. Am I excited? Also, yes.

I've always worried about how I would take this day—when my brother begins his own family. I was scared I'd be sad or lonely. Instead, I'm bursting at the seams.

I shut off the oven and start working on the chicken piccata.

After my call with Ella, I took a long soak with the best bubble bath I've ever used. The water felt amazing on my sore muscles, and I wound up falling asleep. I woke up to a delivery of clothes from Astrid. I felt like a princess.

I hope I don't turn into a pumpkin at midnight.

A smile slips across my lips. *I won't. I know that won't happen.*

"It's Renn," I say simply, as if that explains my conclusion.

The music stops and is replaced by a ringtone. I set the salt and pepper down.

"Hello?" I ask, holding the phone to my ear.

"Is this Blakely?"

"Yes."

"Hi, Blakely. It's Anjelica from Mason Music. How are you?"

Oh. I lean against the counter. "Hi, Anjelica. I'm great. How are you?"

"Not as good as you." She laughs. "Congratulations on getting married. How exciting."

I grin. "Thank you. It's been ... a wild ride."

I giggle, thinking about my *wild ride* last night before falling asleep. My sex clenches at the memory.

"What can I do for you?" I ask, redirecting my thoughts.

"You're not due back in the office yet, but we've been having an issue with photographers camped outside the offices. We assume they're waiting on you."

My stomach drops. A cold sweat breaks out across my skin. "Oh no. Anjelica, I'm sorry. I—"

"Don't be sorry. They're trolls. We've been able to move them off our property, but they're now camped on the other side of the road. It's a bit of a safety issue."

I hold my head in my hands. *Dammit.*

"You're starting a new position, anyway," she says. "It might be a good idea for you to work from home for a week or two—long enough for them to find something else to fixate on. And they will find something else. They always do."

Air fills my lungs again.

"Our CEO, Coy Mason, is adamant that we offer employees the ability to work from home as much as possible," she says.

She drops the name of one of country music's biggest names like we're talking about a clerk at the local grocery store.

"If you want to explore the possibility of moving your position remotely, we can look into that. But that's absolutely up to you. We're here to facilitate as much as we can to keep our employees happy and with their families as much as possible."

"Wow. Okay. Yes," I say, releasing a breath. "I'd love to try to work from home—at least as long as this paparazzi thing is happening. I don't want my life to affect anyone else."

"That's great. Let's go ahead and write off next week entirely. That will give our IT Department time to get you set up remotely. If you need anything in the meantime, reach out to me. You have my number."

"I will. Thank you, Anjelica. Truly."

"You are very welcome. We'll talk soon."

"Goodbye."

I end the call, and the soulful voice plays again.

Turning back to the chicken, I pick up a knife. Just before I touch the poultry, Renn buries his head into the crook of my neck.

I smile, setting the knife down, and move to give him all the access he needs to place kisses against my skin.

"Hey, you," I say, wrapping an arm around the back of his head. "I missed you today."

He spins me around and holds me against him.

If I thought Brock looked tired today, Renn is nothing short of exhausted. His eyes are puffy. The lines around his mouth are prominent. His skin is dull and lacking the glow I've seen every day since we met at the pool in Vegas.

"Hey," I say, running my hand through his hair. "What's wrong?"

His grin is crooked. "I'm just glad to be home."

"That's really nice of you to say, and I'm glad you're here too. But what's wrong?"

He plants a loud, wet kiss on my lips before letting me go. "Jet lag is a real thing. What are you making?"

"Chicken piccata. A salad is in the fridge, and a cake is cooling on the counter."

"How are you up to cook? Aren't you beat?"

I grin. "It makes me happy to be here, cooking for you. And I had all day to relax."

He moves to the cabinet and pulls out two wineglasses. I turn back to the meat.

"Foxx scared the shit out of the grocery delivery guy," I say, laughing at the memory. "Then he and I—Foxx and I—had a small ... skirmish, about the tip."

"Oh, really? Who won that one?"

I lift my chin. "Me."

"I would've paid a lot of money to watch that."

"I'm not sure how you do business around here. But if there are reports filed or something, don't believe anything he says about me without hearing my side of the story."

Renn chuckles.

"First, I don't think he finds me entertaining. He's also rather perturbed that I have visitors. Brock and Ella were here—*oh*!" I swing around and point the tip of the knife at him. "Did you know my brother is retiring?"

He takes the knife from me and puts a glass of wine in my hand. "Is that a done deal?"

"*Of course, it is.*"

He hums before taking a drink, watching me over the rim.

"I would've thrown a fit about it," I say. "But now he's going to be a daddy ..."

Renn's eyes hood.

I set my glass down and rest my back against the counter's edge, smirking. "What's that look for?"

He places his wine next to mine before caging me against the counter.

"*Oh*," I say, trailing a fingertip down his face. His stubble bites against my skin. It only adds to the heat building in my core. "Did you not know Ella and Brock are having a baby?"

"I just found out this evening on my way home."

"So you didn't know and withheld that information as you did about Brock's physical—something we will discuss later."

He nips the tip of my finger. "I look forward to it."

"Back to the baby ... you didn't know?"

"If I knew, I would've used it to talk you into letting me knock you up."

I throw my head back and laugh. "You don't really want a baby."

"Try again, cutie."

My breath stills as I lift my head. "Don't mess with me."

Our eyes lock, and the space between us is charged. He leans forward, pressing a sweet, almost reverent kiss against my lips.

I sag against him. I'm not sure what's happening, and it scares me a little ... but thrills me, too.

He rests his forehead against me. "Tomorrow, after we go to dinner at Mom's, let's sit down and talk."

"Okay ..." My breathing is shaky. "Is everything okay?"

With the news of Brock's medical issues still so fresh in my mind, the sound of *let's sit down and talk* sounds like its foreshadowing a dark moment.

"I hope so." He grins, standing tall. "I'm just dead tired, and you have to be, too. Foxx said you were very active today."

I gasp. "Did he tattle on me? That fucker."

Renn laughs. "I guarantee no one has ever said that to his face and gotten away with it."

"Just wait until I see him." I pull his head against me and hug him. "How was your physical? I need to know you're okay, and whatever you want to discuss has nothing to do with that. Humor me."

"I'm good." He pulls away. "Healthy as an ox. Very capable of giving you a baby, if that's what you're worried about."

I smack him. "I'm worried about your other head, thank you."

"It works good enough to know a damn good thing when I see it."

He holds my gaze, my words from the night on the plane to Australia returning to me.

"A nice man knows a damn good thing when he sees it."

I reach for his hand, entwining his fingers in mine. His eyes are soft and full of an emotion that melts me from the inside out.

"He knows a damn good thing when he sees it. And ... he loves me."

My eyes search his, begging him to tell me what I want to hear. *Tell me you love me, Renn. Please.*

"My brain is fine," he says softly. "But I love it that you worry about me."

The irony of him using the word *love* in the wrong context is not lost on me.

I sigh. "Of course, I worry about you. I'll worry every time you take the pitch. How long is your contract? A year? Is that right?"

He brings my hands to his lips and kisses them. Then he lets them go.

"Dad bought the Arrows today." He lifts his wine and downs the whole glass. I watch him curiously as he refills it. "I just thought you'd want to know."

I start to ask him why I'd care ... but stop.

My stomach hits the floor.

If he had his meeting today and it went well, and if his father's deal is done—and if the media isn't as bad as we expected—then our marriage isn't really needed anymore.

My lips part, assisting my brain with keeping me alive by allowing my lungs more oxygen. Still, it feels like the room is void of it. Like I'm quietly suffocating.

"So," I say, clearing my throat. "Does that mean ..."

"No. That's not what that means."

I grip the edge of the counter. "Renn—"

"We're both tired. Today has been stressful—for me, at least. All I've looked forward to since I left the house this morning was coming back to you tonight."

My sight grows cloudy.

He stands between my legs, tipping my chin up with his finger. "Tomorrow night, we talk. Promise me you won't panic until then."

"Should I plan on panicking then?"

He holds my face in both hands and kisses me slowly, deliberately. This isn't one of his hungry kisses. It's not fueled by lust. It's triggered by something else, something deeper and more meaningful.

Something I'm too scared to name.

"How hungry are you?" he whispers against my lips.

"Not much."

"Come to bed with me. I need you, Blakely. More than I've ever needed anything else."

That's all he has to say.

Because even though I'm worried, scared, and unsure about the future, I know I'll be there if he needs me.

And really—I need him too.

CHAPTER 24

Blakely

"What's wrong?" Renn reaches for me across the middle console. "Are you okay? You've been quiet this evening."

I let him have my hand but stare out the window. The community we entered a few minutes ago, one that's a short drive from Renn's, is more upscale than his. *And I don't know what to do with it.* Mansions that must expand into five digits in square footage make the luxury cars in the driveway look like toys. It's overwhelming.

I'm intimidated.

My stomach has been upset all day—since last night, really, when Renn said we'd talk after his mother's dinner. He's acted normally toward me, more or less. He's a little on edge. Jumpy. His brows pinch together when he thinks I'm not looking. I'm confident it's not a health issue like Brock's, but I don't know what's bothering him.

And I hate it.

The unknown screws with my confidence and messes with my heart. I feel my walls going up, readying to protect me from impending doom. I'm aware of this reaction; it's a weakness. I know I should give Renn the benefit of the doubt, especially because he hasn't given me a real reason not to.

But pain is pain, and I'm unprepared for the heartbreak he could deliver.

"You look beautiful," he says, removing his hand to downshift.

We pull onto a circular driveway in front of a three-story home. The sun's final rays give the home a backdrop of amethyst and ruby. It's as though Mother Nature feels compelled to contribute to the wealth of this family.

Renn turns off the main drive and around a half wall. On the other side is a line of cars that cost more than the GDP of small nations.

Holy fuck.

"It's just my family," he says, warily. "Remember that. These are just my parents and siblings. It's not a big deal."

"If these machines are their daily drives, this is a big deal."

He cuts the engine. "What's the worst that could happen? Give me your worst-case scenario."

"I don't know. I make a fool out of myself?"

He grins. "Impossible. But let's say you manage it. You'll still be adorable."

I smile as he kisses me.

"Now, come on," he says, opening his door. "The sooner we get this started, the sooner it's over."

"Amen."

I round the front of his car, taking in his good looks. His hair is fixed in his *I woke up like this* style. He wears dark denim jeans and a checkered button-up that he refused to tuck in. The sleeves are rolled to his elbows.

"Did you keep everything Astrid sent?" he asks, snatching my hand again.

"No. Did you see the price tag on some of those clothes? It's outrageous."

He chuckles as we walk to the door. "Did it all fit?"

"That's not the point."

"I'm adding this to our talking points for later."

I roll my eyes. "You can shove your talking points up your ass."

He chuckles.

"I'm not being funny. I'm scared shitless over here, and ..."

I hiccup a breath, refusing to look at him. *Fuck. I just made it perfectly clear that I'm afraid of what he will say.*

213

Way to be transparent, Blakely. Not your best move.

He withdraws his hand from the doorknob and turns to me. "Hey."

"Yeah?"

A burst of laughter comes from the other side of the door. My stomach drops, and my palms sweat.

He squares his shoulders to mine. "I had things to take care of—things that I didn't want to talk about until I found my way through them. Things I didn't want you to worry about."

I search his eyes. "That doesn't help."

"Blakely, you have to understand—"

"There you are!" The door flies open, and a tall, dark-headed woman stands like a model on the threshold. "We're waiting on you. Get in here."

Renn kisses the woman on the cheek and leads me in behind him. My cheeks flush as I take in the ornate furnishings in what's more of a museum than a home. There's a bust of someone important, I assume. Large paintings hang proudly on the walls and chandeliers the size of compact cars hang from the ceiling.

I'm out of my league.

"Easy, Mom," Renn says, stepping to the side. "Blakely, this is my mother, Rory Brewer. Mom, this is my wife, Blakely. Don't smother her."

"Darling, hello." Rory pulls me in for a hug. The medallion attached to her necklace presses sharply into my chest. I try not to wince. "It is so nice to finally meet you."

"It's nice to meet you too, Mrs. Brewer."

"No. I'm Rory or you can call me Mom." She smiles brightly. It's the same smile Renn uses when he's happy. "You can set your purse right there unless you want to keep it with you. Let's introduce you to the rest of our brood."

I hang my purse on the hook Rory indicated and clutch Renn's hand like a lifeline. We make our way into a massive kitchen. It's all gray and white marble—the floors, backsplash, and the countertops. Copper pots and pans, which I doubt have ever been used, hang over the middle of the island.

But around the island—that's the most fascinating part of the scene. By far.

They're attractive. Stunning. Jaw-droppingly beautiful.

All of them.

"Blakely, this is my family," Renn says. "That's my sister, Bianca. She's a child genius."

Bianca grins, her perfectly red lips showing off perfectly white teeth. "I'm only a genius compared to these baboons."

"It's nice to meet you," I say.

"That's Gannon. He's a dick."

"Renn!" Rory gasps. "Where are your manners?"

He shrugs, smirking at his mother.

Gannon holds a glass of amber-colored liquid. He does a quick assessment of me and winks. I smile back politely but withhold judgment. I'm not sure what to think about him.

"That's Jason," Renn says, pointing at his brother, whom I met briefly on the plane home from Australia. He's tall and thin—strikingly like the man beside him. "That's Ripley."

"Welcome to the family," he says warmly.

I instantly like him. "Thank you. I appreciate that."

"And that is *Tate.*" Renn enunciates Tate's name in a way that amuses his brother. "Tate, this is *my wife.*"

Tate smiles broadly at me, obviously working to annoy his brother. "Hi … *sis.*"

"Hi, brother," I say, playing into the opening Tate gave me.

"*Don't,*" Renn says just before his siblings start laughing. "Fuck y'all."

Rory shakes her head like she's given up.

"Sorry," I say, sliding an arm around Renn's waist and laying my head on his shoulder. "I've heard a lot about you all. It's nice to meet you."

Tate walks toward us. He's the same height as Renn but without the bulk. He's strong but leaner—not a professional athlete. His eyes are kind and playful. His swagger, complete with a hand in one pocket, makes me laugh.

"Wanna see my bedroom?" Tate asks me, teasing his brother.

Renn punches him in the shoulder. Hard.

Tate shakes his arm. "Don't make me take you down right here."

"You can't take me down," Renn says, scoffing.

Tate grins. "I wasn't talking about you." He moves just in time before Renn reaches for him. "All those muscles are slowing you down, old man."

I laugh at their antics.

"And last but not least. Blakely, this is my father, Reid Brewer," Renn says, the words cooler than he used with the others. "Dad. This is Blakely."

"Hello, Mr. Brewer," I say.

"Hello, Blakely." He flips his attention from me to Renn and then to Gannon.

The chatter begins in earnest again, with everyone talking at once. It's quite a spectacle—eight people talking simultaneously but somehow carrying on a conversation.

My nerves settle as I watch them and have a moment to acclimate to the situation.

Upon closer inspection, I spot pictures of all of them in various stages of their lives sitting on a mantel and pinned to the refrigerator. Fresh flowers that look freshly picked fill a Mason jar next to a tray of vegetables. A cutting board with the lyrics of a hymn leans against the backsplash next to the sink.

It's not cozy like Renn's house. *But it's their home.* It's where they all congregate and come when they need help. For family dinners or to watch the big game.

"So, Blakely, tell us about yourself," Rory says, taking the tops off various foil pans.

The sound lessens a few decibels.

Oh. I tuck a strand of hair behind my ear and try not to fixate on all their attention landing on me. *Why does this feel like a job interview?*

"I graduated from college with a bachelor's in business management," I say. "I work for Mason Music Label and love what I do. My brother is Brock Evans, but I'm sure you all know that."

I love cooking, like the color peach, red roses, and fall weather. Oh, and I love your son, but it's not reciprocated.

"That's exciting," Rory says. "And ironic."

"Why?"

She looks at me and smiles. "Well, Mason Music Label is owned by Coy Mason. He is one of my good friends, Siggy Mason's son." She laughs. "What a small world."

I glance at my ring.

"Yes, that's her," Bianca says. "The jewelry designer. Mom has the hookup."

"Do you like your wedding ring?" Rory asks.

"We sent Renn fifty or sixty options," Bianca says, laughing. "He was so picky—wouldn't settle until he found the exact one." She makes a face at her brother. "You're so cute, Renny."

"Wow," I say, smiling at my husband. "That's really sweet."

It wasn't Astrid. He chose this for me. That makes me love it even more.

"Don't buy into the bullshit," Ripley jokes from across the room.

Renn points at him, walking his way while firing a retort. Ripley's smile never leaves his face.

"I do love it," I say, returning to Bianca and Rory. "It's gorgeous. I can't imagine anything more beautiful."

Rory takes a stack of plates out of the cabinet. "He did do a good job. I was very proud. Raising a boy with taste is so hard."

Bianca looks over her shoulder at the men at the island. "One out of five sons isn't bad."

Rory laughs. "I have hope for Jason."

They chatter back and forth among themselves, working me into the conversation at every available opportunity. It's an effortless interaction, and I laugh with them like old friends. Every now and then, I feel Renn's eyes on me. And each time, I look at him and smile. Without fail, he smiles back.

Yet there's a wobbliness between us. I don't know if it's my doing—my fear that somehow, he'll want to back away from me—or if it's a true gut reaction that something is amiss.

I want to find my spot here. I want to blend in with the others and share their jokes. Of course, I do. This is all I've ever wanted.

They are warm—Reid excluded. Inviting. Kind. Rory turns me

loose in her kitchen to look for her serving spoons, something many women won't allow. And the fact that she accepts me into her fold and the rest of them makes my nerves even worse. Not to mention her ability to *mom hug* like a champion. I've missed those. A lot. Imagine getting them regularly. Yes, please.

Ugh, why does that make me emotional?

And why do emotions have to be so hard to navigate?

"Rory, may I use your powder room?" I ask.

"Of course. It's down the hall. The fourth door on your right."

"Thank you."

I need to settle down. To catch my breath.

I slip into the hallway and count doors, blatantly ignoring the vases and gold candlesticks. My steps tap against the stone floor. *Tap. Tap. Tap.* I reach for the handle but stop when I hear my name.

"Blakely."

Coming toward me is Reid. I have no idea where he came from, but that doesn't change the fact that he's approaching me with a look of displeasure in his eyes.

I gulp. "I was just going to use the powder room."

"Why don't you step into my office for a second?" He opens the door across the hall. "I'll only take a few moments of your time."

My heart pounds at an alarming rate. *Do I go in there and talk to him?* Logic says it can't hurt anything ... but my gut says otherwise.

Still, I find myself walking into a room with a giant stately desk and bookshelves lining the walls.

"Do you want to sit?" he asks, placing his drink on top of a stack of folders.

"No. You said it would only take a second."

He moseys around the room. I think he's trying to make me relax, but all it does is put me on edge. I feel my heart beating in my throat. I have to override the screaming inside my head telling me to leave.

No, I'm going to make a good impression. The door is open behind me. I can leave anytime I want.

"What can I help you with, Reid?" I ask. *Renn—please come find me.*

"Can I trust that you will keep this conversation between us?"

"That depends on what it's about."

He chuckles angrily. He stops walking and faces me, his jaw set. "What will it take to get you out of Renn's life?"

My mouth falls open.

I shiver as cold chills snake down my spine.

"My son may be dim-witted, but I'm not," Reid says. "How much will it take to make you go away?"

"I'm sorry, Mr. Brewer. I don't understand."

"Cut the shit, Blakely."

What? "Don't talk to me like that."

He plants his hands on the desk with a loud thud. His eyes are narrowed, the pupils nearly slits.

"I've been at this game longer than you have," he says. "I know what little whores want when they come around. I can see them from a mile away."

His words catch me so off guard that I fail to respond.

"Name your price," he says. "How much are you after? Quarter million. Half? Give me a number."

I draw in a breath and gather my wits. "You think I want money from you?"

"Don't play the damsel in distress card, girl. It isn't cute."

"What's not cute is this arrogant, disrespectful, abhorrent language you're using with me. I don't know where you get off thinking you can insult me like this, but—"

"Because I'm Reid Brewer. I can get away with anything I want."

I stand taller, meeting his gaze and refusing to blink. "I don't give a fuck who you are."

"So what do you think, then?" he asks, smirking. "Do you think you can get my son all liquored up, marry you, and then—what? What's the endgame? Convince him that you're the one? To start a family with you? To let you be a part of this empire that *I* have created?" He laughs like I'm a joke. "Think again."

"I don't want a damn thing from you—"

"Of course, you do. It's mine. *It's all mine.* And I'm not about to allow some little whore with a nice ass and great tits swindle my son out of his future."

The shock is gone. Rage settles in.

"You are a disgusting excuse for a man."

"You didn't sign a prenup. Explain that."

"I don't have to explain anything to you."

He storms around the corner of his desk, stopping inches from my face. Liquor is hot on his breath, and he breathes down like a demented dragon.

I want to run out of the room. I want to run into Renn's arms and beg him to take me home. But I don't want to give this asshole the pleasure of thinking he hurt me ... and, *this is Renn's home. How is Rory married to this egotistical monster?*

A fissure cracks through my chest.

"You will never fit in here," he says, scowling. "You are not a Brewer. *You will never be a Brewer.* Even if you have Renn's child, it will be a bastard. It'll receive a check every month, and that's it. It won't belong here just like its mother doesn't."

"You don't know him if you think that's true."

"Honey, I know him. *I raised him.* He might be weak—deluded from fucking you—but he has Brewer blood in his veins." He cuts the small distance between us in half. "Your little stunt cost me millions today. I had to pay millions of dollars to expedite my deal before you and my dipshit son ruined it for me."

I stare at him.

"You might've cost him his Royals contract, but I can't help that," he says.

What? I take a step back. *What's he talking about?*

"Oh, didn't you know?" he asks, mocking me. "Your 'husband' is *this close* to losing his contract—*because of you.*"

My brain scrambles with this information. *Is it true? Why didn't Renn tell me?*

Is this why he's acting so odd?

I hiccup a sob.

That must be it. He lost the contract ... because of me.

"Let. Him. Go," Reid says, glaring at me. "Do that fuckup of a son of mine a favor and walk away from this fake marriage before I figure out how to end it for you."

"Say what you want about me. But don't talk about Renn like that."

He looks at the ceiling and laughs.

"He's a good man. He's nothing like you."

He drops his gaze to my face. "And how would you know? Because he fucked that little ass all weekend? Huh? That makes him a good man?"

My hands shake. "Go to hell."

"How about this?" He looks me up and down. "Let me fuck that little ass, and I'll let you keep Renn for a while longer."

Before I know what I'm doing my fist is in a tight ball, flying toward Reid's face. It grazes the tip of his chin, sending splintering pain down my wrist.

"You little cunt." He reaches for me. "Get over here and let me—"

"Don't fucking touch me. You're a piece of shit, and I hope you burn in hell." My voice trembles with anger.

"What's going on here?" Renn asks, making me jump.

I look at the doorway. He fills the space with his broad shoulders, piecing together the scenario before him.

I push around him and bolt down the hallway, tears flowing down my cheeks. I snatch my purse off the hook and make my way outside.

"Blakely," Renn calls after me.

My hand finds my phone in my purse. I rip it out and find Foxx's number, thankful that I listened to him today and saved it into my contacts list.

"Blakely!"

"Blakely?" Foxx's voice is gruff through the phone.

"Foxx. I'm at Renn's parents' house." I choke back a sob. "Can you come and get me?"

"I'm on my way. Sit tight. I'm three minutes out."

"What the fuck happened in there?" Renn grabs both of my shoulders and pulls me into him. "Talk to me."

My shoulders bounce as I cry into Renn's chest.

I don't want to tell him what his father said. *I can't.* Renn is a good man ... and he might have lost his contract. *Because of me.*

"Do that fuckup of a son of mine a favor and walk away from this

fake marriage before I figure out how to end it for you. Let me fuck that little ass, and I'll let you keep Renn a while longer."

No. Renn won't want to hear that.

"What's going on?" Ripley asks, walking across the driveway.

Fuck. I hope the rest of the family—Rory—doesn't come out here, too.

"I don't know," Renn says.

I pull away, wiping my eyes and nose with my hand. Pain shoots up my wrist, and I jerk it back, crying.

"What's Foxx doing here?" Renn asks as a black SUV slides up the driveway.

The vehicle stops, and Foxx climbs out of the driver's seat. He wastes no time getting to me.

"I called him," I say.

"Why?" Renn holds out his hands. "What is going on? What happened? I'm so fucking confused."

"Can we talk about this later?" I ask.

"No. We can't. I just heard my wife fighting with my father. Then she runs out of the house, having called another man to come and get her. What the fuck is going on?"

My face heats.

I look between Renn, Ripley, and Foxx. They all look at me expectantly.

"Fine." I hold my wrist with my other hand, wincing. "What just happened was ..." I force a swallow. "Your father tried to buy me off."

"*What?*" Renn spits.

Ripley bristles beside him.

"He called me a little whore and offered me a half a million dollars to let you go," I say, anger flooding me again. "Pointed out that I didn't belong here and was ruining your life ..." I lock eyes with my husband. "And that I caused you to lose your contract."

Renn's jaw drops. "Blakely ..."

"That motherfucker," Ripley says.

I can't see Foxx, but I watch Renn shake his head.

I gather myself. "Your father tried to grab me to *fuck my little ass—*"

"*I'm gonna kill him,*" Ripley says through clenched teeth, turning on his heel and storming toward the house.

Renn flinches.

"Want me to go?" Foxx asks.

"No." Slowly, my words sink in. The disbelief twists into a menacing snarl. "Take her home, Foxx."

"Yes, sir."

Renn runs back to the house.

"Come on, Blakely," Foxx says, reaching for my arm.

"Renn!"

He ignores me, disappearing around the wall.

Tears wet my cheeks again. Foxx takes my hand, but I yank it back, yelping.

"Explain," Foxx orders.

"I threw a punch."

He fights a smile, refusing to look me in the eye. "Let's get you home."

Home.

I'm not sure I have one anymore.

We climb into the car and pull down the long driveway.

I feel like I just left my heart behind.

CHAPTER 25
Renn

I burst through the door and race into the house. Tate meets me in the hallway.

"*Go,*" I say, jamming my thumb over my shoulder. "Go to my house. Foxx took Blakely there."

"You got it."

He slaps my shoulder as he darts behind me.

Adrenaline is coursing through me.

"He called me a little whore and offered me a half a million dollars to let you go."

Rage snakes through my veins like an old friend.

I jog down the corridor toward Bianca outside Dad's office. Shouts filter from the room in front of her. Screeches of furniture being dragged against the floor. Voices shouting, growing louder the closer I get to them.

"What's going on? Where's Blakely?" Bianca asks, but I can't hear her.

My heart is racing, my head spinning.

He tried to buy her off?

Called my wife a whore?

I want to be with Blakely ... but I have to deal with this piece of shit first.

Ripley has Dad pinned against the wall, his forearm pressed against his neck. He shouts inches from Dad's face. Despite his unfavorable position, Dad glares at my brother—unwilling to back down.

"I'm going to murder you," I say, stepping into the room with Bianca at my heels.

Gannon cuts me off, blocking me from going any farther. Jason watches from the side, taking in the scenario before deciding which side to take—which side is right.

"Don't make me do this, Gannon," I say, clenching my fists. "This isn't between us."

Ripley looks over his shoulder and sees me. Slowly, he lets our father go.

"*Dammit*," Dad hisses, sitting in his office chair like he didn't just assault Blakely. *Pompous, arrogant asshole.* He adjusts his collar. His right eye starts to swell. "Get the hell out of my office. All of you."

"Fuck you," I seethe, shoving Gannon out of the way.

He steps in front of me again. "Stay calm, Renn."

"Stay calm? Fuck that. I'm not staying calm until I kill that son of a bitch."

Mom marches into the room, her heels clicking against the floor. She takes in the room, letting her gaze settle on my father for a searing moment before switching it to me.

"What happened? Don't pussyfoot around it," she says. "Tell me what happened in this room with Blakely."

Ripley and I look at one another.

Our entire family, minus Tate, is surrounding us. Dad's actions have changed the landscape between us all forever. Ripley and I know that. And we also know that the news will break our mother's heart.

"That little bitch came in here and—*oof.*"

A commotion breaks out again as Ripley grabs our father by the front of his shirt, and I attempt to get by Gannon again.

"Stop it!" Mom shouts. "Renn, what happened?"

I glare at Dad. "You wanna know what happened? Your fucking husband called my wife a whore and offered her a half a million dollars to leave me."

Bianca gasps. Gannon's eyes go wide. Jason's arms drop to his sides. Ripley shivers with anger.

Mom lifts her chin. Her throat bobs as she swallows.

I level my gaze with the man across the desk. "*If that's not enough*, he then tried to grab her and told her he was going to fuck her ass."

Bianca covers her mouth. Mom's momentarily blindsided but recovers quickly.

Dad glares at me.

I grin mercilessly. "*Run.*"

I push my way through Gannon and lunge at my father. He slips against the leather as he tries to avoid my swing and falls to the floor. Ripley grabs him as I leap across the chair, ready to rip his throat out. Dad's computer crashes to the floor at Ripley's feet.

Gannon pulls on the back of my shirt. The fabric rips. He slides an arm around me and hauls me away from Ripley and Dad.

I pant, dragging in a lungful of air—seeing red.

"You can only save him for so long, Gannon," I say, laughing angrily.

"I'm not saving him. *I'm saving you.*"

"*Please.*" I spit the taste of blood at his feet. "No matter what you do, he's not getting out of here alive." I look at the old man over my shoulder. "You went too far. Too far. *You're done.* How's it feel to know you're a dead man walking?"

Gannon side-eyes me but turns to Dad. "You give Renn hell every day about being an embarrassment to our family. And look at you. *It's you.* I'm disgusted to be your son."

Mom steps toward our father.

"Now, listen, Rory. Before you get all pissed off and jealous—"

Crack!

Her hand connects with the side of his face. He reaches up like he's going to hit her back, but Ripley is quick to end that.

"How could you do this, Daddy?" Bianca asks.

Dad glares up at Ripley, then at Gannon. "Where is your loyalty, boys?"

"With Renn," Ripley says, switching his attention to me. "He always has my back."

I nod his way.

"What do you want to do, Mom?" Jason asks, giving me a look to be patient.

She pauses. "Let your father go, Ripley."

Ripley releases his arm.

"You little shit," Dad sneers. "You all get the hell out of my house."

"Excuse me." Mom laughs. "I'm not finished." She looks over her shoulder. "Gannon, Jason, please keep your brother from going to jail. I'd love to see your father writhing in pain, but he's done enough damage for one evening."

"No. I'm not leaving here until he pays for what he did," I say, clenching my fists.

Mom turns to me. "You need to take care of your wife. Let me take out the trash." She looks at Bianca. "Will you help your father, please?"

"Do what?" she asks.

Mom turns toward the door. "Help him pack his shit."

"Oh, Rory," Dad says, blowing her off. "Stop it."

Mom stops in the doorway and spins around. She takes in her family. Then she nods.

"I want you out of my house in twenty minutes. Take your car and clothes. The rest is mine."

"Rory—"

"You will not disrespect my children. You will not talk to another woman like you spoke to Blakely, and you will not threaten anyone and expect me to sit back quietly. Did you forget who I am, Reid?"

He trembles with anger.

She smirks. "You came into this marriage with nothing. You'll leave with nothing. I've let you slide by with your bullshit too long. Tonight, you crossed a line you won't return from."

"Where are you going?" he asks, as if he has the right to know. *Bastard.*

"I have a lot of calls to make." She points at me. "Go home. I know you sent Tate, but ..."

Blakely's face flashes through my mind.

The tears rushing down her cheeks.

Her swollen wrist.

The pure destruction in her beautiful eyes.

"Make sure he leaves," I say to Gannon. "Keep him away from Mom."

"He won't get near her. Don't worry about that."

"This isn't over," I say, looking at my father. "Mark my words."

With that, I run to my car.

* * *

Blakely

"Yeah, Troy," Foxx says softly on the other side of the door. "I need a medic to meet us at the airport to look at her hand. Pretty sure it's broken."

I glance down. I'm pretty sure it's broken, too.

The side of my hand down to my wrist is swollen. The skin is tight and hot, and the pain is intense. When we got back to Renn's, Foxx gave me a pain reliever, but it hasn't kicked in yet.

Foxx helped me throw my clothes and toiletries into my suitcase. I made him take the llama, which irritated him. *Many things irritate him, I've learned.* And he tried to talk me out of leaving, but I refused to listen. *That also went over well.*

I can't think clearly. I know my thoughts are jumbled, and I'm terrified I'll say or do something I'll regret later. I waffle back and forth between wanting to puke, needing Renn, and being swamped with embarrassment. *How will I face his family?*

"You will never fit in here. You are not a Brewer. You will never be a Brewer."

Out of everything Reid spewed at me, that bothers me the most.

My eyes cloud with unshed tears.

Renn is a good man—*a nice man.* The kind of man I've been looking for all along. But maybe there's some truth to what his father said. Maybe our worlds are too different for me to fit into his.

Maybe that's why he didn't tell me about his contract.

Maybe that's why he's been acting so differently today.

Maybe he realized I'm not worth the hassle. I'm not worth the fight.

"He might be weak—deluded from fucking you—but he has Brewer blood in his veins."

Maybe he got swept up in the sex and novelty ... and remembered this isn't real. And, if he did, my heart will shatter beyond recognition.

"If either of us start to develop real feelings for each other ... Then we walk away immediately. No questions asked."

I look at myself in the mirror. "There's a reason you made that rule. Trust yourself, Blakely."

I take a final look around his bathroom and his bedroom. Then I step into the hall.

Foxx looks at me with his brows pulled together. Tate stands next to him.

"Stay, Blakely," Tate says. "Renn will fix this. You gotta stay."

"Tate ... I can't."

"Yes, you can." He steps closer. "We're family. Families work their shit out. Come back with me and let us ... well, we'll probably have to clean up Dad's blood first. Then we can talk."

"We're family. Families work their shit out."

I wish that were true. I wish I really was a member of their family. But this whole marriage is a farce. And they don't know. If they did, they'd want me gone as well.

Renn and I never chose to be husband and wife. Not really.

My shoulders fall.

At the end of the day, when it's all boiled down—that's the truth.

This marriage was built on a lie.

Lies always fall apart.

"Foxx, I'm ready," I say. "Tate, thank you for coming here. I'm ... sorry for tonight."

He pulls me into a hug. "No, don't be sorry. This isn't on you." He pulls back and looks me in the eye. "If you need to go think, go think. But take Foxx because I can't deal with Renn if I tell him you left alone." He grins. "But think and then come back. Come home. I need someone to team up with me. You seem cool. It can be us against Renn and Bianca."

My cheeks are damp again, and my heart burns.

I just want to go home.

Except ... I don't have one.

"Let's go," I say, heading for the garage. "Goodbye, Tate."

"No."

I stop and look at him.

He smiles. "I'll see you soon."

My tears fall harder as I enter the garage, climb into Foxx's SUV, and am whisked to the airport.

CHAPTER 26

Renn

"Why can't anyone answer their fucking phones?" As I try Tate again, Foxx's name flashes across the dash. I click a button on my steering wheel. "Talk to me, Foxx. What's going on?"

My heart pounds, aching for Blakely. I need to get to her. Need to see her. I need to hold my wife and ensure she's okay—that she knows I love her.

"We're sitting on the tarmac at the airport," he says.

"*What*?"

"I know you're going to be pissed, Renn. But it was me taking her on your family's plane or watching her call a car service and fly domestic."

"You couldn't stop her?"

He laughs. "Yeah. I could've. But you don't pay me enough for that."

I want to smile. I want to see the humor in it. I just can't.

"We're going to Vegas," he says. "I have—"

"Vegas! Why the hell is she going to Vegas?"

"I have a doctor on board now, putting her hand in a soft cast. She has a boxer's fracture, I think. Someone needs to show her how to punch."

"You really think that's a good idea?"

"Fair point."

I sigh. *What the fuck is going on? Why is she going to Vegas?* "She's okay, right? It's just her hand?"

"Physically, she's fine."

My heart breaks. "Can I talk to her?"

"She's with the doc. I think she talked to Brock and Ella on the way here and then turned it off."

"I'll come to the airport and fly out with her."

He groans. "Look, I'm no relationship expert. But experience tells me she probably needs to process tonight."

This is not what I want to hear. I want him to tell me to hurry. That they'll wait. That she wants to see me, and I need to hustle to the airport. *But no.*

Fuck. Fuck my fucking father. Fuck the fucking Royals.

Just ... fuck.

"Will you stay with her?" I ask. "Don't let her out of your sight."

"Got it."

"And thanks, Foxx, for taking care of her." *When I didn't.*

I should've left with her. I should've cared for her and said to hell with my dad. But if I had done that, God knows what Ripley would've done. I had to stand up for my wife.

Let Dad know hell is coming his way.

I've known he's an asshole for years, but this ... *I cannot get over this.*

My jaw pulses at the thought.

I can't deny I was glad to see Mom put the bastard in his place. My stomach clenches. *What if Dad had hit Blakely or Mom?*

Thank God Ripley was there.

"It's no problem," Foxx says. "My phone will be on if you need anything or want to check on her. I think the doc is giving her a little pain medicine so she might be drowsy afterward."

I nod. "Okay. I have some things to do tomorrow, but I'll check in."

"You got it. Talk later."

"Goodbye."

I fly up my street and slide into my driveway. Tate's car sits off to the side. I'm happy to see Tate at my house for the first time ever.

The garage door lifts, and I pull in. But before I get out, I take out my phone.

> Me: I'm worried about you. I know you want space, and I understand. I can't imagine how you feel, and it kills me that I don't know. I'm trying to balance honoring your wishes and following my heart. I need to hold you. Please, call me.

* * *

Blakely

"I'm so tired," I say, shuffling inside the suite.

Foxx carries my bag and the llama behind me. "Where do you want these?"

"I'll get them."

"With a cast on your right hand?"

"Fine. Please take them upstairs."

He disappears up the staircase without another word.

It's odd being here. The last time I was here, it ended with chaos. The last time I arrived here, I wasn't married. I was celebrating my thirtieth birthday. *Such a shitty birthday, after all.*

It seems like forever ago.

The suite is silent and cold. I don't even know where the thermostat is to adjust it. Instead, I walk into the kitchen to see if there's something edible.

"Foxx?" I call out. "Where did all of this food come from?"

The fridge has a few yogurts, a little fruit, milk, and cheese. There are a few choices of water, soda, and juice. Bread, cookies, and crackers have been placed in the pantry.

He comes around the corner. "Tate had Astrid take care of it."

"Aw." My heart warms. "He seems like a nice guy."

Foxx shrugs.

233

"What's that about?"

"What's what?"

"That shrug. What does that shrug mean?"

He lifts a brow. "I think your pain meds are making you mean."

"No, I'm not *just* mean. I'm stressed, Foxx. I've had a night. I'm tired. I've been traveling. I'm not sure my husband wants to be married to me anymore, and his father tried to buy me off, and ... *ah*!"

He holds his hands up. "Easy."

"Just explain the shrug."

"I have an NDA."

"And I'm your employer now, basically. So NDA me in."

He groans. "You are a pain in my ass."

I gasp. "Is that any way to talk to me? I'm on the verge of a nervous breakdown. Where is your compassion?"

"On the tarmac."

I make a face. He almost smiles.

"I have four brothers," Foxx says. "I have a predisposition to dislike younger brothers."

"Then why do you dislike me?"

"Because I also have a sister."

"Oh."

I take out the cheese and a few crackers—anything to keep my mind occupied. Foxx watches me. It's the most uncertain I've seen him.

"How do you know the Brewers?" I ask.

"I've known Jason for a long time."

"But you work with Renn?"

"Mostly."

I glance at him. "You're a man of few words."

He shrugs.

Grrr.

"Well, I'm trying to have a conversation with you to keep from thinking about my father-in-law talking about fucking my ass tonight. Humor me." I slap a piece of cheese on a cracker and offer it to him. "Do you live in Nashville?"

He declines the snack. "Kismet Beach, Florida."

"Then why are you here?"

"Because someone decided to take a last-minute trip to Vegas."

I narrow my eyes. "Why are you in Nashville if you live in Florida?"

"Because I work for a company called Landry Security. I get assigned to wealthy clients who require my services."

"Kind of sounds like you're a prostitute, Foxx."

He shakes his head. "Are you ready for bed?"

"Almost. Where do you sleep when you're here?"

"There's a room down the hall. I'm sure you'll shout if you need me."

I smile. "Yup."

"I'm going to bed. Don't drink any wine. You're already loopy as fuck."

"This is just my charm."

"God help us," he mutters, disappearing around the corner.

I gather my snacks—a task made more difficult by my broken hand —and head upstairs, trying to decide whether I'm loopy. *I might be.* My body is warm and fuzzy, and I can't quite access all the reasons I'm upset.

It's rather nice.

I climb into bed and drop the goodies. As soon as my body hits the mattress—*how did this get cleaned?*—my eyes feel heavy.

Very, very heavy.

I slip into a world where Renn is on a surfboard next to me, telling me to paddle ...

Blakely

Something crunches beneath me.

I rummage under my stomach and pull out a sleeve of crackers. *Whoops.*

It's dark outside, but the open curtains allow enough light to see around me. I grab my phone and check the time. It's three in the morning.

My screen is filled with texts. I ignore them all except for the top one.

> Renn: I'm worried about you. I know you want space, and I understand. I can't imagine how you feel, and it kills me that I don't know. I'm trying to balance honoring your wishes and following my heart. I need to hold you. Please, call me.

Renn.

I want to talk to him. I want to make this all okay between us. But I don't know what to say ... or if I can make it work between us.

I can't imagine how you feel, and it kills me that I don't know. I'm trying to balance honoring your wishes and following my heart. I need to hold you.

That's what I want too. Renn's arms.

I've never wanted to be held more.

We'll have to talk. I know that. I want that. But not at three in the morning. Not when my hand is throbbing. Not when my eyes are so heavy.

Texting is hard, but I manage.

> Me: I'm confused and scared. That's honesty. My hand hurts. My pride is bruised, too. I'm sorry for whatever happened after I left. I know I'm not responsible, but my heart hurts for you, anyway. Maybe I am responsible for leaving. I'm just trying to do the right thing. We haven't been alone since we got married. Maybe we should think about this. In the words of the great Ella St. James, there's a difference between a fling, feelings, and forever. I'm just not sure where we fall. Good night, Renn. Xo

I drop the phone and fall back asleep.

CHAPTER 28

Renn

I reread her text.

> Blakely: I'm confused and scared. That's honesty. My hand hurts. My pride is bruised, too. I'm sorry for whatever happened after I left. I know I'm not responsible, but my heart hurts for you, anyway. Maybe I am responsible for leaving. I'm just trying to do the right thing. We haven't been alone since we got married. Maybe we should think about this. In the words of the great Ella St. James, there's a difference between a fling, feelings, and forever. I'm just not sure where we fall. Good night, Renn. Xo

I've read it so many times that I can recite it from memory. *I'm confused and scared.* I close my eyes. *Me too.*

"Here you go," Gannon says, shoving a cup of coffee before me. "You look like you need it."

"Thanks."

I sit up and breathe in the aroma as Mom and Bianca enter. They settle around my dining room table.

We're somber. I don't think we slept much—all for individual reasons. Bianca stayed with Mom. Gannon went to the office at Mom's bequest. I was up all night worrying about Blakely.

I called her twice this morning, forgetting the time difference. She didn't answer anyway.

"Where are Tate and Ripley?" Bianca asks.

"They flew to Miami this morning. Tate has a meeting this afternoon, and Ripley tagged along. They should be back tonight," Jason says.

Our sister nods.

Mom slips on her glasses. They do nothing to hide the circles under her eyes. She picks up a legal pad. "Okay, let's get to it. I have a locksmith headed to my house this morning, as well as the security company. All keys and codes will be changed by lunchtime."

"Good," Gannon says.

"I have a meeting with my attorneys at noon," she says. "Your father will try to maintain some stake in this company, but I assure you, he has no leg to stand on. Gannon, would you be able to attend with me? And do you have the financial reports from the last quarter?"

"I can, and I do."

"Excellent." Mom turns the page. "Bianca, you're the interim president. Everyone will report to you. That's a lot, I know, and I'll get you help. You won't have you as backup."

She smiles. "Take a look at Daniel Blue. He might be a good candidate."

"I'll note that." Mom scribbles on the page in front of her. "Jason, is there anything outstanding with Brewer Air? How are things on that front?"

"We're fine. Dad had little involvement with our operation. We're good to go."

"Love that for us," Mom says. "What am I missing?"

Gannon leans back in his seat. "We bought the Arrows yesterday."

"Shit." Mom takes off her glasses and pinches her nose. "Who is the lead on that?"

"Dad had Bobby Downing working on it with him. Let me see what I can dig up today," Gannon says.

"We aren't keeping Downing around," Mom says. "Let's meet about this first thing in the morning. That'll give you time to get the paperwork over to me, Gannon."

"Sounds good."

Mom looks at me and smiles. "Do you want to manage a baseball team, Renn?"

"No, I do not."

She rolls her eyes. "Fine. Don't contribute."

"Look at Mom, turning into a CEO on day one," I joke.

She laughs, wagging a finger at me.

"What about Lincoln Landry?" Gannon says. "He used to play for them. I have no idea if he'd be interested, but I know his brother Graham. I could give him a call."

"Call them and see if there's any interest," Mom says. "That's a good start. We need to get a name behind it as soon as possible."

"I'm just going to cut in here really quick," I say, sitting up. "I'm retiring today."

"*What?*" Bianca asks.

My family exchanges a bewildered look. All I can do is shrug.

It was my late-night epiphany—*I need to retire*. It's the only solution that makes sense.

I can't play for the Royals. Not after my last interaction with Galecki. *Fuck that guy*. And after having a hard conversation with Brock last night about the Royals stance and the events at dinner, he agreed. *Fuck. That. Guy.*

As I lay in bed and thought about Blakely and our marriage, my job, my dad—and the war that broke out with him—Brock and his health, and his and Ella's baby ... and my future and what it looks like, it all became crystal clear.

The only thing that matters are my relationships with the people I love.

I don't need my job—not the money, the stress, or the potential to hurt myself. I have no use for my father. I don't want to be away from Blakely for long periods.

I want to travel with my wife. I want her to be proud of me and feel loved and wanted every minute of her life. Hang out at home and learn to garden. Nurture my relationships with my siblings and support my mother in her badass return to business. *She's gonna kill it.* I want to be around to spoil Brock's kid rotten ... and have as many children as Blakely and God will allow us to have.

I want those things so badly that it takes my breath away.

"I'm retiring," I say again. "I have my team working out the details this morning."

"Why?" Gannon asks.

"I'm done. That's really it. I'm done."

Jason lifts his chin. "How is Blakely? Have you talked to her?"

My spirits sink.

"Actually, no. I haven't. She flew to Vegas last night. She texted once but that's all I've heard from her."

"What are you going to do, Renn?" Mom asks.

All eyes are on me.

I get up from the table and grip the back of my chair. "I don't know, Mom. I don't want to pressure her or worsen it, but I'm not walking away. It's not over."

Bianca smiles. "I didn't have you pegged to be the romantic, but I'm here for it."

"Who did you think it was?" Gannon asks.

"Tate."

"Makes sense," Gannon says, sighing.

"I love her, guys. Somehow, I must convince her we're the real deal —the forever kind."

Bianca makes a face. "Why would she doubt it?"

"Because we were kinda drunk when we accidentally got married."

"Oh, Renn," Mom says, groaning.

Gannon chuckles.

"Look, *Mother*," I say, pointing at her. "You could be a doll and say something sweet like it's kismet. Or that the universe knew what it was doing, forcing us together. You're not even trying."

Bianca laughs.

"I'm sorry," Mom says, holding out a hand. "You're right. Clearly, this was meant to be."

"See? That didn't even hurt, did it?"

Mom shakes her head. "Oh, my child ..."

Gannon sits back and crosses his arms over his chest. "I hate that I'm even getting involved in this, but let me get this straight—you want to prove to her that your accidental marriage was real?"

"Or that he wants it to be real," Bianca counters.

"I want Blakely to know I might've married her while inebriated, but I meant my vows. I'd marry her all over again sober. How do I convince her of that?"

Bianca grins. "I have an idea ..."

CHAPTER 29

Blakely

"Why do these women just fight all the time?" I dig the spoon into the tub of chocolate ice cream. "Oh, my gosh. *Stop it*. Don't say that about her. You were just on a yacht with her two days ago."

I stretch out in the bed. My foot hits my phone. I consider just kicking it off the end of the bed, but I don't. It would be a bit more effort than I'm willing to give.

"Are you talking to yourself again?" Foxx's voice tears me away from the television.

"You're never going to believe it. Adria is pissed at Camille *again*."

"The horror."

I take a big scoop of ice cream and look at him. "Do I sense sarcasm?"

He just stares at me.

"Ugh," I groan, going in for another scoop. "I'm trying to distract myself, Foxxy. You aren't helping."

He lifts a brow.

"I'm heartbroken over here," I say, shoving another heaping spoonful of chocolatey goodness in my mouth. "Does this qualify as me leaving my husband? I mean I did, but—"

"You're dripping ice cream down the side of your mouth. Swallow first."

"That's what he said."

Foxx sighs, shaking his head.

"That was funny." I point my spoon at him. "Come on." I shove the spoon into the container, my spirits dwindling again. "What am I going to do?"

"I'm unsure why you think I'm here to give advice."

"Because you're the only friend I have here with me. You win by default."

"Yay."

I glare at him. "Do you even have friends in real life?"

"Blakely, I'm going home."

"What? What do you mean?"

"I mean, I'm going home. Someone will be coming to replace me today."

My bottom lip trembles. *Great. Now I'm getting emotional over the security guy.* "You can't leave me. We've bonded."

"I'll let you know before I go."

"Fine. But do I get a say in your replacement?"

He holds his hands out, confused.

"I request Troy," I say, lifting a glob of ice cream into my mouth.

"How do you even know him?"

"Ways."

He points at me. "You missed."

"What?" I look down at my shirt. A drop of melted ice cream is smack dab in the middle of my chest. "Oh. *Shit.* Eating with my left hand sucks."

He takes the opportunity to sneak out. *Bastard.*

I flop back against the pillows and search for the remote. I can't take any more of the arguing ... that or it's getting harder to be distracted.

Channel surfing doesn't deliver a viable alternative to thinking, so I give up.

My head is a little clearer this morning ... or afternoon. I'm not sure what time it is. Sleep helped. A long bath this morning assisted. But the quiet, the space to decompress—that's what I really needed.

It's made things evident that were cloudy.

I'm in love with Renn Brewer.

Since I'm in Vegas, if I were to make a wager, I'd put my money on the fact that he loves me too.

I can see a future with him. I can see a family—lots of babies and adventures. I can see us building on our marriage. Even if it started poorly, we could save it.

If he wants to.

What I haven't worked out for certain is if we can return from yesterday's nightmare.

Is he mad at me for leaving? Was it wrong for me to bolt like that?

Will his family be willing to accept me after the fracas? Because Renn can't live without them, and I won't ask him to. I'd never put him in that position. I'd walk away first, no matter how badly it hurts.

What happened to his father? I can't be near him again.

Did Renn lose his job? Does he blame me?

Does he miss me like I miss him? His text last night said he did, so I have hope. But did he wake up this morning without me and realize his life is better when he wakes up alone?

"I'm too busy. I can be selfish. To be honest, I like my independence. I can spend my money on whatever I please. But probably the biggest thing is that I don't have to wonder about hidden motivations."

My questions can be answered by calling him. But I don't feel like I'm mentally prepared for it just yet.

I grab the ice cream again. I'm about to scoop another glob of dessert when the television grabs my attention.

Renn's face is on the screen. Beneath his picture are the words *Brewer Retires.*

What?

I drop the spoon and scramble for the remote. A talking head comes on the screen. I pound the volume to turn it up. My heart beats so fast that I have a hard time catching my breath.

"Thank you, Jeffrey," the blond woman says. "Shock waves rippled through the rugby community this morning as superstar Renn Brewer announced his retirement. A joint statement between Brewer and the Tennessee Royals was released moments ago. Brewer, who played internationally and here in the US for ten of the last eleven seasons, is heralded as one of the best openside flankers of all time. The Royals wish him well. Brewer, for his part, has asked for privacy." She looks at Jeffrey. "If you keep up with pop culture, you'll remember that Brewer got married last week. Some are speculating this is the motivation behind the abrupt decision."

"*Oh no.*" I turn the volume down, panic setting in. "Foxx!"

His footsteps hit the steps. He appears in the doorway.

"Renn retired."

"I know."

My eyes bulge. "*You know?* You didn't think to mention that to me?"

"NDA."

I glare at him. He shrugs.

"I hate your shrugs," I say, my voice breaking. A well of emotion breaks, and the pressure builds in my throat. "Was it because of me?"

Foxx looks at the ceiling. "Why me?"

"*You might've cost him his Royals contract ...*" Was Reid right?

"No ..."

I rip the blankets off, thankful I'm fully clothed. With shaky hands, I scramble to find my phone. I press the sides—bobbling it in my left hand, waiting for it to turn on. The battery sign flashes on the screen.

Tears fill my eyes as I search for a phone charger.

"Blakely ..."

I whip around. Foxx walks toward me, carrying a manila envelope.

The look in his eye has me backing away. "What are you doing?"

"This is for you."

"What if I don't want it?"

He holds it in the air between us. "It's from Renn."

I take it from him and toss it on the bed like it might bite me. It's a Wild West standoff—Renn facing me, me facing the envelope, and the envelope threatening to explode.

"It's from Renn?" I ask, just to be sure.

"It says Renn on the front."

"I'm not emotionally stable enough for this. Can you open it?"

"No."

"Come on, Foxxy. Help a girl out. I only have one hand." I'm wearing him down. I can tell. "Just open it. You don't have to look at it or anything. Just open it for me."

He's not happy but takes the bait. He undoes the fastener and then puts the envelope back on the bed.

"Do you need a phone charger?" he asks.

"Yes. Do you have one?"

"Give me your phone."

I fork it over. I'm too preoccupied even to crack a joke.

"I'm going to get this taken care of," he says.

"Okay. Thank you."

He walks out, leaving me with the mystery delivery.

I take a long, deep breath and pick it up. The papers, a chunk of them, slide out onto the bed.

And my world falls apart.

District Court
Clark County, Nevada
Joint Petition for Divorce (with no children)

A deep, raw sob spills from the depths of my chest. "*No!*"

Tears blind me. I wince from the pain of having my hopes and dreams ripped from me. I hunch over to prevent my whole heart from shattering on the floor.

My hand hits the mattress. The motion bobbles the papers just enough for me to see Renn's signature in black ink at the bottom of the last page.

I crawl to the middle of the bed and curl into a ball. The force of the heaves is so strong that it's nearly impossible to breathe.

It's my fault. I shouldn't have left him. I should've stayed.

I want to think we should've gotten an annulment right after our wedding, but I can't make myself believe it. The last few days have been the best days of my life. I wouldn't trade them for the world.

"*Renn ...*"

My eyes squeeze shut, tears leaking from beneath my lashes anyway.

All the visions I had for us—morning coffee in the sunroom, vacationing in Australia, evenings in the pool while we share all our secrets—are gone.

There won't be nights that turn into mornings while we forget to fall asleep. Dark-headed babies racing down the hallways with Renn chasing after them. Telling our grandkids that we accidentally got married on my thirtieth birthday.

"I'm so sorry," I whisper through my tears. "I'm so, so sorry."

The mattress dips.

I swipe behind me. "Leave me alone, Foxx," I say, hiccuping. "I don't want my phone. Just take it."

Instead, the mattress dips more. And slowly, a body lies behind mine.

My sobs shudder as an arm with a number seven tattoo stretches across me, pulling me into him.

What?

I roll over as fast as I can with one hand and a heart on the verge of exploding.

"Hey, cutie," Renn says, his head resting on his hand.

"What are you doing?" My mind races. "You can't … You just …" I scramble to sit up, confused. "You just served me divorce papers and come here like this?" My throat squeezes. "I can't do this. I don't know what you're doing, but I can't—"

He grins. "Do you want to know what I'm doing?"

"In the words of Foxx …" I shrug.

His laughter shakes the bed. *I'm so confused.*

"I didn't want you to leave," he says in his casually cool way. "I was mad. Worried. You didn't let me take care of you. You deprived me of that, and it hurt me."

I watch him, too scared that I'll read things wrong to say anything.

"But it's not just about me," he says. "And you needed to be alone, and I have to give you what you need."

I mean, you didn't have to …

"But all I can give you is one night because I miss you too much." He reaches for me. "Let me hold you."

Slowly, I fall into his arms. He holds me so tight I almost can't breathe.

He presses a kiss on the top of my head. "I love you. I love you with all of my heart and soul. And I will never not love you, Blakely." He kisses me again. "We aren't getting out of this bed until we're on the same page."

I close my eyes and absorb the peace. The love. *He loves me? But he doesn't want to be married to me? How cruel. How does that make sense?*

I smile. "I love you, Renn. I love you in ways I didn't know were possible. But if you love me, why did you give me divorce papers?"

He lets me pull away. "Because you said our marriage wasn't real. It's the realest thing in my life. But if I need to divorce you and remarry you, so we remember it, let's do it. I'll do it tomorrow. But I can't love you more than I do right now. Nothing will ever be any more real than our marriage."

"Really?"

"Really." He takes my broken hand gently and inspects the cast. "Are you okay?"

"It hurts."

He pulls me into another hug. "My mom is divorcing my father. None of my siblings will have anything to do with him. Ripley got a pretty good shot off on him before I returned to the house."

"I'm sorry."

"Never, ever apologize for that, baby. I'm sorry my father put you in that position. And I'm proud as hell that you stood up to him." He presses his cheek against my head. "Thank you for giving me and my family another chance."

"Your family?"

"Not my fucking dad. But the rest of them ... they hope you'll get to know them. That they can be a part of our family."

My brows pull together. "You mean that I can be a part of your family?"

"Nope. It's me and you now. And all ten of our kids."

My heart swells. *Although, ten kids is a stretch. I was thinking maybe four ...*

"You are my family," he whispers. "Whatever we do, we do

249

together."

I hold on to him. *Just one more question.* "What about your contract? Did you lose that because of me? I need to know the truth."

He takes a deep breath. "No. I didn't. I walked away after a meeting that made me realize I no longer need to play. I won't sacrifice things I might've sacrificed before. And with Brock and all that ... my heart wasn't in it. My heart is yours. So let's start fresh together. No outside bullshit."

My smile turns into laughter, which turns into a burst of energy. I roll over, straddling him. He holds my waist looking up at me, laughing.

"You do realize I'm lying in melted ice cream right now, don't you?" he asks.

"Oh, crap!"

"At least you're consistent."

My giggles are captured by his mouth, and his touch restores my dreams.

"Renn?" I ask between kisses.

"Yeah?"

"Let's not get divorced."

He chuckles against my mouth. "We were never really getting divorced anyway. I was making a point."

"Ah!" I yell as he flips me onto my back. I look up at him, beaming. "Is this a good time to tell you that I've been thinking ..."

He looks at me nervously.

I bite my lip. "And I want to take you up on your offer."

"What offer?"

"Let's make a baby, Mr. Brewer."

"Foxx!" Renn shouts, stripping his shirt off. "Don't come up here!"

"Yeah, Foxxy!"

Renn laughs, his eyes sparkling. "I love you."

"I love you more. I've missed you and never want to spend another day away from you."

We ruin the divorce papers in the melted ice cream. My shirt lands on the llama—again. We wind up on the floor, laughing and touching, kissing and fucking.

And this time, we make love.

CHAPTER 30

Blakely

"What are you guys doing?" Ella asks.

"Renn is making a fire," I say.

"She's into caveman kinks—*ouch*!" Renn laughs, rubbing his rib where I jabbed him with my elbow.

I make a face at my husband. "Actually, Renn served me with divorce papers yesterday."

Brock bristles beside Ella.

"I was making a point," Renn says, lifting a brow at Brock. "And I've spent the past two days trying to get Blakely to let me give her the wedding of her dreams."

"Are you going to do it?" Ella asks.

"No. I don't need another wedding as long as the first one counts."

Renn smiles. "It better count, or you're guaranteeing yourself a redo."

I try to play it off, but his insistence makes me feel special.

Renn, Brock, and Ella get into a conversation about weddings. Now that my brother and best friend are getting married, it's a hot topic around here. Ella wants to wait until after the baby is born. Brock prefers to do it before the baby is born. It's a whole mess ... but a mess stemming from love.

To say I'm relieved that they're going the distance is an understatement. I've never seen him ... dote, but it's adorable. *And will probably drive Ella crazy very soon.* I grin. But that's their jam. It works.

The fire roars as it catches in the fireplace. Renn leans back, proud of his handiwork.

"There you go," he says. "Look. I made fire."

"Good job." I roll my eyes, handing him the manila envelope filled with ice cream-stained papers. "Burn these."

He drops it unceremoniously into the flames.

It's satisfying to watch the papers turn into ash.

"My retirement will be announced tomorrow," Brock says. "The Royals had a complete meltdown when they realized that Renn and I were both leaving. Serves them right."

"Are you going to play in the charity game next weekend?" Renn asks him.

"No," Ella and I say together.

Brock sighs. "It sounds like I'm not."

"You have no business out there," I say. "We are no longer a rugby family."

"We have to find something to do with our time," Renn says. "We can't sit here all day staring at our beautiful wives. We have to do something."

"You can golf," Ella offers.

"Actually," Brock says, sitting and pulling Ella onto his lap. "We were thinking about starting a podcast. We don't need the money; we need to have something to do. And who knows what a podcast can turn into."

"There's zero chance of getting hurt," Renn chimes in.

The doorbell rings. I excuse myself and head to the foyer. I turn the handle, swinging open the door.

My heart skips a beat. *Okay. We're doing this.*

"Hi, Blakely." Rory Brewer steps inside, offering a hug but nervous, I think, that I won't accept it. *Of course, I do.* "I hope I'm not interrupting anything."

"Absolutely not," I say, pulling out of her warm, motherly embrace. "Come on in."

"I'm not staying long. I just wanted to come see you face-to-face and ensure things are okay between us."

I smile at her.

As terrible as Renn's father is, she's the opposite. He's disgusting and vile. She's genuine and kind. It's hard to believe they ever worked as a couple. I can only figure that Reid must've changed a lot over the years —for the worse.

"I'm happy you came by," I say. "I've been wondering how to break the ice and hoping it wouldn't be awkward between us."

"Why should it be awkward? My soon-to-be ex-husband is to blame for this—not us. We must stick together. Family always comes first."

Does that mean she sees me as family? She accepts our marriage?

"Reid and I had problems long before you came along," she says. "Nothing like what he did to you, or I would've left him years ago. But he crossed a line with you. It's unacceptable. So please know you are welcome at my home any time you'd like to swing by. You are as welcome as my other children. Brock, too. He's also a part of our family now."

I smile. "Thank you, Rory. You will never know how much that means to me."

She pulls me in for a quick hug. "And you will never know how much it means to me to see a smile on my son's face. I can never thank you enough for that."

She takes a step back. "Let your husband know I was here, please. I'd like to have a family dinner again soon. Maybe we can sync schedules?"

"I'd love that."

"Okay, sweetheart. Goodbye."

"Goodbye, Rory."

She lets herself out quietly.

I make my way slowly back to the others.

"My soon-to-be-ex-husband is to blame for this—not us. We must stick together."

I can't imagine the pain Rory must be experiencing. Yes, she said her marriage hadn't been great for a while, but her life has still been upside down. And she must love him on some level. That must hurt. Still, she radiates peace and ... strength. Maybe even joy.

Mom would have loved her.

Her strength, kindness—her resilience. She puts family above all else. Differently than my mother, but the same, too.

For many years, I was afraid I'd never find the person I was supposed to be with. *Or if I was going to marry at all.* I felt like time was passing me by—that there was a window of opportunity and, if I missed it, I'd be out of luck. *And alone.*

I didn't realize that my timetable isn't necessarily the same as the universe's.

Renn—*the bad boy troublemaker extraordinaire, my brother's best friend.* The man who said he'd wanted me from the first day he laid eyes on me. Someone my mom knew and loved. And now the man I'm going to spend the rest of my life with.

Seems we just needed to wait until the time was right. Maybe, if we'd gotten together earlier, it might have failed. Between Australia and the United States?

No. Our time is now.

I grin, making my way back into the living room. I stop in the doorway and take them all in.

Renn's by the fireplace, laughing at something Brock said. My brother's on the sofa next to Ella, rubbing her shoulders. Ella glows as she basks in Brock's attention.

How did I get here? How did this happen?

How did I get so lucky?

I walk in and sit on Renn's lap. As usual, he puts his arms around me and holds me close.

My protector. My passionate, kind, sexy man—the one who loves me.

The only man I'll ever love.

I might have missed the proposal—*and I might not remember the ceremony, just the llama*—but I know I'll have many amazing years with this man, making incredible memories filled with love.

Epilogue

B lakely

5 months later ...

"Can you imagine living here?" Ella sighs, pulling her sunglasses down and squinting into the Australian sunlight. "And, since we're dreaming, we might as well have our houses next door."

I lie on the chaise next to her and smirk. *If she only knew that Brock and Renn have talked about building beach houses next to each other ... just not in Australia.*

I won't be shocked if they go through with it. I won't be mad about it, either.

Nothing surprises me anymore.

Renn is happily unemployed. He and Brock have taken up wood-working ... and neither of them are good at it. So far, they've made a chair that broke during its first use, a dresser with drawers that won't close, and a huge mess. But they're happy. And that makes me happy.

Thankfully, knowing woodworking won't be enough to keep their bodies and minds satisfied, the two of them are in the process of creating a training program designed for teens. It focuses on holistic health, is affordable for low-income families—therefore not lining some rich asshole's pockets, which was imperative for Renn—and builds mental strength as well as physical.

I love and respect the hell out of them.

And love they gave up the idea of podcasting, too.

Ella suggested she and Brock forgo wedding planning and get married in Vegas. We hopped on a plane, *perks of marrying into a family with their own private airline*, and flew across the country. Renn and I watched our best friends get married at the King and Bling Chapel. We reenacted ours to see if it rang any bells. *It didn't.*

We've spent a lot of time with Renn's siblings. I didn't know them pre-Reid, but from what I can tell, they're closer than ever. The boys go golfing once a month. Gannon always wins, much to Ripley's dismay. Tate takes selfies with the club. I'm not sure he ever uses it to hit a ball. Jason is still his quiet self. But the more time I spend with him, the more interesting he becomes. His stories are the best—especially the ones he shares about Foxx. I'm determined to make Foxxy my buddy. Renn says to let it go, but I can't. I'm not making progress, but I'm not a quitter. Bianca told me to manage my expectations. I like her delivery better than Renn's.

There has been so much change—so many things flipped upside down—that nothing can surprise me.

But I bet I can still surprise my husband.

"Here comes trouble," Ella says, grinning.

I follow her gaze down the beach.

My brother is oblivious to the eyes trailing them. So is my husband. *Now, anyway.*

Secretly, I think he still loves the looks he receives—the man has an ego, after all. But it does nothing for him anymore. After all, I'm his singular focus these days. Having Renn Brewer's full attention leaves me a very, very satisfied woman. *Likewise, as his reward, he's a very, very satisfied man.*

Renn slides his Aviators off, his lips twisting into a smirk.

A flurry of goosebumps rushes over my skin, intensified by the love shining in his eyes. It makes him more attractive, more desirable—*my dream.*

"What are you two doing?" Brock asks. Without missing a beat, he bends down and quiets Ella's potential response with a long, deep kiss.

I shake my head. "Some things never change."

Renn removes his hat, stopping beside me. He woke up, grabbed a shower, and tucked the strands under the cap without a second thought. The unruliness makes my fingers itch to comb through the tangled mess, digging my nails into his scalp until he moans—*again.*

He watches me intently as he tugs the brim over his head again.

Once upon a time, I wondered if I could ever get used to a man like him. He was overwhelming. Tall, muscled, and swagger for days. But now, I know the answer. *You can't.*

What I didn't know then was the heart behind the heat—the sweetness beneath the sex appeal.

It's how he charges my phone for me every night because he knows I forget. I notice it when I overhear him talking about me to strangers and when he invites strangers over for dinner because of his wife's amazing chicken piccata. I see it in the way he takes care of his mother, lets Tate borrow his car, and insists Astrid overtip *everyone.*

His heart is as big as ... *other parts.*

Nope. I'll never get used to him. He'll overwhelm me in the best ways every day.

"Hey, cutie," he says, pressing a soft kiss against my lips. It's barely deep enough to hint at the ideas floating in his head for later.

I hold his cheek in my hand. "Hey, Daddy."

He laughs. "New kink?"

"You better hope it is."

Ella and Brock stop talking.

Renn's forehead pulls together. His brows slowly raise. His eyes grow wider as his mouth falls open.

"*Blakely* ..."

I laugh, my heart swelling in my chest. "*Renn* ..."

He gulps, his eyes dropping to my stomach.

I place a hand over the spot where I assume the little bean is growing.

He raises his eyes to mine, a hopeful sparkle shining brighter than the sun.

"We're having a baby," I say softly.

He sucks in a breath, then blows it out in disbelief. It takes a long few seconds for it to settle in. Watching it register is the most precious thing I've ever seen.

My eyes fill with happy tears. A slow smile breaks across his face.

"We're having a baby?" he asks.

I nod.

"*Oh, my God*. We're having a baby." He looks up at Brock and Ella. "We're having a baby."

Ella claps. She figured it out before I did, but thankfully kept it a secret ... from everyone but Brock. *Naturally.*

My brother pulls Renn into a big hug, wishing him congratulations while winking at me over my husband's shoulder. The scene fills me with more happiness, more pure joy than I ever dared to dream for myself.

Renn steps back and takes my hand. "Come on, Mama."

I giggle and get to my feet. "Where are we going?"

"I don't know." He laughs. "I just want you to myself for a little while."

He turns me to face him, his face as happy as I feel.

"You get me to yourself for as long as you want me," I say over the lump in my throat.

"Forever, then."

"Forever."

He kisses me softly, still chuckling in disbelief.

"Guys, we'll see you later," he says, leading me to the house we rented for our honeymoon. "I need to have sex with my wife, find out when the baby's due, and do a lot of research because, I don't know what the hell I'm doing."

I giggle. "You're going to do great."

Our eyes lock as I run through a litany of things that qualify as *things Renn does great.*

His tongue caressing every part of my body. His hand wrapped around my ponytail, pulling my head back while he slams into me from behind. The taste of him as he comes in my mouth.

Mischief floats in his eyes. *He can read me like a book.*

I grin. "Yes. All of that. Now."

A low, throaty chuckle is his response.

My laughter trails us as he picks me up and carries me toward the house.

To our happy ending.

To *forever.*

Want more **Foxx Carmichael**? His story, **Flame**, releases Fall 2023. Flame is available for preorder.

Another Brewer Family book, The Arrangement, releases December 7, 2023. It is also available for preorder.

Read on for Chapter 1 in Flirt, Book #1 in the Carmichael Family series ...

More from Adriana

Foxx Carmichael's family has their own series, starting with Flirt. This is the first chapter. Enjoy!

Chapter One
Brooke

WANTED: A SITUATION-SHIP

I'm a single female who's tired of relationships ruining my life. However, there are times when a date would be helpful. If you're a single man, preferably mid-twenties to late-thirties, and are in a similar situation, we might be a match.

Candidate must be handsome, charming, and willing to pretend to have feelings for me (on a sliding scale, as the event requires). Ability to discuss a wide variety of topics is a plus. Must have your own transportation and a (legal) job.

This will be a symbiotic agreement. In exchange for your time, I will give you mine. Need someone to flirt with you at a football party? Go, team! Want a woman to make you look good in front of your boss? Let me find my heels. Would you love for someone to be obsessed with you in front of your ex? I'm applying my red lipstick now.

If interested, please email me. Time is of the essence.

My best friend, Jovie, points at my computer screen. The glitter on her pink fingernail sparkles in the light. "You can't post that."

I fold my arms across my chest. "And why not?"

Instead of answering me, she takes another bite of her chicken wrap. A dribble of mayonnaise dots the corner of her mouth.

"A lot of help you are," I mutter, rereading the post I drafted instead of pricing light fixtures for work. The words are written in a pretty font on Social, my go-to social media platform.

Country music from the nineties mixes with the laughter of locals sitting around us in Smokey's, my favorite beachside café. Along the far wall, a map of the state of Florida made of wine corks sways gently in the ocean breeze coming through the open windows.

"Would you two like anything else?" Rebecca, our usual lunchtime server, pauses by the table. "I think we have some Key lime pie left."

"I'm too irritable for pie today," I say.

"*You* don't want *pie*? That's a first," she teases me.

Jovie giggles.

"I know," I say, releasing a sigh. "That's the state of my life right now. I don't even want pie."

"Wow. Okay. This sounds serious. What's up? Maybe I can help," Rebecca says.

Jovie wipes her mouth with a napkin. "Let me cut in here real quick before she tries to snowball you into thinking her harebrained idea is a good one."

I roll my eyes. "It *is* a good one."

"I'll give you the CliffsNotes version," Jovie says, side-eyeing me. "Brooke got an invitation to her grandma's birthday party, and instead of just not going—"

"I can't *not go*."

"Or showing up as the badass single chick she is," Jovie continues, silencing me with a look, "she wrote a post for Social that's basically an ad for a fake boyfriend."

"Correction—it *is* an ad for a fake boyfriend."

Rebecca rests a hand on her hip. "I don't see the problem."

"*Thank you*," I say, staring at Jovie. "I'm glad someone understands me here."

Jovie throws her hands in the air, sending a napkin flying right along with them.

Satisfaction is written all over my face as I sit back in my chair with a smug smile. The more I think about having a *situation-ship* with a guy—a word I read in a magazine at the salon while waiting two decades for my color to process—the more it makes sense.

Instead of having relations with a man, have situations. Done.

What's not to love about that?

"But, before I tell you to dive into this whole thing, why can't you just go alone, Brooke?" Rebecca asks.

"Oh, *I can* go alone. I just generally prefer to avoid torture whenever possible."

"I still don't understand why you need a date to your grandma's birthday party."

"Because this isn't *just* a birthday party," I say. "It's labeled that to cover up the fact that my mom and her sister, my aunt Kim, are having a daughter-of-the-year showdown. They're using my poor grandma Honey's eighty-fifth birthday as a dog and pony show—and my cousin Aria and I are the ponies."

"*Okay.*" Rebecca looks at me dubiously before switching her attention to Jovie. "And why are you against this whole thing?"

Jovie takes enough cash to cover our lunch plus the tip and hands it to Rebecca. *Perks of ordering the same lunch most days.* Then she gathers her things.

"I'm not against it in *theory*," Jovie says. "I'm against it in *practice*. I understand the perks of having a guy around to be arm candy when needed. But I'm not supporting this decision ... this *mayhem* ... for two reasons." She looks at me. "For one, your family will see any post you make on Social. You don't think they'll use it as ammunition against you?"

This is probably true.

"Second," Jovie continues. "I hate, hate, *hate* your aunt Kim, and I loathe the fact that your mom makes you feel like you have to do anything more than be your amazing self to win her favor. Screw them both."

My heart swells as I take in my best friend.

Jovie Reynolds was my first friend in Kismet Beach when I moved here two and a half years ago. We reached for the same can of pineapple rings, knocking over an entire display in Publix. As we picked up the mess, we traded recipes—hers for a vodka cocktail and mine for air fryer pineapple.

We hung out that evening—with her cocktail and my air fryer creations—and have been inseparable since.

"My mom is not a bad person," I say in her defense, even though I'm not so sure that's true from time to time. "She's just ..."

"A bad person," Jovie says.

I laugh. "*No*. I just ... nothing I can do is good enough for her. She hated Geoff when I married him at twenty and said I was too young. But was she happy when that ended in a divorce? Nope. According to *her*, I didn't try hard enough."

Rebecca frowns.

"And then Geoff started banging Kim and—"

"*What*?" Rebecca yelps, her eyes going wide.

"Exactly. Bad people," Jovie says, shaking her head.

"So your ex-husband will be at your grandma's party with your aunt? Is that what you're saying?" Rebecca asks.

I nod. "Yup."

She stacks our plates on top of one another. The ceramic clinks through the air. "On that note, why can't you just not go? Avoid it altogether?"

"Because my grandma Honey is looking forward to this, and she called me to make sure I was coming. I couldn't tell her no." My heart tightens when I think of the woman I love more than any other. "And, you know, my mom has made it abundantly clear that if I miss this, I will probably break Honey's heart, and she'll die, and it'll be my fault."

"Wow. That's a freight train of guilt to throw around," Rebecca says, wincing.

I glance down at my computer. The post is still there, sitting on the screen and waiting for my final decision. Although it is a genius idea, if I do say so myself—Jovie is probably right. It'll just cause more problems than it's worth.

I close the laptop and shove it into my bag. Then I hoist it on my shoulder. "It's complicated. I want to go and celebrate with my grandma but seeing my aunt with my ex-husband ..." I wince. "Also, there will be my mother's usual diatribe and comparisons to Aria, proving that I'm a failure in everything that I do."

"But if you had a boyfriend to accompany you, you'd save face with the enemy and have a buffer against your mother. Is that what you're thinking?" Rebecca asks.

"Yeah. I don't know how else to survive it. I can't walk in there alone, or even with Jovie, and deal with all of that mess. If I just had someone hot and a little handsy—make me look irresistible—it would kill all of my birds with one hopefully *hard* stone."

I wink at my friends.

Rebecca laughs. "Okay. I'm Team Fake Boyfriend. Sorry, Jovie."

Jovie sighs. "I'm sorry for me too because I have to go back to work. And if I avoid the stoplights, I can make it to the office with thirty seconds to spare." She air-kisses Rebecca. "Thanks for the extra mayo."

I laugh. "See you tomorrow, Rebecca."

"Bye, girls."

Jovie and I walk single-file through Smokey's until we reach the exit. Immediately, we reach for the sunglasses perched on top of our heads and slide them over our eyes.

The sun is bright, nearly blinding in a cloudless sky. I readjust my bag so that the thin layer of sweat starting to coat my skin doesn't coax the leather strap down my arm.

"Call me tonight," Jovie says, heading to her car.

"I will."

"Rehearsal for the play got canceled tonight, so I might go to Charlie's. If I don't, I may swing by your house."

"How's the thing with Charlie going? I didn't realize you were still talking to him."

She laughs. "I wasn't. He pissed me off. But he came groveling back last night, and I gave in." She shrugs. "What can I say? I'm a sucker for a good grovel."

"I think it's the theater girl in you. You love the dramatics of it all."

"That I do. It's a problem."

"Well, I'll see you when I see you then," I say.

"Bye, Brooke."

I give her a little wave and make my way up Beachfront Boulevard.

The sidewalk is fairly vacant with a light dusting of sand. In another month, tourists will fill the street that leads from the ocean to the shops filled with trinkets and ice cream in the heart of Kismet Beach. For now, it's a relaxing and hot walk back to the office.

My mind shifts from the heat back to the email reminder I received during lunch. *To Honey's party.* It takes all of one second for my stomach to cramp.

"I shouldn't have eaten all of those fries," I groan.

But it's not lunch that's making me unwell.

A mixture of emotions rolls through me. I don't know which one to land on. There's a chord of excitement about the event—at seeing Honey and her wonderful life be celebrated, catching up with Aria and the rest of my family, and the general concept of *going home.* But there's so much apprehension right alongside those things that it drowns out the good.

Kim and Geoff together make me ill. It's not that I miss my ex-husband; I'm the one who filed for divorce. But they will be there, making things super awkward for me in front of everyone we know.

Not to mention what it will do to my mother.

Geoff hooking up with Kim is my ultimate failure, according to Mom. Somehow, it embarrasses *her,* and that's unforgivable.

"For just once, I'd like to see her and not be judged," I mumble as I sidestep a melting glob of blue ice cream.

Nothing I have ever done has been good enough for Catherine Bailey. Marrying Geoff was an atrocity at only twenty years old. My dream to work in interior architecture wasn't deemed serious enough as a life path. *"You're wasting your time and our money, Brooke."* And when I told her I was hired at Laguna Homes as a lead designer for one of their three renovation teams? I could hear her eyes rolling.

The office comes into view, and my spirits lift immediately. I shove all thoughts of the party out of my brain and let my mind settle back into happier territory. *Work.* The one thing I love.

I step under the shade of an adorable crape myrtle tree and then turn up a cobblestone walkway to my office.

The small white building is tucked away from the sidewalk. It sits between a row of shops with apartments above them and an Italian restaurant only open in the evenings. The word *Laguna Homes* is printed in seafoam green above a black awning.

My shoes tap against the wooden steps as I make my way to the door. A rush of cool air, kissed by the scent of eucalyptus essential oil, greets me as I step inside.

"How was lunch?" Kix asks, standing in the doorway of his corner office. My boss's smile is kind and genuine, just like everything else about him. "Let me guess—you met Jovie for lunch at Smokey's?"

I laugh. "It's like you know me or something."

He chuckles.

Kix and Damaris Carmichael are two of my favorite people in the world. When I met Damaris at a trade show three years ago, and we struck up a conversation about tile, I knew she was special. Then I met her husband and discovered he had the same soft yet sturdy energy. All six of their children possess similar qualities—even Moss, the superintendent on my renovation team. Although I'd never admit that to him.

"I swung by Parasol Place this afternoon," Kix says. "It's looking great. You were right about taking out the wall between the living room and dining room. I love it. It makes the whole house feel bigger."

I blush under the weight of his compliment. "Thanks."

"Did Moss tell you about the property I'm looking at for your team next?" Kix asks.

"No. Moss doesn't tell me anything."

Kix grins. "I'm sure he tells you all kinds of things you don't need to know."

"You say that like you have experience with him," I say, laughing.

"Only a few years." He laughs too. "It's another home from the sixties. I got a lead on it this morning and am on my way to look at it now."

"Take pictures. You know I love that era, and if you get it, I want to be able to start envisioning things right away."

"You and your visions." He shakes his head. "Gina is in the back making copies. I told her we'd keep our eye on the door until she gets back out here, so it would be great if you could do that."

"Absolutely," I say, walking backward toward my office. "Be safe. *And take pictures.*"

"I will. Enjoy the rest of your day, Brooke."

"You, too."

I reach behind me to find my office door open. I take another step back and then turn toward my desk. Someone moves beside my filing cabinet just as I flip on the light.

"Ah!" I shriek, clutching my chest.

My heart pounds out of control until I get my bearings and focus on the man looking back at me.

I set my bag down on a chair and blow out a shaky breath. "Dammit, Moss!"

He leans against the cabinet and smiles at me cheekily.

"We're going to have to stop meeting like this," he says. "People are going to talk."

Continue reading ...

About the Author

USA Today Bestselling author, Adriana Locke, writes contemporary romances about the two things she knows best—big families and small towns. Her stories are about ordinary people finding extraordinary love with the perfect combination of heart, heat, and humor.

She loves connecting with readers, fall weather, football, reading alpha heroes, everything pumpkin, and pretending to garden.

Hailing from a tiny town in the Midwest, Adriana spends her free time with her high school sweetheart (who she married over twenty years ago) and their four sons (who truly are her best work). Her kitchen may be a perpetual disaster, and if all else fails, there is always pizza.

Join her reader group and talk all the bookish things by clicking here.

www.adrianalocke.com

Acknowledgments

The end of a story is such a bittersweet feeling. I reflect on all the talented, kind, generous people that helped make the idea in my head a reality and feel immense joy. Then I remember the journey is over and a brief sadness takes its place.

Until I begin the next book.

I have so many wonderful people to thank for helping me get this passion project into the world. This story has been marinating in my head for the longest time. I finally found a spot on my calendar to write it and I did ... for me. Now, I'm sharing it with you. I hope you enjoyed Renn and Blakely.

First, I would like to acknowledge my Creator. I'm eternally grateful to have been given the tools and skills to be a storyteller.

My family is my reason and my rock. They're my heart and soul. I love you, Saul, Alexander, Aristotle, Achilles, and Ajax. I love you more than you'll ever know. Also, I would like to thank Peggy and Rob for always being in my corner. I appreciate you both. You know I love you.

I was lucky to work with two talented designers on the cover of this story. Kari March, my first friend in the book world, designed the delicious cover for the ebook and paperback. Her talent astounds me. Staci Hart, an author and creator who is truly one of the sweetest people I've met, brought her skills to the special edition cover. I'm obsessed with both.

I scored the perfect photograph from Regina Wamba for this cover. She was a delight to work with and I'm thrilled to have her work on mine.

Emma Nichole jumped in last minute to assist with graphics design. You're a gem!

Atlee Breen from Atlee Breen Designs went to work designing logos for the Brewer businesses (and more). I love working with you.

I want to thank Marion Archer for content edits (the llama made it just for you!), and Jenny Simms for copy edits. Also a huge hug to Michele Ficht for proofreading. You are an amazing team, ladies!

My author friends rallied around me during the production of this book. Mandi Beck provided levity, inspiration, and no-nonsense feedback. (Sometimes even about books—ha!) Rachel Brookes delivered awesome Aussie knowledge and answered all of my questions (and there were many!). Chelle Sloan brainstormed King and Bling (and her characters might have had a cameo—did you catch it?). Anjelica Grace stayed up to read chapters way passed her bedtime. Kenna Rey talked this out with me, beta read, and was a general shoulder of friendship. S.L. Scott talked me through many a meltdowns and I sprinted with my sweet friend Jessica Prince. You all are amazing. I'm lucky to call you friends.

My assistant, Tiffany, kept the wheel turning while I turned out this story. Brittni Van cheered me on from the sidelines, and Erica Rogers jumped on board and left all the emojis. Also, a big hug to Melissa Panio-Petersen for her swift save and averting a newsletter crisis.

Last but certainly not least, thank you, friend. I know you have a million choices to read and I'm honored you chose mine. I hope you enjoyed it.

Made in the USA
Monee, IL
26 May 2024

58977618R00157